CITY OF THE
MIND

Also by Penelope Lively

CITY OF THE
MIND

A Novel

PENELOPE
LIVELY

GROVE PRESS
New York

First published in Great Britain in 1991 by André Deutsch Ltd.

This edition is printed by special arrangement with HarperCollins Publishers, who printed the first U.S. edition in 1991.

Printed in the United States of America

FIRST GROVE PRESS EDITION

Library of Congress Cataloging-in-Publication Data

Lively, Penelope, 1933–
    City of the mind : a novel / Penelope Lively.
      p. cm.
    ISBN 0-8021-4020-3
    1. Architects—Fiction. 2. London (England)—Fiction. 3. Identity (Psychology)—Fiction. I. Title.

PR6062.I89C5 2003   2003057125

Designed by Alma Orenstein

Grove Press
841 Broadway
New York, NY 10003

03 04 05 06 07   10 9 8 7 6 5 4 3 2 1

For Adam and Diana

ONE

Night. Lights on. The lights that glide in jewelled columns, red and white, that make glowing caverns of the windows opposite, that rake the bedroom ceiling in long yellow shafts. And in the sky, the dead and dancing sky, there are a million yesterdays. "Why are there stars?" the child asks her father. He shakes his head, pulls the curtains to, and goes. It is late; she should sleep. And in any case he has no answer.

London; Monday; eight-thirty. Matthew Halland, delivering his daughter Jane to his estranged wife, waited in the car, engine running, until he saw the front door open. He sat watching, one hand on the gear lever. He glimpsed Susan. He saw the door close. He accelerated away, carrying the child with him in his head—the sound of her voice, that downy cleft in the back of her neck, the small milky crag of her new front tooth. She was eight years old, and amazed him. And then as he turned from the side street into a busier one, as the traffic gripped and slowed him, as he halted for the lights, she began to slip away. The twinge of loss was swallowed in a rising tide of impatience—twenty to nine, the morning at his throat. The city had him in its current; yesterday withdrew. He switched on the car radio, rummaged with one hand in his briefcase. He made plans and decisions—get to Blackwall in time for a good look round before the site conference, have a session with Jobson about that staircase at Cobham Square. Jane returned for an instant—her sleepy voice, "Why are there stars?"—and simultaneously he caught sight of the moon, a pale morning moon hanging above the city, sinking, drowned out by day. And at once time dissolved and he flitted to a moment when, as a boy, he saw the surface of the moon through a telescope, pitted and shadowed, a tangible landscape. That same moon, then and now.

And thus, driving through the city, he is both here and now, there and then. He carries yesterday with him, but pushes forward into today, and tomorrow, skipping as he will from one to the other. He is in London, on a May morning of the late twentieth century, but is also in many other places, and at other times. He twitches the knob of his radio: New York speaks to him, five hours ago, is superseded by Australia tomorrow and presently by India this evening. He learns of events that have not yet taken place, of deaths that have not yet occurred. He is Matthew Halland, an English architect stuck in a traffic jam, a person of no great significance, and yet omniscient. For him, the world no longer turns; there is no day or night, everything and everywhere are instantaneous. He forges his way along Euston Road, in fits and starts, speeding up, then clogged again between panting taxis and a lorry with churning wasp-striped cement mixer. He is both trapped, and ranging free. He fiddles again with the radio, runs through a lexicon of French song, Arab exhortation, invective in some language he cannot identify. Halted once more, he looks sideways and meets the thoughtful gaze of Jane Austen (1775–1817), ten feet high on a poster, improbably teamed with

Isambard Kingdom Brunel and George Frederick Handel, all of them dead, gone, but doing well—live and kicking in his head and up there guarding the building site that will become the British Library. And then another car cuts in ahead of his, he hoots, accelerates, is channelled on in another licensed burst of speed. Jane Austen is replaced by St Pancras.

Thus he coasts through the city, his body in one world and his head in many. He is told so much, and from so many sources, that he has learned to disregard, to let information filter through the mind and vanish, leaving impressions—a phrase, a fact, an image. He knows much, and very little. He knows more than he can confront; his wisdoms have blunted his sensibility. He is an intelligent man, and a man of compassion, but he can hear of a massacre on the other side of the globe and wonder as he listens if he remembered to switch on his answering machine. He is aware of this, and is disturbed.

The city, too, bombards him. He sees decades and centuries, poverty and wealth, grace and vulgarity. He sees a kaleidoscope of time and mood: buildings that ape Gothic cathedrals, that remember Greek temples, that parade symbols and images. He sees columns, pediments and porticos. He sees Victorian stucco, twentieth-century concrete, a snatch of Georgian brick. He notes the resilience and tenacity of the city, and its indifference.

He sees, too, that the city speaks in tongues: Pizza Ciao, King's Cross Kebab, New Raj Mahal Tandoori, Nepalese Brasserie. And he hears another clamour, a cacophony of sound that runs the whole gamut from Yiddish to Urdu, a global testimony reaching from Moscow to Sydney by way of Greece and Turkey and remote nameless birthplaces in Ireland or India or the Caribbean. The resonances of the place are universal. If the city were to recount its experience, the ensuing babble would be the talk of everytime and everywhere, of persecution and disaster, of success and misfortune. The whole place is a chronicle, in brick and stone, in silent eloquence, for those who have eyes and ears. For such as Matthew. Through him, the city lives and breathes; it sheds its indifference, its impervious attachment to both then and now, and bears witness.

He climbs the heights of Pentonville Road, listening to Manila, seeing the fretwork of wrinkles on an old man's neck, the tiny horned plaits on the head of a black baby, suspended between intimacy and invisible distance. He is exposed to everything: to what is here, and not here, to what is no longer here but only in the mind. And now it is nine-fifteen and he is impatient, restless at the hindrance of metal, tarmac and humanity that lies between him and his office, between him and the day ahead. He drums his fingers on the steering-wheel, achieves another hundred yards, halts and drums again. At the Angel crossroads he contemplates the airy wasteland of orange cranes, scaffolding, hoardings and battered buildings clinging to their last days of existence, everything coming down and going up simultaneously, it seems. He notes a late Victorian façade—red terracotta Gothic arches, capitals with acanthus—what has it been? Bank? Pub? Glassless, backless, one-dimensional, it has weeks or months left, at most. Its columns are plastered with torn posters: Uriah Heep, The Dog's d'Amour, Boxing: Anthony 'The Terminator' Logan, Jazz & the Brothers Grimm. In front of it two children cling to balloons like silver cushions, a man with Rasta hair crowded into a roomy beret waits to cross the road. For thirty seconds Matthew is at one with all this, and everything that it implies, and then he is off down City Road. The moment is gone, irretrievable, and with it the conjunctions, the jigsaw of time and reference.

He liked to be at his office by nine-thirty, and today was not. At twenty to ten he dropped his briefcase beside his desk, shuffled through the mail, reached for the phone, scowled sideways as the door opened.

"Matthew, I'd just like to . . ."

"I'm not here."

"Forgive me, I must be hallucinating. I'll come back when you are."

"I've got a site conference at Blackwall. I'm off again at once. I only came in to collect stuff and make some phone calls. This afternoon, Tony, OK?"

"I'll come to Blackwall with you," said Tony Brace. "Too long since I took a look. Knock on my door when you're ready." He went.

The architectural firm of James Gamlin and Partners occupied the top three floors of a renovated nineteenth-century warehouse in Finsbury. On the ground floor was a row of shops—stationers, newsagent, locksmith, dry cleaners—and a dental surgery. The partners, five of them, along with associates and other staff, made regular use of the stationers and newsagent but would only have patronized the dentist (grimy windows of opaque green glass, eroded brass nameplate) in desperate circumstances. Up aloft, in their empire, all was sweetness and light, the carpets smelt new, the pot plants, sprayed twice daily by the receptionist, gleamed with well-being. The chairs for waiting clients were of discreetly good design; on the walls were striking black and white photographs of the firm's most valued projects. The junior members worked in an open-plan area, bright, light, airy, quietly humming and clacking with new technologies. The partners, such as Matthew and Tony Brace, had individual offices. James Gamlin, once an *enfant terrible* of post-war architectural innovation and now something of a grand old man, was in semi-retirement and tended only to pay infrequent and interfering visits which required tactful handling and a certain amount of self-control all round.

Matthew made three phone calls, had a word with his secretary, gathered up papers and alerted his colleague.

"Why the interest in Blackwall? I thought you hated the place?"

"It has a certain awful fascination."

Tony, one of the original partners, specialized in restoration and conversion. His interest in the firm's big commercial developments, of which the Blackwall site, in Docklands, was perhaps the largest they had ever taken on, was tinged with genteel disdain, but sensibly pragmatic. James Gamlin and Partners had to make a living.

"I want to see how they're dealing with that sill detail in the cladding on the upper levels," he explained, as they got into the car.

"The fixing fillets spring back if you're not careful. Quite exciting. They nearly had a nasty accident last week."

"I hope everybody's insurance is in order."

And so long as it is, thought Matthew, striking out into City Road again, give or take the odd Irish navvy is really of no consequence. Not that that is what Tony means at all—he is no more cold-blooded than the rest of us, merely prudent. Well, there hasn't been a fatality on a Docklands site yet, and if and when there is, it won't be the first sacrificial blood shed in this city. He saw for a moment, in the mind's eye, a sequence of bodies toppling from buildings, squashed under brick and stone and timber—Roman slaves, squat medieval peasants, eighteenth-century labourers. Uninsured, poor sods.

"Maybe we should have tucked a spare criminal under the foundations."

"What?"

"A Roman custom. To placate the gods."

"How very unpleasant," said Tony, after a moment. Matthew, who had known he would say that, or something similar, accorded himself five points on a private scoring system. He both liked Tony and was intermittently exasperated by him.

The conjunction with workmates is a curious one—associates as randomly achieved as neighbours or relatives-in-law, and frequently as crucial to well-being. You spent more time with the people you worked with than with your friends. Or with your child. Matthew had known this man for ten years, day in, day out; he knew his opinions on everything, the extent of his wardrobe, the way he combed his hair. He knew his way of life. Tony Brace lived in Richmond, in circumstances of impeccable domestic content. Matthew and Susan had visited, in the early days of their marriage; driving home, they had mocked the décor and the connubial complacency. Thinking of this, Matthew felt ashamed, and faintly envious.

They were moving now through one of the city's most turbulent areas of metamorphosis. Gaunt shells of nineteenth-century buildings, delicately shrouded in green netting, stood alongside huge spaces bright with the machinery of construction: yellow cement-mixers, orange bulldozers, immense elegant cranes in yellow, red, green, blue—dinosaurian monsters unleashed to wreak their mechanical will upon the London clay.

"Bishopsgate Jurassic," said Matthew.

"Sorry?"

"Nothing. An association that sprang to mind. Silly, really."

"Oh, I see—the bulldozers. Yes, they are rather, aren't they?"

They were stationary again, at a big junction, at the hub of things, crowded by cars, buses, pedestrians nipping through where they might, crowded by brick and stone and concrete and by glass which soared here into the sky. A sky loaded with rain, against whose grey surface there shone on one side the white spire of a church, across which crawled, soundless, a glinting aircraft.

"This city," said Matthew, "is entirely in the mind. It is a construct of the memory and of the intellect. Without you and me it hasn't got a chance."

"It seems to me to be managing quite well. This bloody traffic is real enough. What time did you say your meeting was?"

"Eleven. I'll be all right. What I mean is that significance is in the eye of the beholder."

"Shouldn't you be taking a right at these lights?"

"I'm going to try some creative back-street work. Now, for example, what does that wall mean to you?"

"Well—Georgian brick. Probably once the churchyard wall, now gracing the private car park for this office block. A rare survival given that all this was flattened in the Blitz."

"Exactly. And here you are bearing witness for the wall, so to speak."

"Are you sure this is going to get you back to Aldgate?" said Tony.

"With any luck it will." Matthew swung round a corner and into the traffic again.

"It's this interesting combination of silence and eloquence. Depending on what the viewer happens to know. And the tenaciousness. That particular stack of bricks occupied the same space in, maybe, 1740. The same bricks, in the same place, looked at by different people. That, to me, makes a complicated nonsense of the passage of time."

"Talking of which, it's past ten-thirty. There's no left turn at the end here—had you realized?"

But Matthew, now, is on another level, caught up by his own perception, his fancy, by the reflections in his head of all that is around him. He is, for a few instants, disembodied—aware of himself as subsumed within the crowd, the horde of humanity that has sifted through the city, and died, and been reborn. He is both sobered, and uplifted. He is alone, and at the same time less alone. He sees that time is what we live in, but that it is also what we carry within us. Time is then, but it is also our own perpetual now. We bear it in our heads and on our backs; it is our freight, our baggage, our Old Man of the Sea. It grinds us down and buoys us up. We cannot shuffle it off; we would be adrift without it. We both take it with us and leave ourselves behind within it—flies in amber, fossilized admonitions and exemplars.

He swings the car left (Tony, at his side, bleating on unheard), registers but hardly sees a girl in a red coat, a helmeted wet-suited figure on a motorbike (Pony Express), the rearing black horse logo outside a bank. He thinks only of eyes seeing, million upon million pairs of eyes, recording the same world, the same images. He thinks of all these conjunctions of knowledge and experience, these collisions of what is known and what is felt which flame within the head to create a private vision, but a vision which is coloured by the many visions of other people, by fact and error and received opinion and things remembered and things invented. We can see nothing for itself alone; everything alludes to something else. And Matthew is caught now by the allusion of these streets, as he glances at that blackened brick wall, at the remnant of a Victorian façade amid the office blocks.

Before him is a canyon of fire. The man hesitates—even he, who has trodden the inferno of these streets for hours. He sees the firemen at work on a building at the far end: a figure swarming the black ramp of a ladder, the silver arcs of water against the stark façade and at the windows that bloom with flames. He sees glass shower to the ground; he sees the gas main shooting up in a geyser of white fire, the pavements which creep with scarlet tongues. He sees a tailor's dummy sprawling from a shattered shop front; he sees the defiant white horse of a pub sign; he sees the blackened carcass of a car.

He tilts his warden's helmet down to shield his eyes and walks into the furnace, picking his way through shattered glass, rubble, the tangle of the firemen's hoses. Further down the street, a roof sags, collapses with a roar, and a fountain of flame shoots fifty feet into the sky; a blizzard of orange sparks showers upon him. He shelters for a moment in the lea of a phone box, wipes his burning eyes. He is beyond reaction, beyond thought, he is responding simply to each minute as it comes, to the demands that each minute brings; direct someone to a shelter, visit and encourage those already in another, mark and report a UXB, locate and report each new outbreak of fire. But there are no new outbreaks now—the City is one single fire, from Old Street to Cannon Street, from Moorgate to Aldersgate, the flames jump now from one building to another, they need no bombs to feed them (though the bombs still come, he hears at this moment the great thud of an oil-bomb, and the ground seems to lift beneath him). Above are huge incandescent clouds, choking orange smoke rolls all around, one building spouts flames that are green and blue, another has set free a flock of great black birds, charred sheets of paper that come flapping and dying down the street. The whole place crackles, spits and roars, elemental and unleashed; only the rhythmic throb of the pumps and the clanging fire bells are the faint and desperate reassurance of order, of sanity, of human control.

This is the worst yet. It has risen, the infernal crescendo, since early evening. A bugger of a night, a right pasting we're getting, the bastards have pulled the plug on us all right: there is no language yet to confront it. People are grim-faced, too busy, afraid, exhausted, to assess, to do anything but what has to be done. He has seen sights tonight that will be with him to the end of his days. A four-storey building with roaring crimson windows which suddenly bulges outward and collapses like a house of cards. A cat carrying a kitten, silhouetted against firelight, picking its way along a window ledge. The spire of St Bride's lit from within like a lantern.

He leaves the shelter of the phone box and heads on towards the firemen, to whom he must report the urgent need for more pumps in Cheapside. The black figure at the top of the ladder is still playing a hose into the furnace that yesterday was a bank; the others are damping down a neighbouring building not yet fully ablaze, two men together fighting the heavy brass branch, from which, as he approaches, the fountain of water suddenly dies to a trickle. They curse and swear in frustration; the hydrants are running dry. The man on the ladder is swarming back down, the superintendent is shouting instructions—they will back off, shift to another hydrant. The warden delivers his message; the superintendent bawls back above the din: "Tell them I can't bloody do anything for them—I need everything I've got on this lot." And then for a moment the group of men stands silent, beaten, staring at the building in front of them whose bricks glow, etched in sparks—a building with arched ecclesiastical windows, constructed in the 1860s, maybe, a home to commerce, to insurance companies and to accountancy firms and to banks. The firemen are smoke-blackened, red-eyed; water streams from them, cascades down the waterproof hoods attached to their tin hats which always make the warden think, wildly, inappropriately, of beekeepers. He was a country boy, once, in some other incarnation. And now is Jim Prothero, a thirty-five-year-old print-worker and part-time warden, husband and father. And in the midst of it all there comes into his head, suddenly and wonderfully, a vision of his child—her snub nose, her spare bony little body. There'll be an end to all this, he thinks with sudden clarity, one way or another. It'll be over, in the end.

*   *   *

"What?"

"I said I hoped things were going reasonably for you on the domestic front."

Matthew edged the car into the flow of traffic round Tower Green. He recognized from the delicacy of Tony's tone that they must have entered a different conversational territory. This was condolence time: older man to younger.

"Not too bad," he said briskly. "The flat was pretty ropy when I took it on, but I've slapped paint around and so forth. And it's a decent size. Jane's with me there every other weekend."

"Still, you must miss that house. Lucy was saying the other day how nice you and Susan had made it."

Not the most apt of comments, thought Matthew. Bricks and mortar and furnishings are the least of what one misses. Well meant, though, I don't doubt.

There was a silence. They were in Whitechapel Road now; tower blocks cohabited with the struggling remnants of the old East End. Asian Supermarket; Bangladeshi Welfare Association; The Horse and Jockey. A new development like a clutch of shining white silos rose above a grubby nineteenth-century terrace.

"No chance of a . . . *rapprochement*?" said Tony.

"None whatsoever, I'm afraid."

Tony sighed. In sorrow or disapproval? "Pity. There it is, then. Do bring Jane to see us sometime."

"It was simply that the marriage ran out of steam, you know," said Matthew. He felt provoked to further comment, was exasperated with himself even as he spoke. "Went dead. I don't have anyone else in mind, and nor does Susan, so far as I know."

"Oh, quite," said Tony. "One hadn't supposed . . . Not that it makes the situation any better, I imagine."

12

No, it certainly doesn't. Too right it doesn't.

"As I say, we'd love to see Jane. She might enjoy the deer in Richmond Park."

"I'm sure she would." The deer, the river boat, you name it. This city is laid out for entertainment; that is its function. On alternate weekends we sample the city, Jane and I; parks, museums, funfairs, the zoo. We are instructed and amused. Millions are spent on our edification and our enjoyment. A good deal is spent by me. There must be no time to brood, to regret, to question. And in any case we are both energetic people and inquisitive by disposition. It is just as well I am not obliged to spend this precarious section of my life in the middle of Dartmoor.

"I must say," said Tony, "nothing would induce me to live down here."

They are entering Docklands, the land of promise, the city of the new decade, of the new century. It is a landscape of simultaneous decay and resurrection; glass, steel and concrete rear from the mud and rubble of excavation. The meccano outlines of cranes preside as far as the eye can see, the completed buildings are monolithic glass structures in whose serene surfaces of smoky grey and greenish-blue there float the soft mountain ranges of the clouds. Below them, the few surviving terrace houses of Limehouse, of Poplar, of Shadwell seem to crouch in some other time-band. The docks themselves still glint pewter in the sunshine—that ancient sequence of inlets and harbours: East India Dock, Surrey Docks, Canary Wharf, Millwall. The names alone have resonances that range over time and the globe—the spice trade, India, tea, rice, copra, jute, clippers and schooners, frigates and men o' war, whales, coal and timber. This place is hitched to Bombay and Calcutta, to Singapore and Hong Kong, to Jamaica and Trinidad and Greenland and Suez. In the empty waters lies the beached carcass of a barge, defunct at the feet of the bright cranes.

13

Commerce has always presided here; the place has always looked forward, round the next corner, into the next decade, as men have turned a shrewd gaze upon the world and seen where to put their faith and their investments. Fortunes have been made from pepper and timber and rum and silk and from exploitation. The figures toiling now on scaffolding and cat-walks or down there in the mud have a long ancestry. A place of work; a place of wealth.

Matthew viewed it with increasing ambivalence. He had been involved with the Blackwall project at every stage, some-times with excitement, at others in exasperation. He thought it an effective, efficient and not uncomely building. But now, as it began to rear into the sky, shooting its scaffolding and its concrete up thirty storeys over a matter of months, he found himself thinking incessantly of change and flux, of people as pawns, of the city as some uncontrollable organic force. Some-times it seemed to him as though the building rose despite him, despite all of them, that to commit a pattern of lines to a drawing board had been to unleash an unstoppable power. Which was, at a mundane level, true: the requirements of con-tracts, penalty clauses, insurance policies, labour agreements committed the builders to an inexorable, predestined course.

They arrived at the site and parked the car. Heading for the site offices Matthew said, "Incidentally, I've got a name for this place. I'm going to put it to the client. Frobisher House."

"Sounds quite nice. Why?"

"Because Martin Frobisher, the Elizabethan seaman, set sail from Blackwall to find the North-West Passage. It's one of the epics of Arctic exploration. We'll have a ship done in glass engraving for the main entrance doors."

"You'd better get going on it," said Tony. "They'll be unrolling the carpets in a week or two, by the look of things."

"That's the whole point of fast-track."

Down here, at ground level, there were walls and floors. Up in the sky, they were still pouring concrete. Five hundred workers, on shift-work round the clock; at night the machines continued to roll under arc-lights. Sixty million pounds and one year; the scale of late twentieth-century construction. The building was a great scaffolded tower glinting already with a patchwork of the turquoise glass that would eventually encase it, adorned with thick blue tubes down which roared spasmodic streams of dust and rubble from the invisible activity thirty floors up. At its foot, cement mixers endlessly churned in a wasteland of mud, heaped girders, timber, piping, monstrous cottonreels of coiled flex, a mountain of sand. Cranes swung with slow majesty. A man wheeling a barrow up a ramp seemed an archaic figure, out of place, a throwback.

Down in the site offices, Matthew became involved with the clerk of the works in a wrangle about non-delivery of essential materials. Tony Brace vanished with the site architect for a conducted tour. When they returned the wrangle was resolved, in so far as that was possible, and the site architect proposed a trip to the top of the building in the contractors' lift.

There is wind up here, that you would not have suspected from down below. It tilts their plastic helmets and induces a sudden surge of elation in these three men, who have seen all this before, but are struck with wonder, lording it over the city, which reaches further than the eye can see, swallowed eventually in haze on this bright spring morning: the tower blocks snapping light back at the sun, the muddle at their feet, the old symmetries of streets, tiny creeping cars and buses. In the distance the Tower; beyond it the complex density of the heartlands, punctuated by spires, by soaring columns, a rainbow in pink and grey and white on the skyline. It is a world—entire, complete.

They point out landmarks, exhilarated and possessive. It

is they, after all, who have made this possible—this new occupancy of space, this new claim upon London. They have added their mite—their tonnage of steel and concrete. The site architect is talking technology. Tony Brace peers into the haze in search of known points of reference.

But Matthew's eyes are upon the river. He looks down at the wide, glittering and empty roadway. He sees it reaching away to Tilbury, to the sea, to the rest of the globe. Reaching into time and space.

"The stars are given by God," says the uncle. "That men may find their way across the seas. Look, boy." And he lifts the child upon a stool. "Look carefully. Hold it thus." And the child holds the glass to his eye and sees a spark leap from the dark blue backcloth of the evening sky, and then another, and another. He steps back from the instrument, and the sparks vanish. There is just the sky, and the river, upon which craft are scattered like insects on a pond—twelve-legged, six-legged, and the two-legged skiffs that jostle in their dozens. But the boy gazes only at those with wings, the great, bellying butterfly wings that fill with wind, that take the vessels scudding downstream and out of sight.

TWO

"If you ask me," said Tony Brace, "this whole thing is a bubble that will burst. Docklands. I can see it empty in ten years' time. But it's no skin off our nose, I dare say."

"No doubt they said the same thing about the Bedford Estate, in its day. Stick streets and squares out there in the fields! You must be out of your mind! I'll drop you back at the office, shall I? I'm going straight on to Cobham Square."

"I'm somewhat peckish. Aren't you?"

"I'll stop off and get us a sandwich," said Matthew sternly. "It's going on for half past one already." Tony, a fastidious eater, sighed. Matthew, to placate and distract, made an enquiry about his colleague's own current project, an elegant and ingenious restoration and conversion of a disused late Victorian school building to a restaurant and wine bar. He half listened as Tony expanded upon the difficulties and solutions, thinking of the sour blackened brick of the place (scoured clean to a pristine rust once more), of pinafores and breeches and slates and a cramped, didactic but well-intentioned educational process. From books to claret; from learning to commerce. He thought of the unstoppable force of profit, of wealth flooding down decade by decade, a stream becoming a river, gushing through the city over centuries, bricks ripped down and rising again to the greater gain of Grosvenors and Bedfords, families fattening on houses and shops. People die, but money never does. Most people spend much of their lives thinking of nothing else; the stuff itself, indestructible, pours mindlessly onwards, throwing up streets and factories, obsessing both those who control it and those who crawl through stunted lives for lack of it.

"The problem is the windows. One wants to keep that leaded glass, but the light's bad. I'm toying with the idea of some kind of skylighting."

Matthew pulled in to the kerb. "Here we go. What do you want?"

"Beef," said Tony resignedly. "With mustard. Ham, failing that. Two rounds."

The sandwich counter was busy. Matthew had patronized it on other occasions for its efficiency and the convenient yellow line on which to park. A youth was giving a complicated order for, evidently, an entire office. A young woman in a red jacket waited her turn; Matthew took his place behind her. The order became ever more diversified and extensive. The girl in red half-turned, her glance met Matthew's, they exchanged smiles of complicity and endurance. She had short brown hair that lay in neat wings against each cheek, clear skin with a warm flush, an interesting tilt to the nose; white open-neck shirt, hands thrust into the pockets of the red jacket, a gold chain round the neck. All this Matthew registered with vague detached appreciation, thinking about wealth and poverty, about the light of the nineteenth century falling through leaded windows upon pinafored infants, about the sandwich order (two rounds of beef with mustard, one cheese and pickle, one egg and tomato). He saw a good-looking young woman with a smile that intensified the sense of solitude within which, these days, he lived. It was like seeing sunlight on a distant, inaccessible hillside. He looked sharply beyond her into the street, at passersby, at the traffic, at Tony waiting in the car. And when he turned back the smile was no longer directed upon him but upon the man behind the counter, to whom she was giving her order. Tuna salad; just one round.

"One-fifty."

She fished in her skirt pocket; froze. "Oh God—I came out without my purse."

Matthew stepped forward. "Please let me, then. Stick it on my order," he added, "Beef with mustard twice, please. Cheese. Egg and tomato."

"You can't do that," she said. "It's one-fifty."

"I shall think of it as one-fifty particularly well spent," said Matthew.

"I can't accept one-fifty from a total stranger."

"I don't know why not, really. Plenty would."

Her sandwich lay on the counter, neatly wrapped. She hesitated, then picked it up. And smiled. The sun blazing now on that hillside, gold upon green. "Thank you very much then. It's very nice of you. Goodbye." And was gone—visible briefly stepping away down the street, then blocked by others, cut down to a glimpse of red, until she vanished, swallowed up by the city, quite gone.

"That's six-fifty, then," the man grinned. "I could have offered to put it on the slate, of course. I thought you were going to ask for her address."

"Did you?" said Matthew coldly. He took out his wallet, paid, and returned to the car.

"Sorry to be so long. Here you are—beef with mustard. We'll chew as we go, if you don't mind. I told Jobson I'd be there by two."

*   *   *

19

When Matthew was a child he had watched the trains go by. He had hung over the fence at the bottom of the garden, waiting. The slow processional thump-thump of goods trains. The thrilling roar of the express. The busy to and fro of the commuter trains, with people's heads in profile and sometimes an observing pair of eyes, meeting his for a fraction of a second. The trains charged north; Doncaster, Newcastle, Edinburgh. He learned to recite the litany of names, thought of them as other Londons, up there, out there, with nothing but the shining railway track between. The row of houses was too close to the line, so that strangers stared casually at the intimacies of their back gardens: washing, children's toys, seedlings in a greenhouse. At night, the windows rattled. Matthew's parents, patiently, doggedly, scrimped and counted and put enough by for the move to the leafy suburb for which his mother had always yearned. Turn that light off; don't scuff your shoes; money doesn't grow on trees. When at last the move came his parents were breathless with the achievement, scarcely able to believe their luck. They tiptoed reverently around the pebble-dashed semi in the quiet side-street, with its tiled fireplace, primrose bathroom suite and varnished front door with stained glass yacht in a porthole inset, while Matthew mourned the trains.

He was the only child: their pride, their worry. Fresh vegetables, cod liver oil, clean shirts. Sedate people, cautious, alarmed by excess. Matthew excelled; he did well at school, was noticed, began to stray. He loved them, and fumed to be off. Nowadays, when he went back to that house, to his mother, he saw his childhood as though through the wrong end of a telescope: brilliant and diminished. The same people, the same place; his mother's lopsided smile, the oak settle in the hall, that vase. He saw himself: minute, unreachable. He saw his father: distinct, continuous, gone. His widowed mother sat in the same chair in which she had once knitted him school jerseys and pulled him towards her to measure the sleeve; he could feel her hands and his own irritation. He took Jane to visit her and she drank from the Mickey Mouse mug that had been his. You travelled through time and space to find that the world had caught up with you. "Where is Grandpa?" asks Jane. Grandpa is behind the glass of the photo on the mantelpiece, in his Royal Ordnance Corps uniform, in 1944, alongside the clock that they gave him when he retired from thirty years with Cooper Brothers of Enfield (clerical division). You cannot step twice into the same river, and yet you do. It has carried you away, and yet you stand on the bank, looking at the point of your own departure.

They had wanted him to be a doctor. Our son the doctor. He was a clever boy, and ought to do good in the world. They had a puritanical streak, and mistrusted display. They had brought him up to finish what was on his plate, speak nicely to the neighbours and get through his homework. Now he filled the house with Beatles music, had a girlfriend with her skirt barely covering her behind, and said he wanted to study architecture. They couldn't think where they'd gone wrong. Peering down the telescope, Matthew saw the shimmer of discord, of distress. From far away, his father's voice admonished: money never brought happiness to anyone, when you're born with brains you've a duty to make use of them. He associated architects with builders, with brash commerce, with turning a quick penny. His mother, looking in the opposite direction, saw artists starving in garrets, unemployment and ruin; she remembered the paintbox given one Christmas, and blamed herself. Matthew said (to his father) that architects seldom got rich, so far as he knew, and (to his mother) that it was more to do with maths and science than with art. Today, he found it difficult to trace the origins of the decision. A certain aptitude at draughtsmanship, an interest in how things are made (he had always liked taking objects apart, for the pleasure of reassembly). A gathering fascination with the variety and manipulation of landscape. He began to scrutinise buildings to see how they were put together and what they were made of. He saw that there are triumphs and disasters, and that someone is responsible. The idea formed that there was no reason why that someone should not be himself. Hitherto, almost the only architect he had ever heard of was Sir Christopher Wren. He was a rational youth and doubted if he was going to build cathedrals—you only had to look around you to see that the demand is not high—but the world has other needs. He improved his knowledge of the profession, identified the bottom rungs of the ladder, and pointed his life in a certain direction.

The first building on which he worked after he qualified was a school, the second a hospital, and his parents heaved sighs of relief. Also, he was patently hard up, and seemed likely to remain so. Their fears had been unfounded. The world needs schools and hospitals; our son the architect. ("That Docklands," says his mother. "Someone's making a mint of money down there, if you ask me. What d'you want to get mixed up with that for, then, Matthew?" She has a point. Oh, indeed she has a point.) And besides, the emphasis was changing, year by year. At the time, you were not aware—but peering down the telescope Matthew saw his parents move from the centre of the frame, shunted sideways, grown smaller. That watershed had been reached and passed, when one generation makes way for another. He and Susan, now, were the central figures and, presently, Jane. His parents sat on the periphery, commenting.

Susan. Wearing not a miniskirt because by then the fashion had changed, but something trailing and multi-coloured, with overtones of the Far East—to which Susan, hailing from Gloucestershire and Sussex University, has never been. The telescope showed this garment, and Susan's fair straight bobbed hair (longer these days, caught back at the nape, an

22

older woman's style) and her grey thoughtful eyes (which, today, seldom meet his, as they face each other on the doorstep, making necessary arrangements, no more and no less). The telescope showed her stepping up the path towards the varnished front door, on that first visit, observing, assessing. Matthew's parents, too, had assessed. They had perceived before ever she spoke that she was from an alien world, scenting differences from afar; courteous, uncompromising and wary. "She's a nice girl," Matthew's mother said later, but did not amplify.

His mother, who had her priorities right, and for whom, in the end, first things came first. Never mind that there'd always been the odd reservation ("Susan has her own way of doing things, I know that"); when the chips were down she could only anguish. Her eyes had pleaded, when he and Susan had visited in those last disintegrating days of their life together, when the pretence was being kept up that all might yet be well. Love one another, said his mother's eyes, be reasonable and love one another. To which he could only reply: we cannot. I'm sorry—dear God, am I not sorry?—but we cannot.

He had taken Jane, on a whim, to see the house from which he had watched the trains go by. Ignoring all British Rail's admonitions, they had scrambled over the fence at the end of the row of houses and made their way along the cindery strip of no-man's-land that separated the gardens from the track. "Here," he had said. "This one." And they had gazed down the long funnel of the garden. The back door had acquired a glassed-in porch, the coal-shed was gone, and the scabby apple tree. Jane was interested only in the hutch beside the back porch, in which something moved: "It's a rabbit. They've got rabbits. Did you have a rabbit?" "Certainly not," said Matthew. "Why not?" "Rabbits cost money." "Not *much* money. About two-fifty. Not as much as gerbils." "Money doesn't grow on trees," said Matthew. And then the train came, and they turned and flattened themselves against the fence, and Intercity hurtled past in a blur of red and white, aimed at King's Cross, at the city, at the heart of things.

It is 2.21, and Matthew Halland is at last reaching Cobham Square. It is also, in another sense, 1823, when the square was built, and when a considerable tonnage of bricks was hauled from brick fields not too far away and assembled into walls of Flemish bond, some shrouded in stucco, some not, most of which still stand precisely as they were constructed. Matthew drives around the square impatiently searching for a parking slot. It is 2.25 (and still 1823) when he finds one, locks up, and hurries towards the north side of the square, whose Flemish bond, stucco, porticoed entrances, fanlights and Coade stone surrounds are encased in scaffolding and green nylon netting. The pavement is an obstacle course of cement mixers and skips; a large notice across the front of the scaffolding declares that Gresham Associates regret the inconvenience caused, mentioning also that 25,000 square feet of office space will be available, leasehold, in the spring of next year. Graffiti have been spray-painted along the foot of the notice: SKINS OK KEV AND SID WOZ ERE TERRY 14/3/89. Matthew, who is a connoisseur of graffiti, notes them: nothing very recondite, though the CND sign is new and quite rare, and DOZY MARGE interestingly cryptic. The scrawled fantasies and assertions of a disembodied crowd, shouts of defiance and of egotism, the silent insistent clamour of an invisible horde, not quite unheard, not quite extinguished, their purpose eerily fulfilled. They were indeed here, once, and are still.

For this is the city, in which everything is simultaneous. There is no yesterday, nor tomorrow, merely weather, and decay, and construction. And the passage of hoofs, wheels and feet, the path of fire, the blast of bombs. The city digests itself, and regurgitates. It melts away, and rears up once more in another form. People die, and die, and die again, and from the graveyard float forth reminders and warnings and recommendations. They sift through the place in their millions, leaving this sediment of brick and stone, the unquenchable testimony of their existence by way of pediments and cornices, statues of men on horseback and women in draperies and admirals on the tops of columns. And initials gouged into balustrades or words sprayed onto a wall.

"Sorry. I was held up at our Docklands site."

"Ah," said Jobson. "The never-never land. If you ask me that whole set-up's a . . ."

"Bubble that could burst. Oh, I dare say. And a lot of people are making a mint of money."

"Including James Gamlin and Partners." Jobson laughed, explosively, making passers-by turn their heads. He was a big man, huge in his working boiler-suit, with a voice that could carry up five floors. He ran the site on towering energy and an invincible technical knowledge. Matthew respected him and sparred with him.

"True. But I'd rather do this sort of thing, on the whole." The two men stood in front of the scaffolded terrace, looking up to the roof-line where a man unloaded Welsh slates from a pulley. "That slate came, then?"

"In the bloody end it came. The first lot they sent was rubbish—all had to go back."

"The original roof probably came from the same quarries," said Matthew.

"That so? Well, what we're putting up now will see out the next hundred years. More than I can say for your glass-houses down in Docklands."

"You could well be right. Which is what's satisfactory about this sort of job. My mother used to do something with clothes called making over—turning collars and cuffs inside out, putting in new elbows. We're making over."

"We're making money, too," said Jobson, and roared again. "Making money for other people, that is."

"We're also keeping the place ticking over. Why don't we just pull the lot down and start again, after all?"

"Because of the bloody planning laws." Jobson, momentarily distracted, broke off to interrogate a driver unloading timber. "Talking of which, we've got a real headache with that stair balustrade—you'd better come and have a look."

Matthew continued to stand in front of the building. "This is a pile of bricks. Carefully arranged bricks, I grant you, but a pile of bricks none the less. You may call it a late Georgian house with a neo-classical portico and Coade stone dressings. Others might just call it a house. A Martian would call it a pile of bricks, if he had got as far as identifying a pile or a brick. You can take it to pieces in order to build something else with the bricks. You can pull it down in order to use the space it occupies for another building. Or you can give it a new significance because you have stopped thinking about it as simply a pile of bricks. This is what we're doing."

"I'll tell you what I think of it as," said Jobson. "My bloody wage-packet, that's what. And so do you—never mind all that hoo-ha."

"Oh, quite. So did the lot who ran up this square. The likes of you and me. The last thing they had in mind was immortality, I should imagine."

"They didn't do a bad job. Though they could have left out the Coade stone—looks like bloody fossilized brains, if you ask me."

"It was the last word in architectural chic, at the time. OK—let's have a think about that balustrade, for starters."

They went into the building, which vibrated to a heavy drill somewhere overhead. Cement flooring was being relaid.

Dust hung in clouds. "Another thing," said Jobson. "I'm not happy about that party wall at the far end. I want to have it out after all—it looks dodgy as hell to me. Of course all this lot were war-damaged. Those two at the end were a pretty ropy job. Anyway . . . what do we do about this ruddy balustrade?"

The problem with the balustrade, constructed in 1823 along with the building, is that it is not acceptable to the planning office at the Town Hall. It has been indeed, for many a long year, an illegal balustrade. Its elegant curved iron uprights are two inches further apart than the maximum permitted distance; a child could get its head through there. Jobson runs up and down with a steel measure, irritably demonstrating. "Inch and a bloody half, more like. Why the silly bastards can't turn a blind eye . . ."

"Just nip out and find us a passing child," said Matthew. "Two years old or so will do nicely. Of course, children were considered more expendable in the nineteenth century. Look, I'll go along to the Town Hall tomorrow and see if I can talk them round. If not . . ."

They stand, the two men, in the dust-hung shell of the building, debating the problem of the balustrade. The place has been stripped to its bones, reduced to a frame of brick which still shows, on the inside, the soot-stained column of old fireplaces. The embattled staircase sweeps down from the first floor, which survives only as joists and makeshift boarding. Here and there you can see right up through four storeys to the roof. A West Indian is pouring concrete for what will one day be once more the entrance hall; reggae music crashes from a cassette player. Someone has scrawled the date in the wet concrete—10/5/89—and a crude cartoon outline of a horse's head; the West Indian, maybe, who wears a T-shirt on which capers a pink horse wearing a daisy-chain. His logo, perhaps, his sign, his "I am here." He looks up at Matthew, and grins.

And Matthew, grinning back—a mute exchange in the throbbing screeching building—hears an echo beyond the din, receives the silent signals of the place.

Coming into the square, Jim Prothero sees that the trees have almost lost their leaves. He stands for a moment, tired at the end of his day, the noise of the print works still ringing in his ears, and sees the sparse branches, with the small blunt buds from which, eventually, spring will come. The world is turning still, here in the dishevelled stricken city. There is glass over the road, where windows were blown out last night, and a crater in the next street where the UXB fell a month ago, but the leaves are falling.

The front door of the house stands open; the entrance hall is a clutter of prams and bicycles. Twenty people live here, or did, stacked above and alongside each other in the tall house whose big rooms have been sliced up and pared down to meet the requirements of the age. The Protheros' kitchen is graced with half of an ornate plaster ceiling rose, the rest of it swallowed up into the flat next door. The place is a rabbit-warren of plaster-board partitions and dark passageways; the panel of bells at the entrance bristles with scruffy hand-scrawled name-cards. People come and go, these days; those who have fled lend their flats to relatives, friends, acquaintances. Dozens pass through, stop over, disappear. Goodness knows who may be here, on any one night; a warden's nightmare, as Jim often thinks.

The stairwell is dark, the windows boarded up where the glass blew out last month. He gropes his way up, smelling cabbage from old Mrs Hanson's and something rank from the O'Connors and then toast from his own front door. Mary is giving the child her tea. And he sees, for an instant, in the mind's eye, before ever he goes in, the two of them, his people, his world, and is uplifted.

And later he sits on the sagging cretonne sofa with his wife, and lets the day ebb from him. Another hour, and he must go off down to Aldgate, to his warden's post, but this brief hinge between day and night is his, is theirs. It is quiet. Somewhere a wireless chatters; a solitary car passes. The child is painting; her brush swishes on the paper. They watch her— amused, admiring. "I'm thinking a horse," the child says. Her tongue sticks out in concentration, she scowls over the sheet of grocers' paper and the tray of poster paints. She is attempting the impossible. She is trying to translate what is in the head, that essence of horse that she knows so well, into line and shape. She is having trouble with scale: head is eclipsed by body, the ears have grown disproportionately. The legs are a large problem: there must be four, but how to dispose them? In a row? She dabs angrily with the blue-loaded brush (and why should a horse not be blue?). There is something amiss with legs-in-a-row; the horse in the child's head and the horse she has created do not tally. She cries out in frustration, unable to translate the moving, shining, kicking maelstrom of horses-in-the-head into this wilful recalcitrant horse upon a sheet of paper. She is in the grip of an ancient, abiding and crucial predicament. The distant wireless is playing brass band music; the light is fading, her father has moved to the window, and stands looking again at the drifting leaves.

Three twenty-eight (and 1823) as Matthew Halland gets back into his car in Cobham Square, and starts the engine, gazing as he does so at the great trunk of one of the planes which soar from the garden in the centre: *Platanus X hispanica* Muenchh, the London plane, an immigrant, appropriately, first reaching this country in the late seventeenth century. And doing well, thrusting its roots down into the sour London soil, living off brick dust and cinders, drinking up lead emission and carbon monoxide. *Platanus X hispanica* Muenchh has seen off smogs and soot and will no doubt learn to cope with acid rain—the archetypal adaptor and survivor, taking advantage of its own convenient attributes of a short season in leaf and a glossy leaf surface easily washed clean by rain. Matthew, though, is thinking not of this but that its trunk has the subtleties of an abstract painting—a Braque perhaps—with its patching of peeled bark, yellow, fawn, grey and brown. He looks at the trunk of a tree and is referred at once to a different image, another set of signals; one vision triggers another, in the complex and unique network that is within his head. He is not especially interested in Braque, and cannot recall where or when he last saw a Braque painting—but there it is. The London plane has done its stuff, has served as the prompt whereby the physical world is not just itself but the shadow of a thousand things, is unique to each of us, is a code, a key, a chronicle.

And so, his head filled with Braque, with a Georgian stair balustrade, with Martin Frobisher, with stars and the moon, with his parents, with his child, Matthew slots himself once again into the moving city. He has travelled already today, through time and space, is so many hours older (has grown hair, has sloughed skin), has covered so many miles of tarmac, has set eyes on so many hundred fellow beings, has exchanged words or glances with a few. He heads now for his office, to clear up the day's work, to finish with time in which he is at the disposal of others and enter time that belongs to him.

Thus, seven hours later, he rolls off the body of Alice Cook and lies beside her: spent, somnolent. "Drink?" enquires Alice, companionably, too soon, and Matthew pulls himself together, remembers his manners, and replies that yes, he will have a quick drink. It is late; he will not stay the night; he never does. Alice would not wish it, and nor does he. He lays a hand on her thigh—to propitiate, to quell—but Alice is already bouncing from the bed, into the bathroom, fixing herself up, heading for the kitchen. She will bring him a whisky, with too much water in it.

Matthew dresses, in Alice Cook's bedroom. He has known Alice for many years. She was a friend of Susan's and still is, probably, in a tenuous way. It would never have occurred to him, back then, to make love to Alice, and he only does so now, if the facts are faced, at her suggestion, and out of apathy, availability and need. Alice is a physiotherapist: brisk, self-sufficient and unimaginative. Matthew likes her and, in a curious way, envies her. Alice, at this moment, pouring drinks in the kitchen, is not experiencing the twinge of bleakness that Matthew is experiencing. Alice has short black curly hair, a trim body in the best of health, and many friends to whom she talks noisily on the telephone (sometimes from the bed, when Matthew is in it). She is probably happy. Matthew appreciates Alice's body—indeed at times he lusts after it—but there is a businesslike quality to her lovemaking that has always disturbed him; it is as though she were ingesting a glass of tonic wine. As soon as he has gone, Alice will fall into a deep, untroubled sleep until her alarm wakes her at seven.

Alice returns, with the whisky (which has too much water) and a fruit juice for herself. She sets her alarm, talking about a power struggle between doctors at the hospital at which she works. Matthew drinks his whisky, while putting on his socks. Alice has got back into bed. Matthew has never told Alice that he loves her, nor has she required it. What is between them is not love, but something cordial, mutually sustaining, that can be taken up or relinquished at will, without obligation. It is better than nothing, and entirely unsatisfactory to any who have known better.

THREE

Frobisher House?" said the client. "I'll talk to my Board. I don't see why not—it might be quite a nice gimmick. And a nautical theme for the décor. Yes, I like it."

The client had a name, of course: Charles Sanderling. Matthew thought of him, though, more than of most, as The Client. Their relationship was bleached of any personal flavour. At a working meal such as this one, in a Covent Garden restaurant, they would carry out a ritual three-minute exchange about weather, or current events, and then proceed to business. Business, today, had come to an end, along with the lunch.

"Brandy?" enquired Sanderling: "No? Nor me. Two coffees. Rather quickly, if you could." He had a face as thin as a chopper across which glimmered now, for the waitress, an admonitory smile. Matthew could see, outside, the shining bulk of his chauffeur-driven car, partly blocking the narrow street. Sanderling's time was parcelled out in quarter-hours, bespoken weeks ahead; you could feel its value, as the minutes ticked by in his company. It could not be wasted, nor treated lightly with unproductive conversation. Behind Sanderling was a Group, a hierarchy of other men and women with lightly tanned faces, groomed, polished and glowing with good health, conveying a sense of impregnability and purpose. And behind the Group was money, pure and simple, flickering in green figures on VDUs, stacked up in columns on print-outs, assessed and quantified in sheets of newsprint.

A few nickels of which were disposed of now, as Sanderling signed the bill. He held the door open for Matthew: "Can I drop you anywhere?"

"No, thanks," said Matthew, as he always did, and as Sanderling had known he would. The car slid away into Drury Lane and Matthew walked off in the opposite direction, heading for Soho and Meard Street where he had to look at a couple of decaying Georgian houses under consideration by a potential client for a restoration venture.

First, though, he would allow himself time for a stroll around and a few small shopping errands. He liked Covent Garden. You could not but warm to an area that had so successfully been reborn. The place teemed with people, on this warm spring afternoon. It was international, multi-cultural, eclectic—it was all the things you were supposed to be, in this day and age. It was ecologically-minded (he could have bought a T-shirt that said Protect the Rain Forests, or an umbrella protesting against Acid Rain) and deeply involved with organic foods. Matthew's first purchases were a half pound of goat's cheese from Somerset and some of the unpasteurized yoghurt favoured by Alice Cook. He could also, a hundred yards away, have indulged rather more dubiously in a dried sea-horse or a large conch shell. For of course Covent Garden was also doing what it had always done: selling things. And you sell what people will buy, be it environmentally beneficial eatables or the mummified remains of an endangered species. You could buy, here, Japanese teapots, Indian dhurries, Tibetan prayer wheels, baskets from Hong Kong, silverware from Mexico, clothing from everywhere. You could buy a Margaret Thatcher toby jug or a Ronald Reagan mask or a Michael Jackson poster. You could buy a £500 leather jacket or a £2,000 gold necklace or a tropical fish (Golden Gourami—£3, Lemon Tetra—five for £3.50). Matthew bought a Chinese kite for Jane. He considered and rejected a bamboo flute from the Philippines. He browsed in a bookshop and came out with novels by Gabriel García Márquez and Italo Calvino. He heard half a dozen languages spoken, brushed against French schoolchildren, Scandinavian girls with backpacks, American matrons. He went into the map shop in search of the Ordnance Survey sheet for the Sussex Downs (he intended introducing Jane to the pleasures of long-distance walks, before too long) and was sidetracked by an elegant reissue of the Victorian street map of the city. He turned the pages over, seeking out familiar territories. Here was the Isle of Dogs: East India Dock, Canary Wharf, Millwall. And here was Covent Garden: the precinct, Seven Dials, the same grid-pattern, the same names—Shelton Street, Parker Street, Macklin Street.

He made a quick foray down into the precinct, listened for a couple of minutes to violinists playing a Mozart duet in the forecourt, bought a half pound of Colombian coffee beans. And then was transfixed for a moment by a flower stall—blooming with colour and scent, a luxuriant symposium of tulips, irises, mimosa, gypsophila, lilies, stocks. And, in the front, little posies of violets. "I'll have one of those," said Matthew for no reason at all, except that the violets seemed to bear some freight of reference. And walked away down Floral Street with violets in his hand.

She can smell violets. And dung and sewage and the strong pervading stench of unwashed humanity. But these are the nameless components of the element through which she moves, churning fickle stuff which is also smoke and fog and rain—

rich, raw, cruel and inescapable. She is less than four feet high, and close to the gutter, which is to her advantage. She can dart for a fallen potato, or a cabbage leaf. She can snuff the buns on a baker's tray and, once in a while, snatch one up with a quicksilver, heart-thumping movement. She can scour the mud and the garbage for that other miracle of a dropped coin. There is treasure, down here.

Up above there is the driving purpose of the place: the logjam of carts, beasts, men and women. The stacks of cauli-flower, carrots, broccoli, rhubarb, oranges, lemons; the fra-grant caverns of stocks, wallflowers, roses, carnations, lilies of the valley, mignonette. A catalogue of elsewhere; a chronicle of suggestion.

The child does not know of elsewhere. She could recite the litany of names—language bombards her, she drinks it in without inspection, it is a feature of her element, like the fog or the dirt—but they are sounds, and that is all. They evoke faces and places: the orange-seller who will give her a rotten fruit, that corner of the market where she is struck by gusts of wind laden with the scent of stocks.

She is a pair of eyes and ears, concentrated upon survival. She is also a yawning belly, ice-cold hands and feet, and a crawling skin, but since she has known nothing else she dis-regards these, in so far as it is possible, just as she disregards the rain, the mud, the noise of wheels and hoofs. She knows that her name is Rose, and she knows the year, and sometimes the month, but she does not know how old she is. She knows only that she has always been here, and supposes that she always will be.

Matthew turned into a stationer's in Long Acre for a pen. Waiting at the cash desk, he glanced up and saw, looking in at the window, the girl from the sandwich bar. Or was it? For, once he had paid and hurried out into the street, with a curious upsurge of pleasure, still clutching his violets, there was no longer anyone in sight who resembled her. He stood for a moment searching the street. So? A million to one chance, that the city throws two people thus together twice. And what if it had been? But there was again, for a few seconds, that glimpse of sunlight.

Waiting to cross Charing Cross Road, he forgot her. He walked up Romilly Street gazing at the white clock-tower of St Anne's Soho. The weathervane swung, glinting gold. The former churchyard was screened off by high hoardings, beyond which bulldozers roared. Matthew stopped to peer through the peephole in the woodwork, to find himself eyeball to eyeball with a helmeted construction worker, who opened the gate. "Looking for someone?"

"No. Just curious." There was a wasteland of mud, the bulldozers backing and biting. "What's all this going to be?"

"Paved precinct. Shops and that. We're taking the bodies out."

"Bodies?"

"Churchyard. Thousands of them."

"Where will they go?"

"They're to be re-interred in a big cemetery out Wembley direction."

"Ah," said Matthew. "Glad to hear it."

He headed on into Soho, moving within fifty yards from one landscape to another, crossing one of those invisible frontiers which section the city off into areas, each with its own flavour, its own climate. Festival of Erotica. Eros Books. Pastrami Bar. Double Act Bed show. Cheapo Cheapo Records. Over-18 Cinema. The whole place smelled of food: roasting chicken, frying onions, garlic. Pigeons picked over refuse outside a take-away kebab bar. The classier restaurants displayed menus framed with the reverence due to masterpieces of calligraphy. On a corner stood a derelict in a grimy raincoat, his skin dirt-veiled, blackened trainers on his feet, plastic carrier bag in his hand: See Buy Fly—Amsterdam Airport Shopping Centre.

In Berwick Street market Matthew made further purchases: an avocado and a mango. He hovered in front of a shop selling outrageous toys, and eventually plumped for an imitation dog turd, which would suit Jane's present scatological turn of mind. Outside the shop a balloon skeleton jounced in the wind, white bulbous limbs with stark black painted ribs, skull, femurs and tibia.

He was by now quite laden. The violets were becoming something of a problem. He shifted them from hand to hand, tucked them in one of his carrier bags, where they got squashed, and then took them out again. He had arrived in Meard Street, and stood in contemplation of the Georgian houses, which clung precariously to life, displaying cracks, subsidence, decay of every kind. He took out a pad and made some notes. He thought about eighteenth-century brick, about steel pinning, about money.

One of the houses was in use as offices. A middle-aged woman came out, riffling through a handful of letters, her face puckered in a frown of harassment and concentration that reminded Matthew suddenly of his mother. He stepped forward and held out the violets: "Please may I give you these?"

She stared at the flowers, then at him. "Look, what are you after?"

"I'm not after anything. I'd just like you to have these violets."

"You're some sort of nut, aren't you?" said the woman angrily, and walked off.

Well, if you accost women in the middle of Soho, even today, you are liable to be misconstrued. He put the violets back into the carrier bag and set off for the tube station.

When he was eight or nine his father had warned him against strange men. They had been walking past the little cluster of shops on the main road, and his father paused suddenly outside the tobacconist: "If a bloke ever offers you sweets and that, Matthew, you just push off sharp, do you understand?" Matthew, perplexed, had asked why anyone should do such a thing. Random generosity, in his experience, was rare. "Because," said his father, succinctly. And the matter was closed. When Matthew raised it with cronies at primary school the general feeling was that the sweets might be poisoned; all accepted this as a natural hazard, without questioning why people should wish to poison children. Matthew, conditioned by the black and white vision of his parents, divided the world into good and bad, but badness was a simple matter of theft, telling lies and making an exhibition of yourself. Beyond, admittedly, was a grey area of unspoken and mysterious transgression hinted at by the headlines and photographs in the sort of newspaper banned from the house. Somewhere out there people were sticking knives into naked torsos, defrocked clergymen raped chorus girls. It was all unmentionable and as remote as the lives of that other élite featured in newspapers: the rich. For this was the 1950s. Lady Docker stepped from gold-plated Rolls Royces, aristocratic brides beamed at admiring crowds from the porch of St Margaret's, Westminster. As Matthew grew up he was to see both these obscure but titillating worlds become tawdry realities. There is vice, he realized, and there is sex, and the two are by no means necessarily linked. There are indeed the rich, who are distinguished from others only by fatter wallets. He learned cynicism, discrimination, and indignation. His parents, to be fair, had always been possessed of all three. They were offended by gratuitous display of any kind, by fecklessness and by obscenity. Their defence had been to ignore, with dignified contempt, those aspects of society of which they disapproved. If you read a decent newspaper the naked torsos and rapist clergymen were no threat; the Lady Dockers of this world would no doubt get their comeuppance if left to their own devices. "If you keep your nose clean, young Matthew," his father advised, "you'll find everything usually works out all right."

Perfectly respectable counselling, father to son. It does not, of course, take into account the brutal intrusions of public events or the more insidious influence of a person's own inner drives. Matthew, requiring more of life than had his parents, and taking a more pugnacious attitude towards reversals, came up against both. In the Sixties, as an adolescent, he fell briefly prey to the tawdry aspect of a permissive climate and played about with drugs. In the Seventies, he became more worthily involved with the climate of the times and demonstrated against the American involvement in Vietnam. The first episode was unsuspected by his parents. The second irritated and perplexed them. "The Yanks'll go their own sweet way," said his father. "Them and the Russkies. The best any of us can hope for is to keep out of it. What do you think you're going to achieve?" His mother pointed out that he was allying himself with people who had thrown marbles under the hoofs of police horses, which could not be right. Matthew, trying to meet both objections and remain on good terms with his parents, tied himself into knots.

If you spend your entire adult life within the confines— or the freedoms—of a politically stable country in peacetime the demands and challenges of history tend to be eclipsed by those of private life. Matthew's taste for public affairs was sharp enough, along with his capacity for outrage, but by the time he was thirty work and home life had him by the throat. He parted company, acrimoniously, with the first architectural firm for which he worked, feeling his ideas to be insufficiently appreciated. "Are you being bolshie, Matthew?" enquired his mother suspiciously. "You've always been a bit that way." "No," he said. "They are." His father, with a sudden and uncharacteristic abandonment of caution, backed him up. So, less surprisingly, did Susan. Matthew landed a better job elsewhere.

Susan. Who is both now and then. Who is both the cool and distant Susan with whom he exchanges brief and necessary words on the telephone or over Jane's head, and the lost and vanished Susan whom once he loved to distraction. In his bleakest moments, these days, it seemed to him that the death of feeling is more hideous even than the death of persons. He could cope better, he thought, with a Susan who had died, loved and loving, than a Susan who had survived the extinction of his love, and of hers. Forever, now, there would be superimposed upon the Susan he saw and spoke to that smiling, intimate shadow-Susan of another time. She came to him in his dreams. She arrived suddenly in his head as he worked, and said something she had said ten years ago. Most painful of all, she looked at him, for a split second, out of Jane's eyes. He saw her in the tilt of Jane's mouth, in the curl of Jane's nostril.

"Can I have a Cornetto?" says Jane.

"Not on the boat *and* at Greenwich. One or the other."

She pulls a face, and settles finally for anticipation. They install themselves on the top deck, for the better view. Jane keeps wanting to move to a yet more advantageous position until eventually Matthew calls a halt. They agree on the left-hand side ("Port," says Matthew, "we're at sea." "At river," corrects Jane) and admire Boadicea, with her rearing black horses alongside Westminster Bridge. Jane wants to know why there aren't any other boats, and indeed it is true, the river flows wide and empty save for a busybody police vessel buzzing to and fro and some sleek capsule purring off to the City

Airport. The only vessels moored to the banks are, it seems, nightclubs or restaurants. "That's not proper boats," says Jane, disgusted. But presently there are gulls, and interesting refuse in the water and the archaic splendour of Billingsgate fish market. "Fish! Yuck!" says Jane. "I don't like fish. Not even fish fingers, any more." And the castle fantasy of Tower Bridge and soon the delicate forestry of cranes that marks the Isle of Dogs. Jane kneels up on her chair, her nose to the glass. She is wearing blue denim dungarees, sweater, anorak, and new green trainers of which she is inordinately proud. Her fair hair is scraped back into a ponytail from which tendrils constantly escape to curl against her neck. Matthew finds these peculiarly disarming; observing them, covertly, he can experience an almost unendurable wash of tenderness. The ponytail is held by a pink plastic clip which Jane persuaded him to buy a couple of weeks ago. Susan, he has learned, detests the clip; nevertheless, Jane is wearing it. He decides not to ponder the significance of this.

The boat is crowded with tourists, both foreign and indigenous. The skipper—or someone—gives a commentary over the tannoy as they go. They are told about St Katharine's Dock and about St Mary's Rotherhithe, where the captain of the *Mayflower* lies buried. The commentary is laced with the occasional pungent joke. The pound coin is usually called a Thatcher because it's thick, brassy and thinks it's a sovereign. The American tourists titter but are patently embarrassed. Are they disturbed by the irreverence or afraid to give offence by conniving at it? "Is that funny?" enquires Jane. "Actually, it is quite," says Matthew.

They have rounded the curve of the Isle of Dogs. Matthew is able to pick out, in the far distance, the blue patchwork glitter of the Blackwall building. Jane is impressed. She thinks it would be more striking yet if the glass were pink. "We'll bear it in mind for next time," says Matthew.

She yawns. "What are we going to do when we get to Greenwich?"

"We're going first to the big museum there so that I can find a picture of a ship."

"One like this?"

"Certainly not," says Matthew. "A real ship. An old-fashioned ship with sails."

"What for?"

"Because when I've found the right one I'm going to ask someone I know about to make another picture of it in glass. That's called a glass engraving. And it's going to go over the front door of the blue glass building."

"Why?"

"Because more than four hundred years ago a man called Martin Frobisher sailed from just about where the building is to the Arctic in a ship like that."

"There are whales at the Arctic," says Jane.

"There are indeed. And seals and polar bears."

"It's cruel to kill whales," says Jane, a child of her time. "Did he kill whales?"

"I don't think so. He went there when there were no maps and nobody really knew what there was there. It was all ice and snow."

"Can I have the Cornetto *before* the museum?" says Jane.

"Probably. I'm telling you interesting things," Matthew admonishes. "I'm telling you about this man Martin Frobisher sailing to the Arctic."

"Why did he?" says Jane, scribbling with her finger in a puddle of spilled drink upon the table.

"Because he thought there was gold there, partly. Because he wanted to get rich."

"Why?" drones Jane.

"You may well ask. Because there are always people who

want to get rich. Because a lot of other people egged him on, so that they could get rich too."

But Jane has lost interest. "Look," she says. "I'm drawing a ship. These are the sails." Matthew is left alone with Martin Frobisher and the Arctic, here, there, and four hundred and thirteen years ago.

Martin Furbissher, Ffourbyssher, Frobusher. Write it as you will—but he will leave it here, tacked forever to this inhospitable place, to this treacherous sheet of water. Frobisshers Streights; West Ingland; Cape Walsingham. In the meantime . . . Where are the stars? he cries. He howls to the shuttered skies, the blank and freezing skies that offer not a spark, not a glimmer, no Orion nor Cassiopeia. No Arcturus. No Polaris. The ship spins, becalmed, adrift in a featureless sphere. There is up and there is down; there is north and south and east and west. But there is no here, and no there; they are untethered. Where are the stars?

"We're there," says Jane. "Come on. First we'll find the Cornetto and then we'll go to the museum and find your boat. Right?" She slips her hand into his, ingratiating. When they are ashore she skips, charged with life. She comes to a sudden halt. "I've got a loose tooth," she says. "Feel." She yanks down a lip, offers a rose pink gum. "Later," says Matthew. She points: "There's a ship. A real one. Is that like you want?" He replies that no, that is the *Cutty Sark*, a tea clipper, of another time and place. "I like it," says Jane.

They achieve the Cornetto. Jane is very silent for quite a while. Then, in the park, she does handstands. She wants Matthew to do handstands. "I can't. I'm too old." "You did once," she protests. "On the beach that time." And so he did, he recalls; in both their heads is a summer afternoon, in Cornwall, on another plane of existence. A boy with a kite. Dogs skit-

44

tering in the surf. Susan unpacking a picnic basket. "You were only six," says Matthew. "I'm surprised you remember." And she lifts her face to look at him; "I remember," she says. And he is gripped with unbearable compunction. "Look," he says. "That's the Observatory up there. They have telescopes and things. We'll go there after the museum, if there's time."

Meta Incognita. Out there somewhere in that white fog. *Incognita* indeed. The frozen shores that are paved with gold, which by God's will and pleasure will enrich the nation, Her Majesty and Martin Frobisher. The road to Cathay. Which he will seek out in due course, Martin Frobisher, Admiral of Cathay. But first to make landfall in this hellish *Ultima Thule*, where the men's hands freeze to the rigging, where great islands of ice surge from the white walls within which the vessel spins, and rush down upon it. Where the waters run with fish, and great whales swim. Where the wind roars and snow falls and this, by God, is summer. No man but a fool would come here, unless it were for fame or fortune.

Fifteen ships. The *Thomas Allen*, the *Judith*, the *Thomas of Ipswich*, the *Dennis*, the *Buss of Bridgewater*. Their crews: men, boys. A great carte of navigation at a cost of £5. A great map of Mercator in print. Six cartes of navigation written in black parchment whereof four ruled plain and two round. A cosmographical glass. Twenty compasses of divers sorts. An astrolabum.

"You're not *listening*," she cries. "I said what's that thing for?" She breathes on the glass case, draws a J for Jane in the fog she has made.

"It's an instrument people used to use at sea for finding which direction to go by measuring the position of the sun or the stars."

Jane sighs, massively. "I'm feeling just a little bit sick."

"I told you a second helping of chips wouldn't be a good idea," says Matthew.

"Not *very* sick. Shall we go into the park again? You said you thought there were swings somewhere."

"In a minute," says Matthew. "I want to look round here a bit."

"Why do you?"

"Because it's interesting." There is an edge to Matthew's voice. Jane trails behind him. She scuffs her new trainers on the floor. She swings on a guard rail. "I don't think you should do that," says Matthew. "The attendant's watching you." Jane subsides. She falls in beside her father, a wary eye on the attendant. "Look," says Matthew. "This is a map of the stars. They have names—they've had the same names for hundreds of years. That's Sirius, and that's Polaris, the North Star, and that's Betelgeuse."

"Beetle juice," says Jane. "Silly." She is on the brink of a sulk.

Matthew puts a hand on her shoulder. She makes a half-hearted attempt to shake it off. "Astronomers used to arrange them into patterns, called constellations, and they have names too. There's Orion—the Hunter—and the Plough, which some people call the Great Bear."

"It isn't a bit like a bear."

"In America they call it the Big Dipper. A saucepan. It does look more like a saucepan."

"How can they have got it in America too?" she asks, after a moment. And Matthew, rewarded, explains. At too great length, losing her, so that she drifts off to exchange furtive stares with a child her own age, at the far end of the room, leaving him once more to the inconsequential sequences of his own mind, to an afternoon on a beach in Cornwall, to the terrifying certainty of the stars.

An instrument of brass named *Sphera Nautica* at four pounds six shillings and eightpence. A ring of brass, *annulus Astronomica*. Medicines; viz. *Ambra grisi Oriental, Rubarbi agavise, Turpenti, Calan aromatica* . . . A sea card.

The sea card over which he pores in the tossing stinking cabin, amid the groan of timbers cut in Hampshire, to the flicker of a lantern made in Bow, all suspended there at God knows where. He needs the latitude; he needs a coast. The sea card is a spider web of lines (etched upon the skin of a sheep that once grazed the Berkshire Downs), crisscrossing a waste on which are scrawled, here and there, the uncertain black fringes of coasts that may or may not exist. The sea card is a talisman, a hostage to fortune, a siren voice. He will leave his own mark upon that void, God willing, his own black scribbles to fill in the empty quarter of the globe.

Order and disorder. The order of the heavens, of the points of the compass, of the laws of navigation. The disorder of the world, which is made of wind and rain, rock and water, snow, ice and fog. Which is made of worm-eaten timbers, snapping sails, hemp and iron. Of seals and white bears, seamews, gulls, porpoises. Of foul-mouthed unquenchable seamen, raw brash boys and his own uncertain temper which surges now as he pounds up on deck to survey the awful blank yet again.

And sees beyond and behind the fog a glow, a glimmer, as of the risen Christ. The sun.

"What time is it?" she asks.

"Nearly five. There's a boat at half past—we'd better get that one."

"Why are days different?" Jane enquires after a moment.

"In what way different?"

"Some days are long days and some days are short days. This is a short day."

"Ah," says Matthew. "I see what you mean. I suppose it's that when you're busy, or enjoying yourself, time goes more quickly."

There is a further reflective pause. "Where does it go?" continues Jane.

"Ah." Now it is Matthew who is silent. They are walking beside the river. He looks at the slow swollen flow of the water, at the glitter of the Isle of Dogs beyond. He sees, and also thinks. "Well," he says eventually, "I suppose there's a sense in which it doesn't go at all. Things that have happened are always there, so long as someone knows about them."

"But where do *hours* go?" Jane persists. "And minutes? There's sixty minutes in an hour. And sixty seconds in a minute."

"Do you really want to know?" says Matthew, halting.

Jane, too, halts. "Yes."

"If you're wearing a watch they keep coming out all the time, rather like seeds, and they collect under the glass . . . if you look carefully you can just see them . . . Can you?" He extends his wrist and Jane peers intently at his watch. "And then every so often you have to clean them out. Once a week or so. The same with clocks. And of course the bigger the clock the more of a business it is. They have an awful job with Big Ben. They send men up with buckets, on the first of January every year."

Jane continues to stare into the watch. "I can't see them."

"Dear me," says Matthew. "Perhaps you need glasses. We shall have to fix up an eye test. I can see them perfectly well—those little green specks."

Jane looks up at him. Her expression changes. "It's not *true*," she yells. "You're *teasing* me." And she flings herself at him, butting him in the stomach, her giggles are tinged with anger, they skirmish on the riverside until he lets her push him over and roll him on a patch of grass.

He gets up, hauls her to her feet. "We're making an exhibition of ourselves," he says. "And we're going to miss the boat."

They inhabit time and space. Within the vessel, the hourglass measures out the day, charts the watches, imposes a frail order. Beyond is the space over which they have no control, which shrinks to a wall of fog or comes swirling upon them in cliffs of ice. It is as though these roaring black waters were scattered with great fallen pieces of the moon. He clutches the deck rail and stares now upon one such, sees in its glassy surface caverns and grottoes, caught by the setting sun, flaming with rose and gold. He is wild with sleeplessness, with the awe and horror of the place. He wipes a hand across his face, the ice flames again and now he sees castles, ramparts, pinnacles, and spires. He sees a golden tower, the tower of a cathedral, and is transported, is flown across the globe. He sees the towers of St Paul's, glowing in the evening sunlight beside the river. The world shrinks, within his head, time and space collide. And then the wind shifts, the sails crack and he goes running for the wheelhouse.

FOUR

A cathedral in the ice; a city of the mind. We are hosts to the physical world, the transient purveyors of sequence upon sequence of references. Language sleeps upon the tongue, mutates through generations, survives us all. We see the world, invest what we see with meaning, and send images sifting down from one head to another—a serpent, a lamb, a fish, a cluster of leaves. Sundials and stars and the death's head. The favoured shapes and signs; the archetypes; the things that stalk our dreams. Eagles, gryphons, dragons, lions. Horses. From the caves of Lascaux, from the tombs of the Valley of the Kings, on Celtic brooches and the Bayeux tapestry and by the hands of Uccello and Leonardo and Velázquez and Van Dyke, on to shiny Stubbs thoroughbreds and eventually to the gilt-framed red horses from Boots that hang in the hall of Matthew's parents' house. A picture of a horse always goes down well.

"I want you to dust the top of the picture for me, Matthew," says his mother. "I can't get up there any more." And so, the good son, he gets out the stepladder and wipes a duster across the frame. His mother, from below, directs the operation. When he is through, and down again, she gives him a rewarding pat upon the arm. He waits for her to say "good boy", but she does not. Instead she gives him a glance of roguish triumph; she knew what he was expecting. She can still be one step ahead, his mother.

Her hair is white. Her body, always spare, seems to have withered—there is less of her each year, he feels. But she herself—the voice, the soul—has sharpened. She is a network of opinion, still, but the opinions have blossomed or have faded, have responded to circumstance. Old ones have been adjusted; new ones have been honed and polished. She can surprise. Two weeks ago she asked Matthew if he had a lady friend these days. Matthew, taken aback, equivocated. "I'm asking," said his mother, "not because I'm wanting to see you marrying again, unless it arises, but because a man like you shouldn't be on his own, it's not natural." She meant, he perceived, a man like you should not be without a sexual life; but it was he who was embarrassed, not she. She looked him squarely in the eye, and he mumbled that there was someone he saw from time to time. "I'm glad to hear it, then," said his mother.

She thinks a woman is entitled to the same pay as a man, job for job. If she hears a child use bad language she will threaten to rinse its mouth out with soap. She likes television game shows and detests American serials. She favours the ecumenical movement and environmental campaigners and old-fashioned Tory politicians (she considers the new lot jumped-up nobodies). She would have terrorists hanged, but welcomes abortion reform. She relishes a meal in an Indian restaurant and allowed Matthew to fly her to Paris for her seventieth birthday treat. She mourns her husband with stoical reticence and has booked the plot alongside him in the cemetery she visits each Sunday morning.

They stand in front of the picture, Matthew still holding

the duster. "Give me that," says his mother. "I've half a mind to send those horses to the church jumble, anyway."

Matthew looks at her in astonishment. The red horses from Boots have hung there since the day they moved into the house, since a time when his head barely reached above the oak settle below them, since the beginning of recorded history. "Why?"

"I never cared for them, if you really want to know," says his mother. "Your dad brought them back one Christmas, pleased as punch. I never let on. It can't hurt him now, and there's better ways of remembering a person."

There is mine and thine, and then there is ours. And then eventually, mine again. Objects tend a marriage. They are its toys, its talismans. They chart its progress. Once, Matthew and Susan bought a chair together. They were not married, but soon would be. The chair was in the window of an antique shop: a Victorian nursing chair, high-backed with neatly curving arms. A simple, agreeable, useful object. Susan said, "That's pretty," and Matthew said, "I'll buy it for you." And she said, "No. We'll buy it for us."

Thus, the chair. Which sits today in his flat, pushed into a corner, homeless, adrift. From time to time he notices it; sometimes it is merely a familiar chair and at others it is so invested with meaning that he has to turn away.

When things had reached a point of no redemption, when both of them knew that there was nothing further to be tried, or done, Susan said, "What are we going to do about the house?" Not, I am leaving you, or, You must go. And he looked at her, bleakly, understanding and accepting, and replied, "I've no idea."

The house has passed into other hands. It is a party now to other people's intimacies. Matthew wishes it well. Occasionally he finds himself in the street, and notices that the front door has changed colour, or that it has sprouted window boxes; there is something vaguely reassuring about that. The house has distanced itself, and so it should.

In the parcelling out of objects the Victorian nursing chair fell to him, almost by default, it seemed. Neither of them, in any case, much cared. Like auctioneers, dispassionate and brusque, they surveyed the clutter of their lives, their life; they catalogued and apportioned. You have that, they said, and I'll have this. There were no arguments; all was scrupulously fair, remorselessly polite. Are you sure? they enquired of each other. Don't you want the gilt mirror? Or the Kitaj lithograph? Or the Provençal plates? Or the Beardsley prints or the fake Tiffany lamp or the khelim rug? No, no, they assured each other, you have it, I don't mind. Who cares? they did not say. What does it matter, now? What's the point? All this is just glass, wood, metal, cloth, paper, paint. So much lumber. They dismantled the place, shovelling books, cushions, pots, pictures into boxes and bags. They did it with deliberation and without comment. They ignored, or pretended to ignore, the shimmering haze of reference that hung over each object, intelligible only to themselves, shared and yet profoundly private. Matthew, shoving the Provençal plates into a plastic carrier bag, hardly bothering to shroud them in newspaper, sees Susan in a blue cotton sun dress, with a pink tinge of sunburn across her shoulders, turning to him in a shady street in Avignon, pointing at a stall. He smells garlic, dust and flowers. He feels the ghostly pluck of desire, and cringes.

Carrying the Kitaj lithograph down the stairs, stowing it carefully into the back of Susan's car, he stands again with the picture held up against a wall. "Left a bit," says Susan. "No, to your right now." He feels something on his legs, glances down, and sees Jane's starfish baby hands spread against his trousers. "Standing!" cries Susan. "Will you look at this!"

And what did Susan see, or hear? Their eyes did not often

meet, during those days. They came and went like removal men, passing one another on the stairs, working as a team when necessary for the handling of some large or delicate item. They spoke little, and were careful not to brush against each other. And as the house emptied, it began to echo. The rooms that were becoming shells rang with the hollow sound of their footsteps on uncarpeted floors. The place expanded, grew lighter, as though, relieved of its cargo of furnishings, it breathed more freely. Sunshine flooded through the curtainless windows and lay in slanting geometric shapes across the boards that Matthew had once stripped and stained. Dust balls shifted lazily in the draught; cobwebs swung from the ceilings. The walls were marked with the pale squares of their pictures, the ghostly imprint of their cupboards and chests. Coming upon Susan unexpectedly in one of the bare rooms, Matthew saw her, too, for an instant, as a precarious presence on the brink of extinction. She stood at the window, looking out, wearing jeans and a checked shirt, the person he knew best in the world, and had once loved most, and he seemed to see through and beyond her to a thousand other moments, a thousand other Susans. And then she turned, saw him, snatched herself from whatever had been in her own head, put on the dispassionate mask they both, now, wore with one another: "We've forgotten the cupboard under the stairs. We'd better get going on that next."

And so his mother would send the red horses to the church jumble. It can't hurt her husband now. She is quite right, of course; she was always a rational woman. To continue to live with a picture she had always disliked would be mere sentiment, a secondary emotion, and she has no need for that. There are better ways of remembering a person. His mother, of course, was secure in the stability of love, tolerance, forbearance or whatever had been the substance of marriage. She had to endure bereavement, and loneliness, but not the cruel betrayal of feeling. She can do what she likes with the red horses. They have not the power to turn the knife as does, from time to time, the Victorian nursing chair, for Matthew.

"I looked at those Meard Street houses," said Matthew. "Who is this bloke Rutter, anyway? We don't know him, do we?"

"Hang on." Tony rose from his desk to fetch a file. "No, we don't. He's a developer. Address in Hampstead. Wrote out of the blue wanting an opinion on Meard Street. I did ask around a bit. Apparently he's been operating in the Bristol area and surfaced here recently. Buying up stuff all over the place. D'you mind if I pass him on to you? I'm up to the eyes at the moment."

Who isn't? thought Matthew, with irritation. He took the file. "If I must."

"He's talking about Spitalfields, too. I thought that might be rather up your street. You've got a penchant for that area, haven't you?"

"My penchant," said Matthew tartly "—if that's the right word—is for its interesting historical associations, not for tricking out old houses as pastiche reproductions of the past, if that's what this fellow is after. In any case, there'd be a hell of a lot of problems with Meard Street."

"Better have a word with him. Suss him out. He might make a change from Blackwall and the Group." Tony's grin was both guilty and propitiating, as well it might be.

"Mr Rutter is not available. He would like to see you here tomorrow evening, at about nine-thirty."

The hell he would, thought Matthew. "Mr Rutter seems rather difficult to reach. I wanted a preliminary word."

The voice was male and so thickly London as to seem almost parodic. It was also tiresomely inflexible. "Mr Rutter is not available. He'll see you here tomorrow at nine-thirty."

"So you said. That's not entirely convenient. I prefer to hold business meetings during the day."

There was a pause. Some heavy thinking, evidently, was going on. "Mr Rutter will send a car."

"Transport is not the problem," said Matthew. "I'd prefer another time, that's all. Perhaps Mr Rutter could get in touch with me when he's more available and we can . . ."

The voice cut in, still, apparently, on automatic course. "Mr Rutter will see it's worth your while."

Matthew laughed. The parodic effect was now of a different order. "I'm delighted to hear it. My firm operates a fixed fee system, as it happens, but never mind."

A further pause. Heavy breathing, now. "Mr Rutter will expect you at nine-thirty."

"Oh, all right," said Matthew. Annoyed, but mildly intrigued.

There was a high wall, in which was set a pair of double steel gates with, alongside, a bell and entry-phone. Matthew pressed the bell and at the precise same moment a halogen light snapped on and very large dogs began to bark from just inside the gates. The entry-phone quacked.

"I can't hear you," said Matthew. "On account of those damn dogs. And kindly don't open the gate until someone's got them under control."

The entry-phone quacked again, and fell silent, unlike the dogs, who continued to bay and presently to fling themselves against the gates. Matthew eyed his car and fingered the keys in his pocket. The gates shook and clanged as the dogs hurled themselves against them and bounced off again. The Post Office presumably visited Mr Rutter by helicopter. After a couple of minutes the baying was interrupted by curses. Some kind of terminal struggle took place, with shouting matched by throaty growls, and the gates swung open. One thickset man in an indefinite uniform (olive green blouson, jackboots, peaked cap) stood there while another was trying to haul away a pair of Rottweilers on steel chains and looking as though he might not succeed.

"Mr Rutter's waiting for you." So that was what the voice looked like. Of Italian extraction, built like a side of beef.

"Thanks," said Matthew. "I'll just wait till your colleague's got those things out of the way."

"They wouldn't do nothing."

"I see. Purely ornamental."

Spotlights blazed onto a garden reduced to alternating sections of grass and paving, with a few glass fibre urns and troughs dotted around. The whole frontage of the house was bathed in a glaring white light. It was a Thirties mansion constructed in uneasy imitation of a southern American plantation house, with a flight of steps sweeping up to a semicircular pillared portico, and ranks of green shuttered windows. A Rolls with smoked glass windows was parked on the gravel drive up which Matthew and his companion now advanced.

The front door stood open. A circular hall, floored in black and white marble, curving staircase with marble balustrade. Much gilt furniture. Large, dark, Italianate oil paintings on the wall. An ascending Christ, striking a distinctly false note in this Hampstead Alcatraz.

"Mr Rutter's expecting you in the library," said the voice, with a hint of impatience. One was not, evidently, being given a tour of inspection. Matthew wrenched himself away from an immense silver-gilt seventeenth-century ewer displayed in uncomfortable juxtaposition with a collection of Lalique glass vases. Either Mr Rutter was strikingly eclectic in his tastes, or he needed a new art acquisitions adviser.

The voice tapped at a pair of panelled doors, paused, opened, and stepped aside, with a nod at Matthew.

It was indeed a library, lined from floor to ceiling with ranks of new-looking leather-bound editions of this and that. Encyclopaedia Britannica. The *Connoisseur*. *Whitaker's Almanac*. Mostly that. Marble busts on pedestals. Goethe? Surely not? A distinctly pleasing Dutch painting over the fireplace. Oriental carpeting. French windows giving onto further flood-lit sterile expanses of garden.

And Mr Rutter, seated behind a leather-topped desk of gross proportions and tricked out with all the appurtenances of modern business—fax machine, VDU, elaborate telephonic arrangements. There was also a large television, let into one of the bookcases. Rutter rose, hand outstretched. "Pleased to meet you, Mr Halland. My people been looking after you all right? Take a seat."

Mid-forties, unseasonal suntan, the voice again aggressively of London. South of the river, to Matthew's experienced ear. A square skull that somehow suggested distant Slavonic connections. Spanking white silk shirt with gold cuff-links and grey suit that managed to be both expensive-looking and ill-fitting.

They faced each other, in leather armchairs. "Drink?" enquired Rutter. "Shampoo suit you?"

"Sorry? Oh . . . yes, fine."

A bell was rung. The voice appeared, almost immediately, with champagne in an ice-bucket, and glasses. Matthew looked over Rutter's shoulder into the garden, where one of the Rottweilers was defecating onto a shaven lawn, and spotlights glared from the perimeter wall.

"Cheers," said Rutter.

"Cheers. Quite an impenetrable spot you've got here."

Rutter waved a dismissive hand, weighted with gold signet rings. "There's a lot of villains about in these parts."

Matthew nodded understandingly. An eighteenth-century longcase clock ticked sombrely from a corner of the room, a deeply incongruous sound. Rutter stared impassively at Matthew; the ball, it seemed was in his court.

"I've had a look at those Meard Street houses, Mr Rutter. Just from the outside. As you must know, they're listed buildings—there'd be a lot of problems with a conversion, they look pretty dodgy, but of course that sort of thing is always . . ."

Rutter waved the hand again. "I'm not taking Meard Street. I'm not interested any more. I'm tired of playing silly games with listed stuff. Property in central London—it's a case of build from scratch or forget about it, far as I'm concerned."

"Then I wonder why . . ." Matthew began.

"There's other things we can do business about. Maybe. I'm thinking of Spitalfields."

"Ah," said Matthew. "Plenty of listed stuff there."

"Not that rubbish. Brick Lane area. That's where the clever money's going now. Bishopsgate's played out. Docklands is a waste of time."

"Really?" said Matthew. "I see. A lot of the Spitalfields area is tenanted, you know. Bangladeshi textile businesses, cafés, small shops, that sort of thing."

"That's not a problem."

"Oh?"

"We've had a lot of experience with tenanted property," said Rutter heavily. "It's never a problem, go about it the right way."

"Is that so?" Matthew, now, was impassive.

"You just got to use a little persuasion, haven't you? Make them be reasonable."

"In my experience," said Matthew, "many sitting tenants are elderly people."

"Right. So you got to see they move on, haven't you?"

"If they're old ladies of eighty, moving on might present difficulties. Where to . . . that sort of thing."

There was a pause, in which Rutter appeared to be considering. "Well, basically, that's their problem, isn't it? I mean, I can't get too fussed about that, can I?"

"Oh, quite," said Matthew. "You can't afford to get bogged down in detail, I do see that."

Rutter gave him a hard look. "You wouldn't be taking the michael, would you, Mr Halland?"

"I wouldn't dare."

"Right. That wouldn't be a sensible thing to do. I'm a straightforward bloke to deal with, but I'm touchy. OK?"

"Absolutely. Sensitive—I imagine that's the word."

The next pause was loaded. Rutter stared at Matthew. "I'm not sure about you, Mr Halland," he said at last. "I don't know I've got the right man."

"To be absolutely honest," said Matthew, "I rather share your feelings." He put his glass down and stood up.

Rutter remained seated. "I'll tell you something else. You're no sort of businessman. You've not even heard what I got to suggest."

"I'm an architect. Though as a firm we are indeed in business, as you rightly point out. Incidentally—I wonder why you picked on us?"

"My people made some enquiries. You've got good contracts. You're on the up. You'd be surprised what I know." Rutter now rose. He tapped Matthew on the arm, with a curiously disarming gesture. "I even know what you done, yourself."

"I'm flattered," said Matthew. "All the same . . ."

"Thing is," continued Rutter, "I had a bloke working for me but he got silly—tried to pull off the odd job for himself on the side, that sort of thing, so I had to get rid of him. He did the Arnold Park development for me in Bristol, and Haverfields. You know those?"

"I'm afraid not."

"I don't normally deal with firms like yours. I use my

61

own people. But as I say there's a vacancy at the moment. It's a question of the right man coming along. How much are you pulling in, with James Gamlin?"

"I'm not looking for another job," said Matthew. "If that's the point of your question."

"And I'm not offering you one. Though you never know. I got the feeling we may not be on the same wavelength."

"I think that's a distinct possibility," said Matthew.

"My people say you're into conversions and new stuff, both. Spitalfields I see as a mix, depending on the circs. Sounds the sort of thing you ought to be able to handle."

"I don't doubt it, from a professional point of view. I fancy the difficulty would be one of . . . what shall we say? . . . social delicacy."

Rutter studied Matthew. "I don't get you."

"I feel that I—we—might not be entirely happy about your approach to those unfortunate enough to end up, however temporarily, as your tenants."

Rutter gave himself some more champagne, waving the bottle at Matthew, who shook his head. "You're a sentimental bastard, are you?"

"I suppose that's one way of putting it. One could also call it morally fastidious. Or just plain law-abiding."

"Those old ladies in Bristol was due for redevelopment, in any case. That fucking newspaper reporter was talking off the top of his head. They ought to be grateful, in the long run. There's different ways you can look at tenancy situations. Often as not, people don't know themselves what's best for them. They get it stuck in their heads any change is a bad thing—know what I mean? And another thing—you've got to look at what's good for the country. You can't have valuable inner city development sites standing idle."

"Of course there's the difficulty that a person may not

think of their bedroom, or their corner shop, or their garment factory as an inner city development site."

"Exactly," agreed Rutter. "And those Bangladeshi sweat-shops down there are for the chop anyway. Their turnover's ridiculous, half of them. They don't realize it, but you're doing them a favour."

"Can I ask you something?" said Matthew.

Rutter spread his hands, expansively.

"How actually do you deal with a . . . recalcitrant ten-ant?"

Rutter sucked in his cheeks. "Simplest is you raise the rent, where you can. Five or six hundred per cent. That usually does the trick. If there's some silly bugger nonsense about fixed rent tenancies then you got to be a bit persuasive. The tenants find there's always difficulties with the water and the electric. People don't like being without water and electric. If they go on being awkward you can always move in some kids with ghetto blasters." Rutter laughed. "People soon get pissed off with that, too. Specially older people. Or there's dogs—couple of big bastards that'll bark their heads off."

"I see," said Matthew. "Quite simple, really."

"Mind, you don't need all that, usually. That's just for the odd silly bugger who wants to be obstinate and cause trouble."

"In which case, you really have no choice."

Rutter's expression changed. "I don't think I like your tone of voice, Mr Halland."

"Frankly, I'm not enthusiastic about yours. Tell me—do you ever get . . . how shall we say? . . . the slightest twinge of doubt about your methods?"

"I don't think I'm going to waste any more time on you," said Rutter. He reached out and rang a bell. "You wouldn't be any use in my outfit, I can see that."

"Do you, though?" continued Matthew. "Idle curiosity . . . but at this moment it seems important."

"I don't know what you're on about," snapped Rutter. "It's each for himself in this fucking world, isn't it? If you haven't learned that by now then you've got a problem. I'm a reasonable bloke so long as people are reasonable back. I don't mess about, that's all. You don't get where I am today by messing about, I can tell you that." The voice, now, had appeared and stood waiting. "Mr Halland has to leave now."

"Evidently not," said Matthew, moving towards the door. The voice, who clearly knew a loser when he saw one, stood aside, wearing an expression of fastidious contempt. "It's been interesting to meet you, Mr Rutter."

"Get lost, would you?" said Rutter. Matthew followed the voice out, past the risen Christ and the Lalique and the airy little gilded sofas, down the marble steps, across the gravel (the Rottweilers keening now somewhere offstage) and, at last, into his car.

FIVE

I don't *believe* it!" said Alice Cook. "You've invented him. There can't *be* people like that!"

It was her birthday. They were dining in Soho; a celebration proposed by Matthew, who felt vaguely guilty that most of their meetings seemed to take place in Alice's bed. This was probably an accurate reflection of the nature of their relationship, but still perturbed him from time to time. It did not seem to bother Alice, though she had seized with enthusiasm on the dinner suggestion.

"Apparently there are."

"The police ought to do something," said Alice vaguely. "D'you know, we've got a woman in the hospital who was attacked by a Rottweiler. Eight stitches in her leg and broke her arm when it knocked her over. She said she . . ."

Alice's world was purely referential. It was composed of people she knew or had heard of, places she had been to, things that had happened to her. This quite often made conversation difficult, Matthew found. Alice flew off in a sequence of tangents, pouncing upon the one identifiable reference in a statement to make it the prompt for an anecdote or rejoinder of her own. The effect was somehow disorienting. Dialogue did not progress in the rational and indirectly narrative manner that it should, but leapt all over the place in a way that was unsettlingly inconclusive. It was not so much that you never exhausted a subject, but that it never really left the starting post. The threat of abstraction, in particular, had Alice running for cover. Right now, Matthew wanted to talk about the nature of evil. His encounter with Rutter had left him, in some perverse way, exhilarated. He felt like a naturalist who had been afforded a rare sighting of some creature whose existence he had always doubted.

"It's like talking to a Martian, in a way," said Matthew. "Because you realize you can't make any basic assumptions about how he feels. There's presumably a whole range of emotion he doesn't know about at all—fiddly stuff like compunction, and vicarious distress, and compassion, and moral outrage."

"Mmn . . . Anyway, this woman said all she was doing was visiting a friend, and she opened the door into the hallway of these flats and this animal . . ."

One knew all about it in the abstract, Matthew thought. One knew the effects. Hitler. Stalin. Large-scale historical evil was somehow familiar and, if not comprehensible, at least capable of analysis. On home ground, one had been inculcated in childhood into the simple matter of sorting out right from wrong, of passing judgements. Bullies at school were to be held in contempt. You did not lie or cheat (if you did you would undoubtedly be exposed). You did not kill, steal, blaspheme, say malevolent things about people behind their backs, fiddle the income tax, torment animals, or fornicate. You were considerate of the crippled and the mentally subnormal, you gave money on flag days, you offered your seat on buses to women and elderly men. You assumed that most others behaved the same, and condemned those who demonstrably did not. As you grew older you made certain adjustments to this canon (blasphemy, fornication, flag days . . .) but by and large it continued to condition how you behaved, and expected others to behave.

Which was what made meeting a man like Rutter simultaneously shocking and fascinating. It was brought sharply home to you that you shared the world with those whose every assumption was quite alien. Rutter moved daily through the same city, observed the same landscapes, saw sun and stars and moon, and the processes of his mind were more mysterious than those of some Amazonian tribesman reputedly ignorant of the contemporary world. Infinitely more mysterious, since Rutter was a product of the contemporary world just as much as was Matthew.

"You and I," he said to Alice Cook, "are capable of petty dishonesty, ill temper, the odd burst of malice, plus jealousy, envy, greed and all that sort of stuff. But I doubt either of us could manage to beat up children or animals, or mug old ladies."

Alice giggled. "You don't make us sound very nice. Incidentally, I saw Susan this week. We had a good old natter. She's got a bloke, it seems."

"Really?" said Matthew. Quite cool, quite non-committal. Rutter evaporated, along with the nature of evil. Susan is seeing some man. Sleeping, presumably, with some man. He tested his feelings: a little tenderness there? A twinge of pain under pressure?

"Mmn. I dunno how long it's been going on. Someone she met at work. So I told her we're fucking."

"And what did she say?" enquired Matthew, after a moment. A moment in which he came close to disliking Alice Cook.

"Nothing much. I got the impression probably she thought it was a good idea." Alice reached out to tap his arm, companionably. "So I thought—good. I'd feel uncomfortable if I thought she minded. But you two are so sensible and no nonsense about the break-up. I mean, with some people it's open warfare for ever after, and that's really awkward if you know them both."

"One tries not to be socially inconvenient."

"Don't be sarky," said Alice. She yawned. "Whoops! Sorry . . . A good meal always has that effect on me. You'd better take me home."

And so, presently, they are out in the London night. It is a blaze, a swirl of light and colour, sound and smell. They pass from the intimacies of the Soho streets to the frontier of Charing Cross Road, streaming with people and traffic. Matthew takes Alice's arm; an advancing gang of tipsy youths divides around them, goes whooping into the tube station. Everyone is talking, shouting. Language hangs in the night air and throbs in giant lettering above shops and theatres. A column of buses stands pulsing in a traffic jam: Gospel Oak, Putney Heath, Clapton Pond, Wood Green. Matthew and Alice pause on the pavement and he thinks of the city flung out all around, invisible and inviolate. He forgets, for an instant, his own concerns, and feels the power of the place, its resonances, its charge of life, its coded narrative. He reads the buses and sees that the words are the silt of all that has been here—hills and rivers, woods and fields, trade, worship, customs and events, and the unquenchable evidence of language. The city mutters still in Anglo-Saxon; it remembers the hills that have become Neasden and Islington and Hendon, the marshy islands of Battersea and Bermondsey. The ghost of another topography lingers; the uplands and the streams, the woodland and fords are inscribed still on the London Streetfinder, on the ubiquitous geometry of the Underground map, in the destinations of buses. The Fleet River, its last physical trickle locked away underground in a cast iron pipe, leaves its name defiant and untamed upon the surface. The whole place is one babble of allusions, all chronology subsumed into the distortions and mutations of today, so that in the end what is visible and what is uttered are complementary. The jumbled brick and stone of the city's landscape is a medley of style in which centuries and decades rub shoulders in a disorder that denies the sequence of time. Language takes up the theme, an arbitrary scatter of names that juxtaposes commerce and religion, battles and conquests, kings, queens and potentates, that reaches back a thousand years or ten, providing in the end a dictionary of reference for those who will listen. Cheapside, Temple, Trafalgar, Quebec, a profligacy of Victorias and Georges and Cumberlands and Bedfords—there it all is, on a million pairs of lips every day, on and on, the imperishable clamour of those who have been here before.

"Come on!" cries Alice, tugging him into the road between bus and taxi, and he is jolted back into his own skin and on towards Covent Garden where he has his car tucked up a convenient alley. Alice's thigh rubs against his; he is walking with a comely woman to whom, before long, he will make love. Alice is merry. She chatters, laughs, pulls him back to hover before a shop window: a display of esoteric toys— quivering plastic octopuses, a luminous green dinosaur, a paper mobile skeleton that bobs and turns behind the glass. "I want one," cries Alice. She is lit up, infused with the spirit of the night, an element of the crowd.

And Matthew, all of a sudden, is desolate. He is surrounded by people, and entirely alone. He is brushed by the indifferent glances of a hundred strangers, and looks upon them with equal disregard. Alice Cook is beside him, but he does not love Alice, nor does she love him. He is consumed with his sense of loss, of solitude. There comes surging forth the memory, not of Susan, but of love. Once, he lived within a safe warm capsule of requited feeling; now, he is adrift.

Nothing matters, he thinks, but other people. There is nothing else, for any of us. They have reached his car. He stops, and leans for a moment against a wall of blackened brick, searching for his keys. The smell of food gushes from the back door of a restaurant; the pavement blooms with scarlet rubbish sacks. He feels the harsh cool surface of the brick against his shoulders, and the weight of the place.

The child lies on the bed, in the cold gloom of the room. She can hear the sounds of the street beyond: cart wheels, barking dogs, the wordless maundering of a drunk man, women bawling at one another. It could be day or night.

The child is ill. She is suspended in a timeless black sphere of pain, and fear, and solitude. She swims from a fevered chaos into anxious clarity, and back again. Sometimes she knows her own name—Rose, Rose, Rose—and then she dissolves back into a blank and spinning existence that knows of nothing but its grief. Then, she is no longer in the room; she is untethered, everywhere and nowhere, now and for ever, a concentration of distress that is the world.

And then she arrives back upon the bed, and sees the square of the window, with the six broken panes (she can count, she can count to ten, and back again) and the brown paper that buckles in the wind, and the red rag stuffing up a hole. She sees the wall beside the bed, where the plaster is cracked in the shape of a horse's head. She sees the dark outline of the fireplace. She starts to sob, the child: a fragile human sound that should soak into the bricks and lie there for a hundred years, to be heard again, and again, and again.

Matthew dreams. In his dream, as in all dreams, he has escaped the imprisonment of normal expectation. He is in Docklands, but is unsurprised to see that the place consists of buildings made of some translucent and subtly incandescent material, neither glass nor stone nor steel. He does not know the name of this substance, but is aware that he has himself designed many of these monolithic structures and indeed remembers doing so. As he looks at the great glowing place, spread out before him from some vantage point, he recalls quite clearly the hours at the drawing-board, he feels the pencil in his hand, he recovers precise details of design—the disposition of windows, the curve of an entrance door, a problem with load and stress.

And now, again without surprise or query, he finds himself passing into a different landscape, slipping into some other dimension, just as Alice steps unquestioningly from one square to another beyond the Looking Glass. Now there are fields around him, a pastoral scene with hedgerows, grazing cows and a muddy lane. But there are also, in some of the fields, curious stepped constructions reminiscent of Mayan pyramids, around which toil small, bent and curiously clad figures, some sort of unfamiliar peasantry. Carts process along the muddy lane. His response, now, has changed. He is no longer a detached observer but is in search of information. He perceives that he is in some foreign place, and is anxious to discover where. He accosts a man driving a cart (crudely made, and drawn he sees by oxen) and puts a question. But before the man can reply Matthew's attention is distracted. He has seen a distant hill upon which sunlight pours from a cleft in opalescent masses of cloud. And on the hillside, quite clearly visible though a mile or two away, is a girl. The girl in the red coat, the girl from the sandwich bar. He can see her face, her brown hair that lies in wings against her cheeks. He sees her smile at him across space.

And, inexorably, the dream folds once again and he has stepped elsewhere. He is on a shore now, beside a storm-ridden sea. Waves are rolling in, bringing with them great slabs of pack-ice which break up into smaller pieces, the slabs piling up over each other like cards being dealt. And Matthew watches this, reduced again to a pair of observing, recording eyes.

He woke. The green figures on his digital clock flickered at three fifteen. He surveyed the dream, fresh and clear in his mind, and identified its component elements. The landscape of fields and curious stepped pyramids, the muddy lane and the carts was prompted, he perceived, by Rutter's reference to Brick Lane. Matthew's subconscious, clicking away in his sleep, had supplied the information that this name derived from the road's ancestral function as channel for London building brick, brought from the brick-fields to the north and east of the city. The subconscious, labouring on, had then come up with what it considered to be an appropriate landscape, borrowing the Mayan image when short of something more authentic. Matthew could not recall ever having seen a brick-field.

The seashore with overlapping slabs of pack-ice was a recreation, he recognized, of a photograph he had seen recently in a book of photographs of the London Blitz. He had stood for a long while in the Charing Cross Road branch of Waterstone's, mesmerized by those haunting pictures of St Paul's rising from billowing smoke, of a bus upended in a crater, of a woman being dragged from a cliff of rubble. Other, odder scenes: a bearded Sikh sleeping in a stone coffin; a rescue worker lifting skulls from debris. And there had been one picture, forgotten until now, of a row of bomb-damaged suburban houses, the slates cascading from their roofs like spilled playing cards. Tiles, cards, slabs of ice. Such is the mind's capacity to translate one image into another, to make random connections.

The incandescent version of Docklands was a little more tricky. A reflection, Matthew decided, of one of those illustrations of cities of the future in architectural textbooks and journals that he had studied in his student days—projections of another time that carried with them a curiously dogmatic confidence and precision.

And the girl of the hillside? Oh, that is clear enough. No difficulty about deciphering an image for yearning, for hunger, for seeking the inaccessible. The girl, though, is a real girl. Was a real girl—vanished now into the city, as irretrievably as into a dream.

And so he drifts back into sleep, in pursuit of that hillside, that sense of promise.

"I saw this fellow Rutter. We're not taking him on."

The board meeting had reached the stage of reviewing clients under discussion. "Why not?" enquired Tony Brace.

"He's a crook," said Matthew shortly. He outlined his meeting with Rutter. There was a stir of interest.

"Good grief," said Tony. "Rachman stuff. I didn't realize all that was still going on."

"Evidently it has a new lease of life."

"Well . . . Judiciously phrased letter, I suppose, saying that unfortunately we don't feel the project is quite in our line."

"I feel more like shooting him a bit of his own invariably elegant phraseology and telling him to fuck off. Anyway, he said as much to me. After offering me a job."

There were some grins, around the table. "I hope you hesitated long enough to find out what the inducements were," said Alex Brinton, a recent and junior member of the firm. Matthew, who thought him bumptious and disliked his slavish adherence to any new fad of architectural fashion, gave him a curt glance. "I'm afraid not, Alex. I'll put you in touch, if you're interested."

"Mind you," said Tony, "I've no doubt we've dealt with clients in the past whose business methods might not bear too close inspection. But clearly this boyo is out of the question.

Sorry to have exposed you to such a disagreeable experience, Matthew."

"Not at all. It had a certain awful fascination."

He had become conscious, in the months since he and Susan separated, and indeed in the time before, of how distress blurs the distinction between private and working life. There was an uneasy and disturbing analogy here with happiness. When he had fallen in love with Susan it had taken up all his time. He had drawn up the designs for a primary school while thinking of nothing but her. He had gone daily to work, attended meetings, held consultations with clients, driven from site to site, and thought all the while of Susan. He had seen his drawing board, his desk, his telephone, other people, through the palimpsest of her face. And now that he endured the bleak process of the death of love, he found that its exigencies were the same. It was no longer possible, as in more tranquil passages of life, to separate the working day from personal life. The one spilled uncontrollably into the other, so that as he talked to a site architect, or dictated correspondence, he would be visited suddenly by his preoccupation, he would lose the thread of what he was saying, fall silent.

He went over what had happened, again and again. He tried to pinpoint his transgressions, her mistakes. He tried to see who had done what, and why. He tried to isolate moments at which it might have been possible to halt the process, to cheat what now seemed some hideous unstoppable onset of disease. He set about charting the way in which their marriage had begun to die, in some kind of determined therapy.

"I don't always like museums," says Jane doubtfully.

"You're going to like this one," Matthew promises. "Actually you've been there before—ages ago." This is dangerous territory, but must be trodden; he forges ahead. "You liked the butterflies and the humming-birds."

She ponders. Then . . . "I remember! And I got the shell book and when Mum and I went to the loo there was a lady lying down because she was ill."

"That I wouldn't know about," says Matthew. "And I dare say she's recovered by now. Anyway, this time there's a special exhibition about dinosaurs. You like dinosaurs, don't you?"

"Do you like dinosaurs?" she enquires, after a moment.

"Definitely," he replies.

"Then so do I," says Jane.

And, indeed, the Natural History Museum is doing them proud, they discover. Not only are there dinosaurs, and Chinese dinosaurs at that, but there are also earphones to be hired, and a taped commentary. Hooked up to this apparatus, they pass into the stagy, softly-lit world of the dinosaurs, where the great skeletal forms pose against backgrounds of sand and rock, bathed in a golden glow, while a confiding voice pours out information. From time to time the flow is interrupted by periods of electronic sound approximating, they are told, to the mating calls or aggressive cries of dinosaurs. Jane is entranced by these; she turns up the volume on her set and wriggles in delighted fear. The voice steers them from mamenchisaurus to shunosaurus, inviting them to consider the bone formation, to observe the size of head and length of neck, to make deductions about diet and habitat. These are Jurassic dinosaurs, relatively late in the scale of things, *sub specie aeternitatis*; Matthew and Jane are given a brief run-down of dinosaur chronology, their attention is drawn to a chart on the wall. The earliest dinosaurs of all were short-legged creatures resembling the modern crocodile. There was that Christmas, thinks Matthew, when we quarrelled on Christmas Eve and hardly spoke till New Year. And then at Easter she went on holiday without me, to the Dordogne, with the Hammonds. It strikes him—momentarily—as odd that a confirmed agnostic should chronicle his life by religious festivals.

Scientists are unable to agree about the reasons for the extinction of the dinosaurs. It is possible that there was some global catastrophe—perhaps the earth was struck by a meteor—or there may have been an ecological disaster. If I had asked her not to, thinks Matthew, if I had said, no, please don't, please let's go together to Cornwall, to Spain, to anywhere. But I didn't. I said, yes, that seems a good idea, why don't you? There is controversy also as to whether the dinosaurs were hot- or cold-blooded. Undoubtedly many dinosaurs were swift-moving creatures, not sluggish like the reptiles of the modern world. And then when she came back we had somehow stopped sleeping together, without any decision, without anyone rejecting or prevaricating, we just weren't making love any more.

Some dinosaurs, such as the big herbivores, probably moved around in herds, thus giving themselves a greater chance of defence against the flesh-eating predators. And at about that time I knew that I no longer wanted to, and nor presumably did she. We weren't quarrelling any more. We weren't talking very much. It was then that Jane began to notice. It was then that she used to say the things that she said.

In the Gobi Desert clutches of dinosaur eggs have been found, and fossil nestlings in the nest, suggesting that dinosaurs may have been good parents who tended their young. And now Matthew feels his eyes swim with tears, appallingly, which spill out and gush down his cheeks. He reaches for a handkerchief, and sees Jane's face turned up to his, in curiosity and horror. Matthew blows his nose, with abandon. "I seem to be getting a cold," he announces. "What?" says Jane. He shifts her earphone; "I seem to be getting a cold." "Oh," says Jane.

She looks at him again, with a different expression. "Ssh," she admonishes. "It's making baby dinosaur noises now. Listen."

And so they passed from Permian through Jurassic to Cretaceous. The dinosaurs, roped off, spotlit, frozen in eternal postures, are like iconic objects of reverence in some church or cathedral, past which file the decorous viewers. At one point a vast thigh bone is displayed upon a plinth with a notice inviting visitors to touch; many do so, with the same casual ritual reverence accorded to a holy statue or relic. The exhibition concludes with a display of dinosaur historiography—there are charts and printed commentaries explaining the progress of palaeontological enlightenment. Jane, here, loses interest. The tape is silent; she pulls off her equipment and starts to make enquiries about the cafeteria, to which Matthew does not immediately respond. He is studying a row of portraits with accompanying biographical details—the sombre bewhiskered faces of the founding fathers of the science: William Smith, Dean William Buckland, Gideon Mantell. Richard Owen 1804–1892: anatomist, palaeontologist and compiler of the catalogue to the Hunterian Collection at the Royal College of Surgeons.

"*Please* . . ." moans Jane, on the point of expiry.

"All right, all right," he says. "Philistine. Greedy little philistine."

SIX

We see the city stratified. Decked out according to the times, furnished with costumed figures, with sedan chairs or hansom cabs. A chronology, a sequence.

Whereas the city itself, of course, is without such constrictions. It streams away into the past; it is now, then, and tomorrow. It is as anarchic as the eye of a child, without expectation or assumption. It is we who are tethered to circumstance, not the world we inhabit. Thus Matthew, at the junction of Kingsway and High Holborn, waiting to cross the road, registers buses, taxis, Midland Bank, Thomas Cook Travel, Lunn-Poly, K Shoes, and is not much interested in any of these. Being Matthew, he notices the tops of buildings rather than the bottoms—architectural flights of fancy by way of cornices and window mouldings that have ridden out the winds of change down below. He is also momentarily intrigued by a telephone engineer perched on the edge of a crevasse in the road, hauling out an armful of cables in primary colours, the city's mysterious intestinal life. His attention is caught by a drove of Japanese businessmen with precisely identical briefcases, by a bag lady outside a jeweller's window, ferreting inside a rubbish sack. And then the lights change and he joins the surge across the street.

He passes from this vortex into the calm oasis of Lincoln's Inn Fields, where he has to visit a conversion site. Kingsway is one of the city's frontiers; within a few hundred yards Matthew has passed from the spendthrift hedonistic climate of Covent Garden to the sobrieties of Lincoln's Inn. He is conscious of the effect, as though he were manipulated by his surroundings; he slows his pace, looks around, becomes less pressed for time. Indeed, he is tempted for a few minutes into the gardens at the centre of the great square, where people sit on benches reading newspapers. A flock of pigeons lifts and wheels across the frontages of the Soane Museum and adjoining houses, their wings catching the sun in a sudden brilliance of silver, grey and white. An empty plastic bag dances over the tarmac of the tennis courts like tumbleweed.

Matthew pays his visit to the site, which is a straightforward enough renovation of a late eighteenth-century house for a firm of solicitors. The job is in fact under the supervision of Tony Brace, who has sought Matthew's opinion on a couple of minor problems. Matthew sizes up the situation and has a chat with the foreman. The site is new to him, but it is not the professional aspect which preoccupies him. The problems, in any case, are pretty mundane. He stands with the foreman at one of the glassless windows and looks out at the great green leafy square, where office workers are bared to the sunshine. It is shirt-sleeved, cold drink city summertime. There is the thwack of tennis balls from the courts at the side of the gardens, babies ride regal beneath canopies, girls wear blowing cotton skirts. Matthew absorbs all this, but notes more carefully the majestic façade of the Royal College of Surgeons, with its great classical portico. The foreman, seeing the direction of his gaze, makes a joke about convenient neighbours to have, in case of accidents. "Oh, I don't know about that," says Matthew. "I should imagine they're all theorists, in there." He is looking at the trees now and observes that the London plane reigns here too, in Lincoln's Inn Fields—ancient majestic specimens with immense boles of trunks, knotted, misshapen, like the limbs of monstrous pachyderms, huge grey ribbed feet standing foursquare in the grass. He stares at them, and past them at Dance's Ionic columns, and the city performs its conjuring trick. It folds in upon itself; once, twice.

"They got the shock of their lives. They didn't know where they were, you see—just told there was someone under there, a caretaker or someone, there'd been a direct hit, half an hour before. So they started digging and next thing they knew, they were pulling out these skulls and bones. It was the specimens. Anatomical specimens. They were still at it when I came by—and there was no one buried after all, the caretaker had gone to the shelter. They'd got them all stacked up across in the gardens when I was there—a proper shambles. No end of stuff. Animal bones, too. Bits of elephant and rhino and God knows what all. And fossils. They were joking about it by then. Makes a change, they were saying. You can give me another cuppa while you're about it, love." He looks across the table at his wife, and sees her with relief, with gratitude, as though she were given to him afresh after each of these inferno nights. "You took Lucy down the shelter? I still think it's maybe time you and she should go to your Mum. It could be anywhere now, these nights—not just the docks and the City. All right, all right . . . I don't want you to go, either. What was I saying?" And he wipes a hand across his grimy face. His hair is full of plaster dust; he carries the last hours with him still, in every sense. "Those Heavy Rescue blokes . . . People had brought tea out to them and they'd set up one of these specimens with a mug in his hand. A skeleton. Propped up on a bench in the gardens. That gave me a shock, I can tell you. I thought—that's a bit off, isn't it? And then I thought, no, you've got to get a laugh where you can these days. They've got the worst job of all, those blokes. They start digging into a building and they don't know what they're going to find. It can be like a butcher's shop in there. One of them comes out and you can read in his face what he's seen. And the whole lot can come down on top of them any moment. They know that. And still they go in, if they think there's a chance of someone being alive. So you can't blame them making a bit of a joke of it, when they find it's just bones."

The jawbone of an ichthyosaurus is laid upon the desk in front of him. He draws, with small meticulous strokes of the pen, and makes notes. He reads the history of the world in terms of vertebrae, tibia, teeth and claws. Under his hands, the sauria lift from the rock. When he contemplates a stone, he sees the shadow of the creature it conceals. When he looks out of the window he sees the pigeons that rise from the trees as knots of fragile flying bone, he sees a running dog as a sequence of ingenious hinges. He has worked all his life with death and knows that life arises from an accumulation of decay.

The ichthyosaurus is giving trouble. He frowns and peers. He does not hear the maid knock, and then come in to stoke the fire, to bank it up with another scuttleful of gleaming Carboniferous, mined last month in Northumberland, docked at Tilbury. Nor, presently, does he hear his wife, who is obliged to lay a hand on his shoulder to gain his attention. "My dear," she says. "The men are here with the rhinoceros. Where should they put it?"

The foreman is asking, with a touch of irritation, about some ceiling mouldings. "I'm sorry," says Matthew. "I was distracted by the view."

He concludes his business, and walks out again into the sunshine. It is lunch-time. The square is dotted, now, with sandwich-eaters, which puts thoughts into Matthew's own head. It occurs to him—if indeed it had not occurred before—that he is a few minutes' walk from that convenient sandwich bar.

And so he finds himself once more in front of the glass case laid out with food, and the deft fellow who juggles with slices of this and dollops of that. He grins at Matthew in recognition; one of those who never forget a face.

Matthew gives his order. The man slices and spreads. Matthew fishes change from his pocket, sorts out coins. "By the way," he says, quite casual, quite unconcerned. "Last time I was in there was a young woman . . . She'd come out without her purse."

"Yup!" says the man, grinning further. "I remember. You stood her her lunch. Looking for your money back?"

"Not at all," says Matthew stiffly. "I simply wondered if you'd seen her again . . . if she's a regular. It occurred to me later that in fact by an odd coincidence I think I know her . . . didn't recognize her at the time for some reason . . . thought I ought to get in touch." It does not sound at all convincing, it sounds worse and worse. The man grins the more. Matthew flounders on, trails away, turns in fury and embarrassment to counting out coins from the change in his pocket.

"She's not what I call a regular," says the man. "But she has been in, couple of times. Works round here, I dare say." He is leering, now. "Give her a message for you, shall I? If she shows up again."

Matthew hesitates, unprepared. What to do? He is humiliated, trapped into feeling like some conspiratorial adolescent. And anyway, would any sensible girl . . .? He dithers, and then decides. What does it matter? What would be lost?

It is all fantasy, anyway. He takes out a business card, writes on the back, finds an envelope in his briefcase and puts the card inside. The man watches with amusement, takes the envelope and places it with elaborate care on a shelf behind him. He hands Matthew his sandwiches. He pockets, as instructed, the change for the five pound note which Matthew has hastily substituted for his handful of coins—a move aimed towards shifting the balance of power in Matthew's favour. This, however, does not really work. "Cheerio," says the man. "Good luck. Do my best for you." Matthew, muttering something indefinite, slinks out into the street.

He is now in possession of two rounds of prawn and avocado sandwiches, tidily wrapped in a paper napkin. If you have a sandwich in your hand you are in need of somewhere pleasant to eat it, so it makes perfect sense to head back to Lincoln's Inn Fields. Besides, this is what anyone else would do who worked in the area and was in the habit, on a fine day, of buying a sandwich for her lunch (and not necessarily, after all, always at the same place—the area abounds in convenience food bars).

And so Matthew patrols the paths, casting furtive but systematic glances at each bench. It's possible. All things are possible.

He draws a blank. As he had known he would. He finds a vacant bench and sits down to enjoy his lunch and contemplate the frontage of the Royal College and those impressive specimens of *Platanus X hispanica* Muenchh.

He is able, at last, to return to the ichthyosaurus, invigorated by the distraction and the anticipation of a rare treat, but able to put it immediately out of mind. He is a man capable of total concentration. He retreats once more to the Jurassic while, at the end of the corridor, his wife surveys with resignation the rhinoceros; born somewhere in India, 1820, died London Zoo, 1845. The creature is recently defunct, and the smell is not good. Mrs Owen returns to her husband's study to request that he smoke cigars about the place.

"Have we just come here because it's raining?" demands Jane. "Or because we wanted to anyway?"

"Both," replies Matthew.

The climate, in its petulant way, has served up rain for the weekend, always a problem. The city has switched its mood, gone are the shirtsleeves and the blown summer skirts; the place drips and glistens. But Matthew, expert and resourceful, has, as always, something in reserve.

"We *could* have gone to a film," mutters Jane.

"This is a sort of film," says Matthew. "You wait and see."

For wait they must, along with everyone else, in the straggling unruly queue for admission to the Planetarium show. Meanwhile, they can take in astronomical displays of various kinds while a plummy recorded voice holds forth about the search for the secret of the universe. There are waxwork figures of the great physicists and astronomers, swept in turn by strobe lighting as the voice gives a rundown of their aspirations and achievements. Einstein, wearing a brown jersey and grey flannels, sits perched on a large glass disc, staring without expression at the polyglot and cosmopolitan crowd that shuffles past, eating sweets and sucking Coke through straws. Matthew finds this scene intolerably dispiriting.

At last they are seated in the darkened auditorium. Jane perks up. And when the display begins she is appropriately awed. Above them, the artificial heavens glimmer and sparkle, emphasized now here, now there, according to the subject matter of the commentary. The disembodied voice has a hollow resonance that makes it a pervasive whisper, confiding wonders to the rustling audience. "I like it," hisses Jane. "Good," says Matthew, composing himself to listen.

The stars are distant in both space and time. Even the closest of the celestial bodies is more than four light-years away from us on planet Earth. When we look at the night sky we gaze at the brilliance of the past. How can feelings die? thinks Matthew. And which of us contracted the disease first, Susan or I? Or did we infect one another? I remember that once I could not wait to get home to her at the end of each day, and then somehow it was no longer thus. Once she wanted only to do what I did, go where I went, and then somehow she was always elsewhere.

The word planet means a wandering star. In ancient times astronomers believed that the planets moved around the sky, unlike constellations such as Orion and Cassiopeia. A marriage is not a relationship, it is a unit. Not she and I, but we. Our combined interest was paramount, not hers or mine. When we disagreed, it was a matter of interest and diagnosis, not of resentment. The names of the constellations are of great antiquity and commemorate mythological beings and events. The constellations are composed of stars, many thousands of times larger and brighter than our own sun. She was the centre of my world, and I of hers. Once, I wanted always to tell things to her first, and then I began to realize that she was not really listening. Betelgeuse, the great star in the constellation Orion, is a red giant and has a diameter which could contain the entire orbit of the Earth around the sun. If, at that point, we had said to each other, something terrible is happening, could we have been saved?

"Beetle juice," whispers Jane. "Remember?"

"I remember," says Matthew.

But what I remember is not a narrative sequence, that this happened and then that and then that, leading eventually to this. I remember an expression on her face that was new to me; I saw a stranger look at me out of her eyes. I remember an evening when I did not want to go home to her, when I drove around to put it off. I remember a weekend when she was away and I knew that I was relieved, that I felt as though a load were gone.

Red giants are stars at an advanced stage of evolution, which have swollen up and will eventually collapse. Our own sun, in around five thousand million years time, will become a red giant. White dwarfs are dying stars with very great density. When a massive star collapses it creates the phenomenon known as a black hole.

I know now that the loss of feeling is the worst loss of all. Susan still exists; I see her and speak to her. But she is gone, quite gone, as though she were dead. She died when we ceased to love one another. I have to suppose that her experience is similar, that she sees me, equally, as an absence.

Our own galaxy takes the form of a flattened spiral and measures about a hundred thousand light-years from side to side, with a thickness of some twenty thousand light-years. But it is only one among many countless millions of galaxies, out there in the immensities of space.

All of which, thinks Matthew, should wonderfully concentrate the mind, and place one's own puny concerns within a proper context. Unfortunately, it does no such thing. Or, perhaps, fortunately. The achievement of thought and sensibility, after all, may be unique to this planet. Planet Earth, I should say. This fellow could mention that small point.

The great Andromeda galaxy is more than two million light-years away from us and is the most distant object in the heavens visible to the naked eye.

"Do you think Andromeda is a nice name?" whispers Jane.

"Quite," Matthew whispers back. "A touch pretentious for everyday use, perhaps."

In front of them, a head turns to scowl censoriously. The display of light and sound has now gone into an elaborate convulsion intended to suggest the death throes of a star. Our own sun, the commentator observes, will in its turn meet just such a fate. And in the meantime our galaxy, along with the countless million others, hurtles for ever onward and outward into the darkness of the expanding universe.

The lights come on. The audience gathers up its plastic bags and its cans of Coke and straggles forth once more. "I liked that," says Jane. "I liked the bit when the star got born and then died. Which bit did you like best?" Matthew agrees that that was indeed impressive and they go down the stairs discussing what they have seen.

And so, presently, they find themselves in a Wimpy Bar where Jane falls silent over the ice-cream list, always a demanding matter. Matthew watches her: the scowl of concentration, the lips faintly moving as she works through the text. She is wearing a blue hair-clip today, and her fair hair is more than usually dishevelled. Matthew, looking at her, sees her face as a spectrum of references. Her lowered eyelids have a hint of Susan, there is something in the relation of nose to upper lip that recalls his mother, in her jawline there is an eerie echo of himself. There she is, a unique being, displaying in each feature, each tendency, her connection with various others. She is indeed unique—a fusion of characteristics and capacities that can never be recreated. If I die tomorrow, thinks Matthew, I shall continue to walk the earth a little longer, there.

"Don't look at me," says Jane, squirming. "It's rude to stare at people, anyway. Can I have a vanilla with chocolate hazelnut sauce?"

There had never been a particular moment when he had thought, I want a child. When he and Susan were first married they felt themselves to be too hard up and inadequately housed to consider a baby. Susan was exhilarated by her work as a researcher for a television current affairs programme. Their life was complete as it was: rich and promising. They became more prosperous, and moved from a flat to a house. And somehow, without the matter ever having been discussed, they shifted to a position where a pregnancy would not be disastrous. Susan talked of working part-time. One day she mentioned that she was no longer taking the pill and Matthew, to his surprise, felt a curious uplift, a surge of something that could only be described as excitement. And when she announced that she had missed a period he knew that what he was experiencing was an outburst of triumphant joy such as he had never known.

He saw the birth. He saw Jane emerge from between Susan's thighs, a blotched and bloodstained bundle that made him gasp in shock, relief and something else that he could not identify until, later, he held her in his arms. And then he knew that there is a conspiracy. Half the world is walking around in possession of an insight of which the rest have but an inkling. He had thought himself an expert on love, and saw now that he was only a beginner. He held this little creature—at once infinitely strange and intensely familiar—and glimpsed the rest of his life, and hers. He saw that nothing would ever be the same again, for better and for worse.

"Can we go soon?" says Jane. "I've finished. Why haven't you drunk your coffee? Are you cross about something?"

The years of her infancy were the best of all. They were good parents, they realized. Susan was a calm mother, unruffled by the small crises of babyhood, patient and interested. They shared the chores, relished this mutual concentration of concern. It did not begin then. The corruption of their marriage did not spring from the child. Later, when they knew that there was no more to be done, they held on for her, and her alone.

"*Please* let's go."

They leave the Wimpy Bar, and set forth for what is now called home. Jane discusses alternate means of transport and rejects the tube, of which she is not fond. A child of the city, street-wise in every sense, she is an expert on buses. We can take a 30, she tells Matthew, and then change. Matthew acquiesces. She shoots a look at him—a look tinged with anxiety. She is a child acutely tuned to adult moods; she has had to be. She slides her hand into his. "Love you," she says, offhand, her face averted. After a moment she adds, "I love Mum, too."

"Of course you do," says Matthew.

And so they ride through the city, father and child, seeing, each, a different place. Jane, with the liberation of childhood, without rationality or expectations, sees an anarchic landscape in which anything is possible and many things are provocative. She wrestles with language, scans advertisements, shop-signs, logos on vans and trucks. She pays professional attention to other children, in the way that animals are most sensitive to their own species. She searches out the things that tether her to a known world— a bus with a familiar destination, a hoarding that proclaims her favourite brand of chocolate, Volkswagen cars that are like her father's. Hers is a heliocentric universe, and she is the sun. She is fettered by a child's careless egotism, but freed from adult preconceptions. She does not know what to expect, and can therefore assess what she sees in its own terms. She does not interpret, and therefore can construct her own system of references. The Arabic script on the windows of the Bank of Kuwait becomes little dancing figures. The caryatids outside the church in Euston Road are ladies wearing bath towels with books on their heads. For her, the city is alternately mysterious and familiar, baffling and instructive. She tests her own capacities against the view from the window of the bus; she rhymes and puns, she counts, she classifies. She plays games with words and sounds, she flexes her imagination, she takes the place as she sees it and twists it to her own ends.

Matthew, wiser but inflexible, sees much more and much less. The caryatids, for him, carry a freight not of books but of classicism and all that it implies; he sees so much that the figures themselves are almost obscured. The Bank of Kuwait provokes complex and flying thoughts that run from oil-happy potentates to the date of the Koran. Sometimes he sees nothing at all; the place flows past his eyes as a meaningless panorama while he is intent upon the random sequences within his own head. And then something seizes his attention and he is jolted from the prison of his own concerns and becomes once more—for a second, for minutes on end—responsive and reflective; he joins up with the city and becomes a part of its streaming allusive purpose. He puts a date to a building and sees from what it derives, and how; he looks at faces and sees beyond them to cultures and to histories. The city feeds his mind, but in so doing he is manipulated by it, its sights and sounds condition his responses, he is its product and its creature. Neither can do without the other.

SEVEN

Great architectural concepts are often inspired by sheer utility. London's trademark is undoubtedly the terrace house. Not as executed by Nash but in its humbler manifestations from Clapham to Islington. There can be few more sensible and elegant solutions to the problem of how to concentrate a lot of people into a small area. Matthew, in his daily peregrinations of the city, had become a connoisseur of its various forms, from cheap and basic to lavishly ornate. He had lived for many years in an example of what he thought of as the north London Romanesque size two model, and had been responsible for the renovation of several terraces of the more grandiose estates, such as his current area of responsibility at Cobham Square. He was intimate with the terrace house; he knew the secrets of its construction and of its evolution, but at the same time he retained his pleasure in its effect. The calm perspectives of the terrace, he saw, provide the essentially domestic mood of this city. Whether utilitarian in stock brick or lordly in shining white stucco, it supplies that image of order, of sobriety and of grace which is the essential feature of the London landscape. Here is an efficient machine for living which is also a creative element in the design of a city.

No single architectural genius, of course, can be accredited with the terrace house. Most of them must have been run up by practitioners of varying efficiency who knew a good idea when they saw one. Which is how most architects work. Matthew had abandoned fairly early on in his career the notion of becoming an innovative and controversial star of the profession. It was not that he felt he lacked either the talent or the nerve, but that he knew himself to be short on entrepreneurial gusto and the requisite gift for public relations. In a sense, he couldn't be bothered. This last was patently a deficiency. There is nothing especially honourable about being satisfied with a career as an also ran. It would indeed have been rewarding to know yourself responsible for some seminal instance of contemporary building—some frequently cited university or theatre. Nor would Matthew have been daunted by public obloquy; he rather enjoyed a fight. It was more that the neutrality and anonymity of work within a practice bestowed its own freedom and flexibility. You could be a jack-of-all-trades; you turned your hand to anything and everything. You were out there on the front line.

Contemplating the front line these days, though, driving through Docklands and down at Blackwall, he faced disillusion. The tower block may well have been inspired by utility, but few would claim it as a great architectural concept, at least as expressed in these parts. Manhattan is one thing. The Isle of Dogs looked set to be something else altogether. With rapidly diminishing enthusiasm he watched the turquoise walls of Frobisher House climb up into the summer skies. He still thought the design as satisfactory as could have been achieved within the terms of the commission. He found some of its companion developments agreeable and a few positively appealing. Others were boring or downright disastrous, but even

94

so his quarrel was not with individual buildings. What had gone wrong was both simpler and more cataclysmic. A city is an organic growth and here the profoundly arrogant assumption was being made that you can bulldoze the past, replace it with new constructions and expect the result to be anything other than the semblance of a place.

It was in such a mood that he left Blackwall one day at the end of a site conference. There was a stack of work awaiting him back at the office, he knew, but on a sudden whim he decided to stop off at Spitalfields first. The place had been much in his mind since the encounter with Rutter; it was time he took a look at whatever was going on down there these days. The excuse, if one were needed, could be to pay a call on a colleague, Graham Selway, who lived in and worked from one of those painstakingly restored Georgian houses in the streets around Spitalfields Market.

And so Matthew moves from the *sturm und drang* of Docklands to the haphazard solidities of Whitechapel and Spitalfields. Here is a complex, coded landscape, reassuring in its sense of determined occupancy, an area which has ridden out three centuries of market volatility, an industrial oasis which has cut its cloth—quite literally—to suit the times. Which has mopped up wave upon wave of immigration, from Huguenots to Jews to the Bengalis of today. Which has moved from silk-weaving to cotton and calico and eventually to the viscose, nets and cords offered now on the shop-front of a wholesale textile importer. Skin Centre; Sadik Fashion; Sani and Salim—Bulk Distribution and Sales Offices for Home and Export Markets. A window full of saris displayed on doe-eyed model figures. Another one brilliant with racks of children's party dresses of satin and lace in peach, lime green and fuchsia pink, with accompanying miniature lace parasols and gloves. A pervasive smell of curry—Bengal Cuisine, Imran Restaurant, Halal Meat Groceries and Provisions. This is a world in which business and domestic life are carried on still cheek by jowl; people live here as they would have lived in the eighteenth century—or, of course, as they would live in Dacca or in Calcutta. People move about purposefully—the men with their white skull caps, neat fringes of beard, white cotton tunics, the women in saris, the quick dark children.

But it is also, Matthew sees, a makeshift place, a poor place, a place clinging on by a toenail—the streets cobbled together with corrugated iron and plywood, bristling with For Sale signs. He pauses to watch a lorry being raucously unloaded in a confusion of English and Bengali. The warehouse beside which it is parked has a façade which has been perfunctorily renovated so that the windows are now picked out in oriental style; behind the keyhole shape lies the Romanesque outline of the nineteenth century, and at one end an exposed inner wall shows a column of Victorian fireplaces. Buddleia springs from decaying roof tops; in the hinterlands behind buildings untidy yards can be glimpsed full of broken crates, trolleys and rusting machinery. In some streets a row of weavers' houses, painstakingly revived, face dereliction opposite—embattled sites where a reconstructed past and an inexorable future are fighting it out amid the estate agents' signs and the concrete mixers. And as Matthew looks down the shaft of a street or alley it seems to him that always two dominant outlines meet the eye: the white spire of Hawksmoor's Christ Church and the gleaming blue glass of a new office block with the long arm of a crane stark against it.

He turns from Brick Lane into Fournier Street, and there on the corner is the Huguenot church, the most potent symbol of the versatility of this place. Once Protestant, then a synagogue, and now, of course, a mosque: London Jamme Masjud. And above the sign is a sundial, topped with a little arched pediment framing the date 1743. The sundial's arm is surrounded by Roman numerals; *Libra Sumus*, says the lettering above. The sun is out; a shaft of shadow points to the numerals. Matthew consults his digital watch, and yes indeed, there is agreement between time then and time now, with an effort of adjustment for the anachronism of British Summer Time.

Matthew ponders the façade of the mosque for quite a while, until forced onto the narrow pavement by an imperious lorry. He walks on. Here, in these streets beneath Hawksmoor's spire, the houses are poised on the brink of extinction or transition. Occasionally a sari-framed face glances out from an upper window; a chalked sign outside a door says "Part-time cutter wanted"; a sewing-machine whirrs. But all along the pavements the skips are lined up like small craft hitched to a harbour wall, piled high with splintered wood and chunks of plaster. Some buildings are boarded up, others are already stripped to airy skeletons, corseted in scaffolding, throbbing with Radio One. A thin tenacious frame of brick will soon be all that is left to hitch this place to its origins—a stubborn and eloquent outline.

Crossing Commercial Street, picking his way through the squashed tomatoes and decaying fruit spewed out by the market, Matthew heads for the heartlands of restored Georgian Spitalfields, where frontages are dressed with canaries in cages and, allegedly, the more fastidious residents scorn electricity and live by candlelight. Lorries, vans and fork-lift trucks clatter through the narrow streets in which, here and there, the cobbles have been uncovered. This is the front-line all right; here the warring factions of unbridled progress and entrenched nostalgia face each other across the barricades. There is hardly anyone about; the canaries sing piercingly; drills blast from behind shrouding that apologizes for the inconvenience caused during refurbishment. It is as though people have gone away and left the place to itself, for the opposing forces to get on with hostilities on their own. It is, as it stands, a shrine to opinion and to conflict.

Matthew, refining a few opinions of his own, reaches Graham Selway's house and knocks on the door.

"I didn't attempt to phone," said Matthew. "I assume you spurn anachronisms like British Telecom."

"Naturally I'd prefer to hire a street urchin to take messages across town, but they're hard to come by these days. People will insist on sending their children to school. Anyway, come in and waste some of my time. What brings you to these parts?"

Graham Selway led Matthew into a reassuringly normal office, with decent lighting and appropriate electronic equipment. "How are you? Far too long since I saw you."

They had been at college together, and had kept up the sort of desultory, amiable contact of those for whom acquaintance has never quite overflowed into friendship. In youth, Graham had been solitary, ascetic and self-sufficient—qualities of which Matthew had felt faintly envious. Life must be a damn sight easier for people like that. Moreover, he appeared to be without sexual urges of any kind—also, surely, an inestimable advantage. Now, twenty years on, he had a faded look—a slight stoop, the hairline receding. He was dressed with indulgent shabbiness in baggy cotton trousers and a faded T-shirt. He had operated for the last ten years or so a successful private practice specializing in choice and expensive restoration.

"Coffee?"

"Thanks."

Graham poured out two cups from a percolator in the corner of the room. Drawings spread out on the long table under the window afforded glimpses of unswerving classicism, as though everything since about 1820 were some transient aberration.

"Are you doing a lot round here these days?" asked Matthew.

Graham shook his head. "The best stuff all went some time ago. I did a few then. It's rapidly become too late. The big boys are moving in. City money. How are things on your patch? I took a turn around Docklands the other day. Are you all getting terribly rich?"

"Not personally," said Matthew. "Do I detect a note of supercilious contempt?

Graham laughed. "It's not my line, as you well know. But you're still keeping your hand in with bread-and-butter renovation, aren't you? You personally, I mean. I thought that Cobham Square development was yours?"

"It is indeed." Matthew wandered to the window. The street was cobbled. Opposite, a Georgian number rubbed shoulders with a cavernous shell whose brickwork sprouted a botanical garden of assorted foliage. A fork-lift truck rumbled by, followed by a van whose open windows howled reggae music. "Anyway, you seem to have kept it all at bay here, so far."

"Precariously. And not for much longer. The other end of the street is up for grabs. Maybe you people should be going for that job. There are various interested parties slogging it out over the ruins, I gather. Want to take a look?"

They went outside. Further along, the cobbles gave way to pot-holed tarmac and the Georgian relics to a tottering warehouse, a thicket of estate agents' signs and a length of hoarding which shielded an immense hole in which an excavator was already foraging, its metallic claw picking at a mound of rubble. Matthew and Graham stood watching. "Office block," said Graham. "Of course. We're a suburb of Bishopsgate. There's some sort of battle going on for the last few freeholds, apparently. The money men cutting each other's throats. Good luck to them. Sort of thing you might want to take on?"

Matthew shrugged. "We're not doing a lot of soliciting

at the moment, to be honest. Our books are just about full."

"I'm sure they are. So, in their humble way, are mine."

Above the roof-line Matthew could see the brilliant silhouette of a crane, scarlet in this instance and brilliant against the sky. But it was the sky itself that held his attention—a summer sky in which great luminous masses of pearly cloud seemed to be themselves the source of light, with no sun visible but, here and there, hidden gaps in the cloud cover through which streamed golden rays in which you expected to see a risen Christ. A dramatic, allusive sky—inappropriate and yet, to any Londoner, profoundly familiar.

They walked back towards Graham Selway's office. A svelte black car with smoked glass windows nosed out from the kerb behind them and accelerated past, forcing Matthew to jump for the pavement. A posse of Bengali schoolchildren scampered by, satchels thumping against their backs. The resident canaries poured out an effortless stream of song. Graham was talking about a college contemporary of theirs who was apparently designing futuristic cities in Brazil. "Entirely surreal, by all accounts."

"More so than this?" enquired Matthew.

Graham paused on his doorstep. "This? Oh, you get used to it. It's been going on ever since I moved down here. I've forgotten what static surroundings are like. There's a certain exhilaration about constant upheaval, I suppose. Different of course if one had a family. How's Susan?"

Matthew explained.

"Oh dear. Sorry to hear that." Embarrassment hung heavy. "Come in and have another cup of coffee," continued Graham determinedly.

"No, thanks. I've distracted you for long enough—and oddly enough I have work to do as well."

Matthew headed back to his car, passing once again the

mosque on the corner of Fournier Street, where the shadow of the sundial was now extinguished by the clouded sky. Automatically, he glanced at his own watch, and then was irritated by this servitude to passing hours. Why must we always know what time it is? Once, people wandered through capacious and unstructured days, tipping only from morning to night, and season to season. And there arose suddenly folk memories of his own, in which he had been temporarily innocent.

He is at the end of that long thin garden by the railway track, watching the trains go by. His face is squeezed into the gap where a strut of the fence is broken—he is not tall enough to see over the top. The wood is warm and rough (in his head, his mother's voice warns about splinters); a train hurtles past with that satisfying brief commotion, that rush of displaced air. And suddenly there comes to mind the realization that he does not know what time of day it is. Has he had his dinner or not? He consults his stomach, which is of no help; he is not particularly hungry, nor particularly full. Is it early morning? Afternoon? Evening? It does not occur to him to seek the sun, he simply stands there, adrift, and taking a curious pleasure in his state. It is now, he thinks. I am now. Everything is now. And at the same instant, or so it seems, there arrives the recognition, the revelation that at some other point—at some unknown, unknowable then—he will have this time, this moment, in his head. He will look at it from elsewhere. He will come down here to the fence again, tomorrow, and see his own perception, acknowledge its truth. He feels all of a sudden, infinitely wise.

(And Matthew, unlocking his car in a side street off Brick Lane, pauses for a moment to salute that child, across the decades.)

He wakes. He wakes into consciousness of his own body and, simultaneously, of hers. He is lying on his side; she is lying up against him, curled into him, the curve of her back fitted to his chest and stomach, the front of his knees slotted to the back of hers. He can feel her breathing; her intakes of breath alternate with his. She is asleep and he, now, transiently, is not. It is the dark dead of night, any time and no time. And he is filled with a sense of perfect happiness, of security, of impregnability. He is suspended thus for ever, in darkness and love; there is no age, nor death, nor change. They are immortal, he and she.

(And Matthew, easing himself into the driving seat, stares unseeing through the windscreen, at once enriched and deprived.)

The last three years had been the longest of his life, there was no question about that. Before then, time folded in on itself like a concertina, compacted in the mind as an impenetrable sequence of event and routine. A thousand nights like that night. A thousand days in which he had been busy, angry, tired, joyful, anxious and content. There were landmarks, to be sure—the officially chronicled dates of significance like marriage, the start of a new job, the move to a different place, Jane's birth. And there was the uncontrollable unpredictable maverick record of the mind, in which it all still went on, now obscured and now leaping to prominence, everything foreshortened, condensed, and spotlit.

Whereas the last three years had limped onward with a relentless chronology, from unease that all was not well, through bleak recognition that things were bad, to misery, acceptance, and the slow plod to decision, separation and some sort of eternal convalescence, if that was his present state. There were anniversaries: two years since she went to Spain without him, a year since he moved into the flat. And recently, it seemed as though time had picked up its pace a little, that spring had followed a little quicker on the long dank winter days, the spun-out horror of Christmas. Sometimes, it seemed even to trot again—he came to the end of the week surprised, and a little out of breath. Was this a good sign? Was this what was wanted, that life should hurtle ahead, taking you with it?

"We're none of us getting any younger"; an expression of which his mother was tiresomely fond—including him in the sweep, nowadays. She had granted him, at some mysterious point, admission to adult status, with all that implied: the right to hold opinions, exemption from instruction, mortality. Periodically she enquired about his pension arrangements and appeared to take a sombre satisfaction in the irritation that this caused. She swerved, these days, between treating him as her peer, her associate in wry endurance of the follies and shortcomings of this world, and according him the licence due to youth. He experienced, in consequence, a confusion of identity, blamed her and was exasperated with himself for the immaturity of his reaction. He could not help but note, too, that there is evidently no end to the bizarre complexity and variety of exchange between parents and children.

Jane stands at the window of his flat, running a dampened finger down the glass—a maddening sound.

"Could you not do that?" he says, patiently.

"Why?"

"Because it's a nasty noise and I'm trying to read the paper."

The weekend has come round again. Their weekend.

"What are we going to do today?"

"I've got to do some shopping and then . . . Well, we'll think about it. In a minute."

There is a pause. Matthew reads half of an article in *The Independent*. He glances at Jane and sees that she is chewing the end of her plait. Susan believes that this habit is evidence of disturbance, and is concerned about it; this is one of the few matters they discuss, these days. Matthew's view is that lots of little girls chew the ends of their plaits, and always have done. But in dark moments he doubts his own complacency, and is concerned also. He knows that both he and Susan, alone and helpless, watch Jane with fearful eyes for signs of the damage that they may have done.

Jane says, "Where are you when I'm at Mum's house?"

Matthew, startled and wary, abandons his paper. "I'm at my office. Or here in the flat. Or seeing somebody about something."

She turns from the window to face him. "That's not what I mean," she cries. She is frustrated and intent. "I mean—I can't see you, I can only think you, so you aren't there."

"Oh—I understand." Matthew is relieved. He is also impressed, and floored. She has a point, she does indeed. "Yes, that is a problem. But I am there, I promise you, just as much as you are. You're not really worried about it, are you?" he adds.

"I don't know," says Jane. She puts the end of the plait in her mouth and stares, chomping. And then suddenly she swoops across the room and leaps at him, pummelling him. In play, or so it seems. "We're both here," she says fiercely. "Aren't we? Aren't we?"

"Oh, we are," Matthew replies. "We most certainly are."

"Mr Halland?"

"Speaking."

"Mr Rutter would like to talk to you."

"Why?" enquired Matthew, after a moment.

There was some heavy breathing. "He wants to talk to you, that's all. I'm putting you through now."

A click. "Mr Halland?"

"Yes?"

"I think it might be a good idea if you and I had a little chat."

"I'm surprised to hear that," said Matthew. "I thought we parted fairly conclusively."

"I don't like people nosing around where they've got no business, Mr Halland."

"Sorry?"

"You heard what I said."

"I don't know what you're talking about, I'm afraid."

"Or maybe you're hoping to do business?"

"Mr Rutter," said Matthew. "I am a simple fellow and you are mystifying me."

A pause. For regroupment, it would seem. "You were sussing out the Spitalfields corner site last week. One of my people was watching you."

"I was indeed in Spitalfields last week. And I take exception to being spied on by your henchmen."

There was a change of tone. Rutter became, now, confiding. Propitiatory, even. "And you've got a right to. Sometimes people get over-enthusiastic, know what I mean? You got a lot of staff, it's difficult to keep them all in line, right? Far as I'm concerned, you could be down there for the scenery."

"On the whole," said Matthew. "And all things considered, that's pretty well what I was there for. Not that it's any concern of yours. But I'm beginning to see the point of this phone call."

"I thought you would. You're an intelligent bloke, I could see that when we met. I dare say we got different outlooks, but that's no reason why we can't have a reasonable talk."

"Possibly," said Matthew. "But what about, exactly?"

"That Spitalfields site."

"I haven't the slightest interest in the Spitalfields site."

"I think you was sussing it out," said Rutter heavily. "I think you and your firm's working for Glympton Holdings. And let me tell you something, my friend, Glympton isn't going to get that site. I'm getting that site. So you're wasting your time." Another change of tone; the flexibility was indeed remarkable.

"I'm afraid it's you who's wasting his time. And mine, come to that. I am not interested in the site, and neither I nor anyone else in my firm have any connection with Glympton Holdings. And now, if you don't mind, I'm busy."

"So am I, Mr Halland, so am I. I don't make phone calls to amuse myself. I'm disappointed you're taking this line. I'd hoped we could have a nice friendly sensible chat. You think about it. I may be in touch again."

Click.

Get stuffed, thought Matthew, hanging up.

EIGHT

There's something I want to ask you," said Alice Cook.

Matthew looked enquiringly at her. He felt apprehension—a twinge of panic, indeed. What was coming? Cohabitation? Marriage? Surely not.

"The thing is," said Alice. "I'm thirty-seven. Grey hairs, practically . . ." —she grimaced, forged on, overruling Matthew's frantic protests of disagreement—"Anyway . . . the biological clock and all that. I've decided I want a baby. Of course, in the fullness of time I may find the ideal guy and live happily ever after with him, but right now I'm less bothered about that than the female reproductive process. I don't want to be a geriatric mother. You and I are a jolly good thing but we know it's not for ever. So what I'm saying is . . . I want you to give me a baby. No strings whatsoever. We'll have it all made watertight by lawyers—I don't want you to contribute financially. My responsibility entirely. If you want to see it from time to time, that's fine by me, but if you don't that's fine too. Right?"

No, thought Matthew wildly, not right at all. Wrong,

quite wrong. This was worse by far than anything he had anticipated. He felt horror, embarrassment, and a searing compassion. Dear Alice, you have no idea. That is not how children are made. Except that of course it is—the world is crawling with children made in just that way. But not mine. Not any child of mine. Nor, I hope, before too long, eventually yours, dear Alice.

"Alice . . ." he began. He stopped, scrabbling for words.

She watched him. She was wary now, going onto the defensive. "You don't look as though the idea grabs you very much."

"Alice," said Matthew. "I can't."

"I've never known you have any problems in that department."

"Alice, having a child is . . ." He halted. Is a serious undertaking? Is painful? Is expensive? Is perhaps the most significant thing one will ever do.

"Having a child takes two people," said Alice. "Unfortunately. That's why I need some friendly co-operation. I'm not asking for much, am I?" She gazed at him.

He had to look away. "Alice," he said, "I honestly don't think you've . . ."

"All right. Enough said. You've got your point across. You don't want to. OK then. Forget it. I can always look elsewhere."

He took a deep breath. "Listen. Alice . . . I understand. I really do. At least I think I do. In so far as any of us ever understand what someone else is feeling. I hope you have a baby. But I can't give you one. Someone else might not feel the same and that's fine. I may be being selfish or prissy or God knows what, and I'd dearly like to oblige simply because . . . well, because of you. But I can't. I can't just plant a child as though it was a piece of vegetation."

"What's that arrangement called where you don't need a male?"

"Parthenogenesis, I think."

"Jolly good idea. It's pretty bloody unfair really, isn't it?" said Alice bitterly.

He could only nod.

She grinned, suddenly. "No need to look quite so hang-dog. You didn't personally devise the system. Don't worry—I'll suss something out. Or maybe the mood will pass with a bit of fresh air and exercise. Have I buggered us up, now, suggesting it?"

There was no question of that, he assured her. Absolutely no question. Everything was exactly as it had been. He was glad she . . . He tried to say that he would have been offended if she hadn't asked him, and could not manage to do so. Of course she hadn't buggered anything up. Of course not.

"Hmn . . ." said Alice. "I shan't cheat on you, if that's what you're thinking."

He was creeping with guilt now, for some reason that could not or would not be identified. He felt shabby. Casuistical. Biologically parsimonious. In California, he remembered having heard, there were generous-spirited men who put their sperm on deposit, for any who might be in need. And here was he turning away a nice woman he had known for years, had nothing whatsoever against, indeed was positively fond of. All for some scruple which, when he stared at it in the wastes of future nights, probably would not stand up to investigation. And, for ever more, each time he entered Alice Cook he would experience misgivings. Had she taken her pill? Was she stealing his seed?

"Oh, shit," said Alice. "Wouldn't life be nice and simple without all these bloody urges?"

*　　*　　*

109

Of which the reproductive urge must surely be the most complex, as experienced by late twentieth-century man or woman. Well, some late twentieth-century men and women. The view from Dacca or from Ethiopia was no doubt subtly different. But from the standpoint of urban Western prosperity it was tortuous, or so it seemed to Matthew. Thinking about himself; thinking about Alice Cook. About Susan. About Jane. There was the genetic drive, boiling away unsuspected while you got on with the rest of life, or at least you thought that that was what you were doing. The genes lurked there in the body, determining everything—whether you were six feet tall or prone to sunburn or liable to develop a particular disease—and quite possibly directing your actions as well. Sending you off in pursuit of one kind of mate rather than another. Stirring up an interest in housing and mortgages.

So far, so straightforward. Genetic drive. The compulsion to leave something of yourself behind: your nose, your freckles, your intelligence or stupidity or athletic ability or artistic talent. Except that there of course you ran into dangerous waters—the old nature/nurture controversy. Be that as it may, you were still gene-propelled, driven to ensure your own survival. No, their survival. The gene, of course, does not care about the whole man or woman—it cares only about itself. It is worried solely about the immortality of red hair, or a long nose. Each of us is host to a mindless soup of egotistic tendencies, all in blind and manic pursuit of their own propagation and compelling us in one direction: towards parenthood.

Just the same as any other animal. Except that there the resemblance ends. Animals have it relatively easy. One chick, lamb, cub, kitten is much like another; give birth, wear yourself out raising them, and then start all over again. A taxing process, to be sure, but shorn of the vital element of permanent commitment.

Here, it would seem, genes cop out. People love adoptive children just as much as natural ones. Genes throw in the towel and shuffle offstage, having set the scene. Laughing immoderately, no doubt. What do they care about patricide and matricide, about oedipal complexes and incest? About everyday anxiety and ambition and disappointment and betrayal and rejection? About joy, fulfillment and sacrifice? They've done their stuff. They've ensured continuity, and anything else that ensues is a by-product. If it turns out to determine much of human conduct—well, they can't help that, can they?

When Jane was six she broke her wrist. She also gashed her forehead but that, as it turned out, though messy and initially alarming, was insignificant. She had fallen off the brand new two-wheeler bike and lay, inert, on the tarmac path of the local park. Matthew was not there. He was at the office and there came this phone message. Could he meet his wife at the casualty department of Bart's to which she had taken their daughter with a head injury? And his stomach ran cold. He got up from his desk, went down the stairs, found a taxi and sat in it with his heart thudding. It was the period in which he and Susan had reached their lowest point, living together in silent misery and unrest.

At the hospital, he was directed along a corridor. There were curtained cubicles and, at the far end, a row of chairs and Susan, sitting there all alone. She was very white and when she looked at him there was a vulnerability in her eyes that he had not seen for a long, long time. She said, "I think it's going to be all right. She wasn't unconscious for long. They've taken her to be X-rayed."

He sat down beside her. She told him what happened. She was not looking at him any more now. He asked one or two questions, and then they fell silent. Nurses hastened to and fro.

111

Matthew said, "I'm sorry I wasn't there. It must have been horrid for you."

She nodded. And, suddenly, shuddered. An awful convulsive shudder.

He reached out and put his arm round her. She was wearing a thin cotton shirt; as his hand touched her shoulder he felt her flinch and go rigid. And at that moment he knew that there was no hope, that they were done, that it would have to end.

Jane was brought back on a trolley, and put in a curtained cubicle. Her forehead was swathed in bandages; she was alternately tearful and important, awed by the gravity of her plight. She complained that she felt sick, and that her hand hurt. She wanted to know what had become of her bicycle. Matthew and Susan stood on each side of her. Susan stroked her hair. Matthew said that he would go to the park and find the bicycle. If it was damaged he would mend it.

And then the doctor came with the X-rays. The head injury was superficial. He did not think there was concussion, but Matthew and Susan must watch her, and bring her back if at all concerned. The wrist, though, was fractured, and would have to be set. She would be taken along to the plaster room shortly.

The doctor held the X-rays up to the light. And Matthew saw his child's skull, a small and fragile thing of light and shade—the curve of the cranium, the eye and nose sockets, the jaws, the teeth. That most potent of all images. And her hand—a tiny, delicate fan of bone. He stared, in his numbed state of relief and of grief, amazed and chilled that these structures should be thus revealed, beneath the warm and silken skin that he knew so well.

Matthew's present flat was the top floor of a large mid-Victorian terrace house in north London. When he first moved in he had cared so little about his surroundings that he had simply set down his furniture and lived there as he might have done in a hotel. More recently, partly in view of Jane's weekend visits and partly, he recognized, in consequence of his own slow progress to a more normal state of mind, he had redecorated a couple of rooms, hung pictures and shifted the furniture to more congenial positions. He had put his desk in front of the largest window at the back and began to work there sometimes, at evenings and at weekends.

The view from this window was of the roof-line of the houses in the neighbouring street, and their back elevations. At night, it was surprisingly beautiful. The roof-line made a complicated black silhouette of chimney pots and angles against the ochre-orange city sky, while the buildings themselves were a dark mass brilliantly packed with the squares and rectangles of lit windows. From time to time a plane would creep above them, a firefly winking white and ruby red. And then by day the houses presented a complex of individualities by way of extensions, fire escapes, dormer windows. Someone had a minuscule conservatory in which was a white cane armchair frequented by a ginger cat. Someone else grew tomatoes on a parapet balcony. One penthouse flat with through windows afforded frequent glimpses of its occupant—a shadowy figure who went to and fro and, once, was joined by another with whom he or she stood in an embrace. Matthew had instinctively looked away and when he turned back both were gone.

It was a view, above all, of brick. An extension built onto the house some ten years or so ago jutted out at right angles to Matthew's window, giving him the perfect opportunity, in idle moments, to study in detail the city's system of rebirth. The bricks—laid Flemish bond, headers and stretchers alternating—were all old London stock bricks but of many kinds and colours: rust red, beige, grey, brown, nearly black. Here and there were yellow ones—malm bricks made with an ad-

mixture of clay and chalk. The cumulative effect was pleasing—
the variety gave texture, interest and warmth to the surface of
the wall. The eye approved the range of colour, the uneven
look, the way in which each brick differed from its neighbour
and yet was in subtle harmony. But, more than that, to look
at it was to see the way in which this wall arose from the ashes
of many buildings. Studying it, Matthew saw in the mind's
eye warehouses and churches, factories and shops, terrace
houses like this one, blasted to the ground perhaps on some
furnace night of 1940. He thought of how the city lifts again
and again from its own decay, thrusting up from its own de-
tritus, from the sediment of brick dust, rubble, wood splinters,
rusted iron, potsherds, coins and bones. He thought of himself,
living briefly on the top of this pile, inheriting its physical
variety and, above all, the clamour of its references. The
thought sustained him, in some curious way, as he sat at his
desk in the flat which was not yet a home, or as he moved
through days and through the city, from Finsbury to Docklands to Covent Garden to Lincoln's Inn.

"One prawn mayonnaise and one pastrami, please."

The glance of recognition. "One prawn, one pastrami.
And how's life been treating you?"

"Moderately well, thanks," said Matthew.

"Glad to hear it. Had your holidays yet?"

"Not yet."

"Ah. Anyway, they've got good weather for Wimbledon,
for once."

"Yes. So they have."

It was nearly two. The sandwich bar was empty. Let's
hope most of this chap's customers are better at small talk than
I am, thought Matthew.

"There we are. One-ninety, sir."

"I'm afraid I only seem to have five pounds."

"Not to worry. One-ninety . . . Two, three, four, five. There you go."

There I go indeed, thought Matthew. "Thanks. 'Bye, then."

"Cheerio. Oh, hang on . . . I was quite forgetting. Your friend came in. Last week it was. I gave her your note."

"Ah," said Matthew. "Thank you very much."

"She's not been in touch?"

"No," said Matthew. "She hasn't."

"Ah well. Maybe it wasn't the one you thought, after all."

"Very likely."

"Tell her you were in, shall I? If she's back."

"No need," said Matthew. "Don't bother. Thanks all the same. 'Bye."

Lincoln's Inn Fields is duskier today. The sun is not shining, so the shirts are on and the pram canopies are folded. The sky is high and white (it will not rain on Wimbledon); the girls have flung a jacket or a sweater on top of their cotton dresses; the pachyderm feet of *Platanus X hispanica* Muenchh stand foursquare in the grass but up above their leaves are in continuous motion.

Matthew finds a bench, and tackles the prawn sandwich; the chap has been over-prodigal with the mayonnaise. He opens his paper and reads a couple of articles and an obituary, through errant gobs of mayonnaise.

There is nothing more foolish, of course, than to assess people according to physical appearance. "I thought she looked a nice woman," says his mother—usually recounting some saga of betrayal or disillusion. Well, of course. Physiognomy is a wonderfully unreliable guide to character. Murderers, in newspaper mug-shots, look quite unremarkable folk. The most villainous face in Matthew's newspaper is that of a leading cleric. Women are if anything more impenetrable than men. And then there is the extra complication of sexual allure—absence thereof, or abundance. A woman who is attractive arouses expectations of being agreeable as well. But women who are demonstrably pleasant do not necessarily provoke sexual desire.

The girl in the sandwich bar was not arrestingly beautiful. She would not turn heads. Nice-looking, and for some reason the face stays in the mind: shape of nose, brown wings of hair against the cheeks. And that, of course, is the flaw—*nice*-looking. Whatever leads one to suppose such a thing? She is undoubtedly a nasty little bitch prone to ungovernable rages, unremittingly self-absorbed, whose sole interests are wind-surfing and war-gaming in Berkshire woods. One is well out of it. Let this be a lesson.

Physiognomy may not be an indication of character, but it undoubtedly affects a person's fate. An excess of good looks or sexual appeal will lead to one kind of life rather than another. Beautiful women provoke certain expectations. Handsome men also. Matthew was joined now on his bench by a couple of girls who presumably judged his appearance adequately unthreatening, and who took no further notice of him. He reflected, with detachment, upon his own looks. Shorter than the average male by perhaps an inch, a matter of distress to him in youth, which now seems odd, and a touch disturbing: there lurks still, then, some primitive human belief that size is a measure of potential. Sturdily built, but the build not of an athlete but of a road-mender. Chunky, a mite round-shouldered. As a student, Matthew had taken vacation jobs on construction sites and had had occasion to note that, stripped to the waist, he looked much like everyone else but, mortifyingly, was not nearly so robust.

Dark hair, almost black. Wide face with rather blunt nose; brown eyes set far apart, thick eyebrows. An expression that is apparently cheerful without intention; a woman in a lift last week said to him indignantly, "What are you grinning at me for?" when he had barely been aware of her presence.

So far as sexual allure goes, he would probably register about average. Women had not exactly come running, but neither had they turned aside in droves. His appearance, then, it would seem, was neither off-putting nor particularly magnetic. Women, quite properly, resent being viewed as sexual objects. The difficulty is, of course, that we all in some degree view one another as sexual objects—to the extent of the thought occurring, however subliminally, that one would like to or one would prefer not to. Most people you come across are the wrong age or gender anyway; those who are not are bound to provoke vague responses of inclination or rejection.

And the girl in the sandwich bar? This is purely an academic exercise, since the situation has now been rationally assessed and she is recognized for what she is: ill-tempered, selfish, superficial if not downright perverted. Well, undoubtedly one had registered inclination rather than rejection. In an abstract sort of way. Far more than that, there had been this yearning, this sense of deprivation. The green hill. Not a sexual object, oh no, but an object of desire. A promised land. A naive and irrational impulse.

His companions on the bench had finished their lunch and left. It was twenty past two—high time to get back to the office. Another five minutes. He got up, disposed of the newspaper—now marbled with mayonnaise stains—and began a slow circuit of the gardens, idly studying other walkers. Their faces, their gait, their dress. There were two small girls of Jane's age, whom he watched with benign professionalism; he recognized the skipping game they played, he knew—or thought he knew—what was in their minds. He saw in the distance a young woman whose fair cropped head brought Susan vividly to mind—not Susan now but Susan then.

The first time he ever met her he had barely noticed her. She was brought by another man to a Sunday lunch gathering at a riverside pub. Matthew's sights were elsewhere, in any case; he was mildly besotted with a gloomy and overwrought German girl and had spent the time trying to negotiate the next unsatisfactory meeting, while on the other side of the table Susan chatted with a merrier group. And then he had run into her again at a New Year's Eve party, and talked to her, and noticed. And then he had engineered a group jaunt to Brighton which she had joined, and then he had asked her out to dinner. And then, and then. A conventional enough courtship; banal even.

And the structure, in any case, is now largely forgotten. What remains are those silvered imperishable scenes. He stands by the ticket office at Waterloo, searching the crowds for her, and sees her far off, knows her at once by the way she walks, the way she turns her head, and is swept by joy, by her strangeness, and her infinite familiarity. He looks furtively at her across a room, catches her looking, also, for him, and feels an uprush of excitement. They are walking on the Embankment, in a drizzle of winter rain; they stop under a tree, and he takes her in his arms. They kiss, and over her shoulder he sees the bare branches of the tree black against the sky, with the round balls of the seed pods slinging from them like decorations. The London plane, of course.

But all this was long ago, and in another country. Waterloo is still there, and the Embankment—he passed that precise spot, indeed, just the other day—but the place in which those things happened is the country of the mind. He is elsewhere now, and must make what he can of it.

Two twenty-five, and Matthew heads for Kingsway and the tube station. He looks, as usual, at buildings—and sees, as always, some detail not previously observed. But he looks above all at people. During the last hour the faces of a hundred strangers have passed before him. He thinks of this torrent of flesh and bone, forever replenished, forever renewed. He listens to the sound of that torrent, that flow of death and birth.

It is an incendiary night; they must be dropping them in thousands. You hear them rattle and clatter on the roof tops, and the clunks as they hit the ground, and then a whole street will be sizzling with blue-white fireworks as though they had sprouted rather than fallen. He has dealt with half a dozen already, and has his eye out all the time for that gout of flame from a roof that means one has gone through the tiles and into the rafters. And incendiaries mean the big stuff is to follow, that is the sequence. Get the city lit up with fires, and then come in with the thousand-pounders and the land-mines.

But it is over the docks, as yet. No incidents on his patch. So far. He is able to make the rounds of his shelters unhindered by crisis calls. The tube station is full, but quiet, except for a bunch of soldiers on leave who have stocked up with booze; the self-appointed shelter marshal, a termagant of a woman, will crack down on them if necessary. Branton Street are complaining because their hurricane lamp won't work. The Lunt Square cellar is badly flooded again and they are having to bale out.

He hears the hesitant throb of planes and takes cover in a doorway. He can tell that they are high and heading for the river. They have all become connoisseurs of these sights and sounds that were undreamed of a year ago and will now be for ever before the eyes and in the head. The unearthly, awesome effects of the big fire nights when the whole sky is a brilliant orange, with the plump shapes of balloons floating against it as clear as by day, and incandescent columns of smoke boiling upwards, grey-black touched with red. The scarlet blizzards of sparks, the drifting clouds of red embers; the silver arcs of water jets against the banks of smoke. The shrill descending whistle of high explosive bombs, and then the dull prolonged boom, shuddering away into silence. The shattering thud and blast of a land-mine, after which the pavement lifts under your feet, the whole place rocks. The fire-bells, the high moan of the hooters, the crunch of tyres on glass-strewn streets.

The night skies. In which moon and stars have become a backdrop, eclipsed by the brilliance of a different display. Chandelier flares drifting down like lanterns, drenching streets and buildings in a pure white glare. The long hard beams of the searchlights, feeling around in the black sky, seeming to fence with one another, and then coming together in great tents at the apex of which is the caught firefly of a plane, circled with shining shell-bursts. While down below on the ground people grope about in the dark, feeling their way by the glimmer of shrouded torches, the white-painted landmarks of kerbs and tree-trunks, the thin crosses of colour on blacked-out traffic lights.

There is a torch jerking towards him now, insufficiently muffled, and just as he is about to shout an angry warning he recognizes the voice of a colleague from the ARP post. "That you, Jim? There's a girl having a baby in the Ransome Street shelter."

"Try to get an ambulance down there."

"The phone's gone dead on us."

They meet up in the middle of the black street. "Bloody heck!" he says. "Get to the Casualty Post, then, and ask one of the nurses to come over. I'll go and see what's to be done."

The Ransome Street shelter is one of the small concrete sub-surface ones. There are thirty or so people in there, crowded up on benches in the dim light from the hurricane lamp. They have got the girl laid out on rugs and coats on the floor at the far end. As Jim enters he hears her give a yell, and a rustle runs through the people who have clustered up by the door to make space. An old man is sucking up tea from a tin mug. He says, "Well, here's a fine to-do then." Someone else is murmuring that she shouldn't be here anyway, if she was that far gone, and is reproved by a neighbour.

"She was evacuated, and she come back because her mum was ill, and then her mum was bombed out two nights ago."

He edges down the narrow aisle along the floor gritty with sand spilled from the sandbags that bank the shelter. The girl is not more than twenty or so; fair hair falls lankly from a sweat-stained face. She is gasping and chewing her lip. He says lamely, "Don't worry, there's a nurse on the way." And then another contraction comes; she clutches at the women who are beside her and screams again. And the others in the shelter tut and mutter, in sympathy and in unease, unnerved by that primeval sound of a woman in labour.

"It's all right, my lovey, it's all right." One of the women turns to Jim. "It's not going to be long now. Can't you get us an ambulance?"

He belts out into the night again to see if the nurse is coming, and finds her, stumbling her way on foot, and brings her to the shelter. She is a brisk effective powerhouse of a woman, honed to a fine point of compassionate authority by years on the district in Stepney. She sweeps up the occupants of the shelter, sorts the men into a group by the door, isolates the girl and the self-appointed midwives, despatches Jim back to the ARP post for more blankets, a primus stove, kettles and water.

It is hotting up, out there. He can see a reef of smoke now, to the east; they must be getting it bad in the docks. He picks his way sightless through the darkness, expert now, knowing by feel the siting of kerbs or lampposts, sensing the imminence of breaches in the road surface. He halts for a moment at the end of the road to get his breath, and looks up, as you always look up these days, at the treacherous sky, the sky that was once a simple matter of sun, moon and stars but which now deals out fire and destruction. It is a fine clear night, and he can see stars now, glittering behind the sweeping searchlights and the white blossoms of shell-bursts. And the

121

moon, nearly full, poised somewhere above Greenwich: cold, perfect and inviolate.

Back at the post they are all cursing at the loss of the phone, running hither and thither with messages. When he announces he must take the primus they are further demoralized; the cups of thick sweet tea that punctuate the night are what keeps everyone going. Pleading life and death (an appeal that has perhaps lost its edge, these days) he gathers up primus and utensils, plus all available blankets including that belonging to the post's resident cat. While he is doing this they all pause at the distant crump of a bomb, half a mile away perhaps, and wait for the rest of the stick seconds later—more crumps, and the boom of some buildings in collapse. And then he sets forth once more.

At the end of Ransome Street, yards from the shelter, he pauses, alerted in some uncanny way. He looks down the length of the road, to the wide scoop of sky at the end. And against this darkness he sees a block of even denser darkness, a drifting oblong, something light and wayward as thistledown, that floats slowly and lazily over the roof-line, cruising to earth. For seconds he is mesmerized. He simply stands there, and then his wits respond, he throws himself face down, hands clasped over his head.

There is a great flash of white light. And then a noise like a colossal, supernatural growl that consumes and deafens. And the pavement recoils. It comes punching up at him— once, twice, again. He is sliding helplessly across the road, caught in a current of blast that is like some monstrous tide; he drifts ten yards, and washes up against the wheels of a car. He lies there, battered, his ears ringing. He lifts his head, looks down the street, and sees in the distance that the whole of one of the dark masses of house frontage is bellying out, bulging as though shoved by an invisible hand, and then it simply dissolves, flooding downwards, and now debris is pattering down all around—a building fragmented, reduced to a shower of dust and rubble.

He eases himself onto his hands and knees. The shelter is intact. The land-mine has demolished the end of the street, but the shelter is undamaged, and so is he. He waits till the debris has ceased to fall and then he gets up and hurries for the shelter. It is quiet now. There is a great stillness, as though for a minute the place were holding its breath. He pushes open the door of the shelter and as he does so he hears this sound, this single sound. The thin, determined cry of a new child.

NINE

"Mr Halland?"

"Speaking,"

"Mr Rutter would like to talk to you."

"Well, I'm afraid I don't particularly want to speak to him," said Matthew. "So would you kindly . . ."

"Good morning, Mr Halland," said Rutter. "I got an apology to make to you. I was talking a bit out of turn the other day."

"Don't mention it. And now if you'll excuse me . . ."

"I got a tendency to go straight to the point, know what I mean? I got no time for messing about."

"Quite."

"People can get me wrong and I don't blame them. I get carried away. My girlfriend says I should count to ten before I open my mouth, and she's about the only person can use that sort of talk with me and get away with it. Her and my mum. Eighty-six, my mother is, and treats me like I was in short trousers—you'd laugh, Mr Halland."

Wincing at this unsolicited glimpse of Rutter's private

life, Matthew broke in. "Look, what exactly is the purpose of this call?"

"I'd like you to come up to my place so we can have another little chat. We got off on the wrong footing before."

"No thanks," said Matthew. "I'm allergic to dogs."

Rutter laughed merrily. "All right, then. What about a little lunch at the Caprice?"

"Frankly, no."

"You're playing hard to get, Mr Halland."

"No. I'm being realistic. This is all a complete waste of time."

"Mr Halland, we're both businessmen, right? I got a simple proposition to put to you."

"I really cannot conceive of any proposition of yours that would be of interest, I'm afraid, Mr Rutter."

A sigh. More in sorrow than in anger, it would seem. "I think maybe I've caught you on a bad morning, my friend. I'll be in touch."

Click.

The glass engraver lived and worked in a converted warehouse on the waterfront at Wapping. She was called Eva Burden, and had been recommended to Matthew by a colleague. The address was elusive: he cruised for ten minutes around an area of demolition, of uninhabited new constructions slung about with estate agents' signs and of uncompromising blank façades until at last he found a door with the name scrawled on a card beside the bell.

She was a small dark woman in her late fifties. "Come up. Sorry about all the stairs."

They emerged at last in a bright studio room overlooking the river. Matthew, going to the window, saw the Greenwich ferry and heard the tannoy quacking its commentary. "Very choice view you've got."

"I was lucky—I came here early on. I couldn't possibly afford this place now."

She made coffee, talking about soaring property values, about her neighbours—the original adventuring colonizers of these derelict sites now superseded by the wealthy young of the City. She shrugged: "I'll be dislodged eventually—if only by my own greed. I could make lots of money if I sold, they tell me. But I'd rather stay—where else could I have so much to look at?"

Her speech had an otherness—a suggestion of elsewhere. Vowel sounds; something curious about the *r*s. Matthew said, "Have you always been a Londoner?"

"I'm German by birth. I came here when I was eight, in 1939. The *Kindertransport*."

Of course. That faint unquenchable whiff of Europe. Tenacious and emotive. Looking at her—this middle-aged, oddly vibrant woman in trousers and a sweatshirt—Matthew saw a child with a cardboard suitcase on a station platform.

"Perhaps that's why I'm attracted by the river. Refugee mentality. The way to somewhere else."

"I should think the river draws most people."

They sat at a table by the window, looking out. The City Airport hovercraft, a dapper swirl of white and blue. A rowing eight. Gulls. A piece of drifting timber. Plastic bottles.

"Once I saw a corpse," said Eva Burden.

"What did you do?"

"Phoned the police. They sent out a launch. And it wasn't after all. It was some sacking and bits of wood. I felt very foolish. They said it happens all the time. People expect bodies in rivers."

"No doubt with good reason. But I envy you. If I lived here I'd never be able to take my eyes off it."

"Off what?"

"The water," said Matthew. "Principally."

"Ah, yes. Water. When I was a child they used to take us to this beach, and I would look and look at the sea, knowing that where I came from was somewhere out there. I saw it as an island. A small German island with my town, my house, my parents, exactly as I left it all." She stared across the table—dark intense eyes under a black fringe streaked with grey. "You don't have a map in your head, as a child. Later, you have the globe—the seas and the shapes—and you can't ever get back to that emptiness, that mystery. Knowing that there are other places, but not knowing where they are, or how to get there."

Meta Incognita. The country which has not been discovered and which therefore has no name. The place which lies beyond the sea card, which may be ten leagues off, or fifty, or a hundred. The country of ice and snow, of bears and seals, of savages and of gold. The unmapped, unknown, treacherous coastline which lurks somewhere beyond the mists, over the edge of the seas.

"So you want a ship, for this building of yours? What sort of ship?"

"Something along these lines . . ." Matthew spread his books and photocopies on the table.

"I see. An Elizabethan ship. Fine. Lots of possibilities. I shall enjoy this, I think. How big? And what is the background? I'll have to come and look at the site, of course."

The ship is a pinpoint in infinity, and a universe. It is a fragile thing to be smashed in the ice or swallowed by a wave; it is a great creaking ponderous solidity of oak and iron. It is a defiant statement of ingenuity and order, a challenge flung down to the anarchic wastes of water, wind and ice. Aboard, there is language, a social structure, and the means to manipulate the physical world. An astrolabum. A compass. A sea card. A *Sphera Nautica*. Beyond, there are roaring tides, snow, fog, gales, drifting packs of ice islands, and the blessed elusive certainties of sun, moon and stars. The ship has purpose, and direction. It is powered by human ambition, aspiration, endeavour and greed. And set against this formidable array is the intractable hostility of this blank white quarter of the globe. Which will win? Will the ship vanish into the maw of nature, or will he tame that wild expanse by naming it, by charting it, by giving it position and a shape, by reducing it to a scribble of lines upon a sea card? Martin Furbissher, Ffourbyssher, Frobusher. Frobisshers Streights.

"The sails are the crux of the design, of course," she said. "That wonderful swoop. Three swoops. I shall have to be both accurate and a touch stylized. I shall need to exaggerate the sails, don't you think?"

"Definitely."

"And what about people? Do you want human figures?"

"No. I think the ship says it all."

A monstrous apparition, which comes riding out of the ocean, infested with evil spirits shaped like men. Followed presently by fellow apparitions, large and small, crewed by a devilish horde armed with weapons which spit fire and death.

The people watch and wait. They hide behind rocks. They follow the monsters from inlet to inlet. They dance upon the shore and make signs of friendship. They match trickery for treachery, take captive for captive, shed blood for blood.

"No people, then. Birds? An albatross? A whale?"

"I'm tempted by the whale," said Matthew. "Let's think about that. Albatrosses are Antarctic only, I'm afraid."

"Oh dear—natural history isn't my strong point. What I shall do, of course, is make some rough sketches and then we can go on from there. When I've been to the site and can see how the light will fall on it and how the reflections will work. Mind, I must be honest—I've got pretty mixed feelings about Docklands. From an architectural point of view. Of course, I haven't seen your particular building yet."

"I've got pretty mixed feelings myself," said Matthew.

Eva Burden laughed. "And we all have to make a living, don't we? Actually, I'm rather excited about this commission. Even if it is going to adorn a temple of commerce."

Meta Incognita is inhabited, then. It is populated not only with seals, foxes, wolves, bears and teeming legions of birds, but also with men and women. These people wear animal furs and have skins the colour of a ripe olive which they paint with blue dots. They live in caves in the ground and hunt their food with slings, darts and arrows. They are almost certainly cannibals, and worship some form of magic. They will trade skins for trinkets, knives and bells, but are not to be trusted.

These people are ignorant of the significance of gold. They do not mine the gold-bearing ore from the ground, neither are they able to locate the deposits of ore.

"I'll finish off on site," she said. "But the main work will be done here, of course."

"With the river as inspiration—very appropriate in this case."

"Oh, I'm shuttered off when I'm working—literally." And she reached for a helmet, put it on, became for a moment a motorcyclist, a spacewoman, an alien. "The glass dust—you mustn't breathe it in. This thing has a pump, so you get fresh air. Cumbersome but necessary. So I'm not looking much at the river."

"Ah, I see. Your drill gives me the shivers. It puts me in

mind of visits to an extremely primitive dentist when I was a child."

She laughed. "That's pretty much what it is."

Around the room there were examples of her work. A white and haloed saint-figure floating in a great sheet of glass; goblets etched with delicate lettering; butterflies caught in the curve of a bowl. Matthew prowled—inspecting, approving. He visualized her at work: a Pony Express bike courier creating miracles with a dentist's drill.

"Has this always been your line?"

"What a one you are for questions! No—I was an illustrator originally. I'm self-taught. Anyone can do this who can draw."

"Sorry," he said. "I always wonder about how people get to be what they are."

"And why not? Well, I was a refugee girl who had a certain gift with a pencil, picked up jobs doing commercial graphics, moved into children's books, dust jackets, any illustration work I could get—then saw John Hutton's screen at Coventry one day and knew what I really wanted to do."

"I should think that leaves out a fair amount."

She chuckled. "It does indeed. When I first started to draw all I did was guns, tanks, aeroplanes falling from the sky, burning buildings. It has taken a long time to get to butterflies and saints."

When they show the captive a picture of the City of London, that he may know from whence they come, he displays no interest. But when they show him the portrait of a man he tries to talk to it, and is angry that the image remains silent. He picks up the paper and turns it over, to find where the man is hiding. He can wrestle, climb, and use an oar, but he cannot write or read and looks upon the compass as a toy.

131

But it has substance now, this *Meta Incognita*. No shape as yet, but substance—the inhospitable reality of a barren coast washed by freezing seas, mountains on which the snow lies all summer, and a citizenry of flesh, fowl and a kind of men, one of whom they will take back with them to London, as a token of possession. If, by God's will, they escape from this fearful place.

And in the meantime they must dig for gold. The storms howl down upon them every few days, the bays and inlets start to become thick with ice, and there are those of the company so fearful that the ships will be gripped, grounded, trapped here to face the winter in which all would surely perish, that they argue for departure. He will have none of it. He rants and bawls and sets the miners to dig for gold. He has that great wild silent world ringing with the sound of their pickaxes. They drive and blast their way into the rock; they scrape and scrabble and drag the ore from the ground to be piled into the holds of the ships.

"I like church commissions best," she said. "Funny, isn't it, for a Jew. I like doing memorial windows at cut-price for little country churches where they raise the money with fêtes and jumble sales. I'll go down there and work on site, for people like that. Some romantic concept of the essential England. And here am I living all my adult life in the middle of London. That's what I really know of England. Immigrants' England— bricks and tarmac. That's where I feel at home now. I'm a fish out of water in a country village, but I still think that must be the real England. So I go and make cut-price saints for churches. We immigrants are funny people. But my lot were exceptional, I suppose. Most immigrants are forced into it by something—we were flung, and by our own parents, poor souls. My God, did I hate this country when I was eight years old! Cold, wet, with food I could not eat and a language I could not understand. And then, by some mysterious process that you don't even notice at the time, what is appalling becomes familiar and eventually essential. I hardly ever go to Germany. When I do I am uncomfortable, for reasons over and above the obvious ones. I have to hurry back here. I need London voices and dirty streets and drunks in the tube and bodies in the river." She laughed. "And other things. But the point is that you have been digested. The city has taken you over, in a sense."

The weather becomes daily more treacherous. The wind roars out of the north and the great slabs of drifting ice are closing in upon the ships. He can no longer withstand the urging of his fellows. The holds of the vessels are now filled with ore, and they have with them other tokens by which to prove the existence of this *Meta Incognita*—viz. the skin of a great white bear, the horn of that strange fish known as a sea unicorn, rocks, plants, skins of birds and beasts, and the captive man.

The anchors have been raised, and now it is each for himself. The ships must fight their way singly across the ocean, trusting to God and to the skills of their navigators, to the certainties of the lodestone, the tables of calculation, the moon and the stars: the *Frances of Foy*, the *Dennis*, the *Gabriel*, the *Thomas of Ipswich* and the rest of them. He, the admiral of this fleet, has given instructions that if any vessel should fall into the hands of an enemy then all maps, charts or other references to the newly discovered lands shall be thrown overboard. Equally, upon arrival at the home port of Dartford Creek in the Thames River, all the ore upon each of the ships shall be handed over for delivery to the admiral, and any person taking or keeping to his use any piece of ore shall be apprehended as a felon.

Thus shall the purpose of this great endeavour be fulfilled. And now he commends himself, and all of them, to God, and looks his last upon that barren and brutal land, that obstacle to the road to Cathay, that intransigent barrier within which lurks the North-West Passage and, by the Grace of the Lord, enough gold to enrich Her Majesty, the nation and himself.

"So . . ." she said, "I shall go and have a look at the site, and then get going on some rough sketches. Both with whale and without whale. Which we can mull over together and decide on the final version. All right?"

"Sounds fine. I'll look forward to it."

She extended a hand, with unexpected formality: a small, firm, dry paw. "Goodbye, then, Mr Halland."

"Matthew," he said. "Please. And thanks very much. I've got a feeling you're going to provide the touch of class this building needs."

She laughed. "I don't know about that. Let's see how it turns out first. But you've given me an inspiring subject."

He drove to the Blackwall site, through the tumultuous and discordant landscape of Docklands, thinking of this odd, dogged woman and the small oasis of purpose and conviction she had created there beside the river. Images traced on glass. He thought of the qualities of glass: hard, brittle, reflective. Immensely durable, easily broken, wonderfully versatile. A window or a mirror; a vessel or a screen. Once a cherished and valuable commodity; now one of the cheapest materials going.

And London, he saw, was turning into a glass city. The stuff snapped and glittered all around him, climbing into the skies in columns of smoky grey and aquamarine and turquoise. Sometimes the façades were mirrors of silver or copper, throwing back their surroundings—the movement of traffic, the complexities of other buildings, the flowing clouds. Enigmatic, uncommitted presences; an architecture of deception. All around, glass was soaring above the old structures of brick and stone, dwarfing them, distorting them so that they swam shrunk and misshapen in the shining surface of the new city.

"Would you like to be rich?" Matthew asks Alice Cook.

"God, yes."

"No—think about it. I'm talking about what is inappropriately called serious money. Money that doesn't really exist. Figures on paper. Ballast. Not our kind of money, that you buy a new car with, or have a more expensive holiday than last year's."

"An Alfa Romeo," says Alice. "That's what I'd like. And a month in the Bahamas."

"No, you wouldn't. You'd lose all your friends and feel like a fish out of water. What you want is an extra few thousand a year and a bit off the mortgage. Like me. We're beginners, where money is concerned. Non-starters. The rich are different. I used not to think that, but I'm changing my mind. It's a question of purpose. We could be rich if we wanted to be."

"Then kindly tell me how it's done."

"I don't know. If we really wanted it we would know, you see, that's the point."

"Are there rich architects?"

"Of course. You see?"

"Mind you," says Alice. "You're not exactly skint. You've got a nice flat. And a car that's done less than twenty thousand and you're prepared to lay out fifty quid for a dinner. What was that place called, that you took me to on my birthday?"

"Alice, you prove my point with every word. You don't want to be rich and you wouldn't know how to. You lack the vision. Like me. Like, thank God, most of us. Which is what lends an awful fascination to those powered by financial lust. It's as though you were without any sexual impulse whatsoever and had to try to fathom why other people carry on as they do."

"I've got an aunt like that," says Alice. "My mum swears she's never done it and never wanted to. And if you met her casually you'd think she was perfectly normal."

"I'll tell you one thing," says Matthew. "You may have no talent for serious money, but if you've got a bit to spare I'll give you a tip where to put it, right now. Buy some shares in Pilkington's. Pilkington's Glass."

Jane was given two pounds pocket money every week. Susan gave her one pound on Tuesdays and Matthew supplied a further pound on Saturday. When he was her age he had had a shilling, of which he was required to put sixpence in his piggy bank. The ethos of his upbringing made him feel guilty that he made no such requirement of Jane—but how could you rationally recommend such a course with inflation running at nearly ten percent? On the other hand, children should be taught the virtues of thrift, foresight and financial restraint just as much as that of rational response. Interestingly, Jane appeared to have some kind of natural inclination to save. She liked to be paid in assorted coins, and would hoard at one time ten-pence pieces, at another twenties. These lived in a raspberry yoghurt container and when they had accumulated to her satisfaction she would take them out and spend the lot on a carefully considered item. There seemed to be some totemic significance to the coins being all of one kind; the whole procedure apparently had a ritual quality over and above the process of amassing enough cash for a special purpose. Occasionally, and with faint unease, Matthew wondered if his child was displaying embryonic signs of financial obsession. Were the cherished piles of ten- and twenty-pence coins the precursors of twitching green figures on a VDU? On the whole, given her expressed view of wealth, he thought not.

Jane thought that rich people were probably nasty and poor people likely to be good. She thought that you were justified in taking money away from rich people to give to poor people. Rich people tended to bury their money in secret places or hide it under the bed whence it would be stolen by thieves and serve them right. Poor people, on the other hand, were prone to astonishing runs of luck. They stumbled across bags of gold, befriended beggars who turned out to be millionaires, or married into the aristocracy. Consequently—identifying of course with the poor—one should always keep one's eyes skinned and be charitable. This archaic and judgmental view of the world, which seemed to owe nothing whatsoever to the society in which Jane was being reared, derived, Matthew realized, from the allegorical morality of fairy tales. It said a lot for the power of narrative. Here was a code set up for the comfort and edification of a long-defunct peasantry operating quite satisfactorily among the children of the consumer age. Or is it that it is only children who are able to retain a vision of the world not as it is, but as it ought to be? Matthew, a punctilious parent, had dipped at one time into works on child psychology and had been struck by the salutary tale of the psychologist who told to a group of seven-year-olds the story of the robber who stole a pot of money from a poor old woman. The robber ran away with the money across a wooden bridge over a river. The bridge collapsed and the robber fell into the river and was drowned. When the children are asked, Why do you think the bridge broke?, they do not reply, Because it was rotten, or Because the robber was a heavy man, but Because the robber did a wicked thing.

In the early years of his career Matthew had been involved with the designs of a school, a hospital, a housing estate in a new town and a shopping precinct. Useful and necessary projects—though the shopping precinct leaned perhaps in the direction of Mammon. Nowadays, visiting the Blackwall site, watching Frobisher House take shape by the day, its brilliant, polished tower rising from the mud, that time seemed of a different age. If school and hospital building went on anywhere these days, James Gamlin and Partners were not concerned. Which was of course an effect of the turn his own career had taken, as much as a sign of the times. Professional efficiency and a degree of restlessness had taken him to one kind of firm rather than another. "You've no one but yourself to blame," his mother might have said. He had preferred to work in the front line, to go where the potential seemed to be. And thus, inexorably, as it now seemed, had been propelled towards Docklands. He had pursued the Blackwall contract, indeed, along with his colleagues, had felt challenged and invigorated in the early days of negotiation and then of work at the drawing-board. He still felt frissons of satisfaction at a technical problem overcome, or at having been proved right in some prognostication. But the initial excitement had given way to a sort of weary cynicism. The only thing that really interested him now at Blackwall, he realized, was the glass engraving.

TEN

Matthew's post was seldom promising. It would slither through the letter-box as he was getting himself some breakfast and lie there on the mat in a brightly-coloured drift until he saw fit to pick it up and sort through the accretion of unsolicited envelopes in search of something that might have been intended for him personally. A large number of the missives pressed extensions of credit or goods which he did not want—an American Express card or a set of ceramic thimbles in a velvet-lined case. A few sought his help in saving the environment or alleviating the condition of famine victims, but very many more flourished the lure of free gifts and lucky numbers. To find the gas bill, or a bank statement, lurking amid this vociferous clutch was to feel favoured with a touch of intimacy. A real letter was a rarity.

It was with a certain wonder, therefore, that he came across the hand-written envelope. Unfamiliar writing; a non-committal WC1 postmark. He delayed opening it for a few seconds, with an instinct to damp down expectations.

A single folded sheet of paper: the message quite brief,

no form of address—just "I owe you a sandwich." A phone number. And a signature. Nice and clear: Sarah Bridges.

One had of course been completely mistaken. She is not a nasty little bitch at all and has never been windsurfing or war-gaming in her life. One knew that, of course, really, all along. She is . . .

The phone rang. He leapt to it. "Matthew? It's Tony. I thought I'd better remind you we've got the meeting with the Belgian group at ten. You did take the papers back with you, didn't you? I couldn't lay hands on them last night."

Yes, he said. Yes, I've got the papers, and yes, I've remembered. One eye on the clock—God, nearly nine—the other scanning his desk.

He darts around the flat, snatching things up. Those papers, car keys, jacket. A minute later he is in the car, starting up the engine. It is a quite extraordinarily agreeable day. Sunshine, a light spicy wind. Banks of lilac cloud.

"Sounds delightful," said the client benignly. "I'll look forward to seeing the finished version. You say this woman does small stuff, too? Maybe she could turn us out some decanters for the board room." He made a quick note on the little gilt-edged pad that lay always beside his plate. "Were your langoustines good? I'm always daunted by all those legs."

"Very nice." The langoustines, at £16.50 a throw, had indeed been delicious, and the legs a minor inconvenience. They had moved on to the lemon sorbet now, and Charles Sanderling was skimming through the pile of papers at his side, in case there was anything he had forgotten to discuss. He had not enquired the cost of the glass engraving; a mere bagatelle, in relation to the ultimate bill for Frobisher House.

They finished the meal. Sanderling returned the papers to his briefcase. "I shall be away for the next few weeks. If there are any problems call my office—they'll be in touch with me, of course. My wife is insisting on a spell in the Caribbean—apparently I am considered to be on the verge of collapse." He glimmered the thin smile across the table at Matthew, indulgent and a touch amused. It was the first time a wife had ever been mentioned. Children? No, one would not enquire. Somehow the thought of trading fatherly reflections instead of the ritual two and a half minutes on the weather or the political climate was not appealing.

Sanderling dropped his credit card onto the bill. "So, apart from the possibility of having to invoke that penalty clause, there don't seem to be any major hassles pending. You going away yourself?"

"I'll probably go down to Devon for a week or two."

Sanderling looked faintly perplexed. Possibly he didn't know where Devon was. He ushered Matthew ahead of him out of the restaurant. Once in the street, the chauffeured car appeared, as though at some concealed signal; perhaps the driver spent the lunch period going round and round the block. Sanderling glimmered again, got in, and could be seen immediately at work on the car phone.

Matthew decided to make a quick detour to the Covent Garden precinct to stock up with coffee beans.

He is, as usual, distracted. He buys the coffee; he dips into the Penguin Bookshop for a few minutes; he listens to a group of Malaysians playing reedy, plangent music on some esoteric kind of wind instrument. He wanders past windows displaying skimpy impractical clothes at remarkably high prices, covets for a moment a Chinese silk kimono with dragon motif, but comes quickly to his senses, settles for a jar of honeycomb. The place is dizzy with people, of course—buying and selling, getting and spending. Most people, though, by the look of things, do not want sober goods like honeycomb or coffee beans (and both of these, come to think of it, one could quite well get by without); they want thatched cottage teapots and Union Jack tea-caddies and shell-embossed photo frames and silver lurex tights. There are droves of them, old and young, drawn from far and wide, apparently, in search of these delights. And why not? It is a good place, Covent Garden. Not a great good place perhaps, but a place where people are at ease and enjoying themselves.

He makes his way up James Street, through the crowds. There is such a throng, indeed, that when he is forced to a halt it is a few seconds before he is aware that a girl is addressing him—a dishevelled girl in jeans and T-shirt, clutching the handle of a push-chair in which sleeps a small child. The girl is asking for money, he at last realizes, she is saying that she has nothing with which to buy food for herself and the baby, that she has nowhere to live, that she slept rough last night. She is begging, in other words.

Matthew experiences a confusion of feeling: mistrust, distress, incredulity, embarrassment. Stalling, he asks the girl where she comes from, but in fact that is already apparent from her accent. She replies that she comes from Northern Ireland. Why did you come over here? Matthew asks. To get away from the Troubles, the girl promptly answers. She launches into a spiel about the DSS, about lodgings that cost twenty pounds a night, about some letter that has gone astray. How old is the baby? Matthew asks, still playing for time, still trying to sort out his feelings. Two years old, replies the girl. The baby, Matthew notes, appears clean and well-fed. As indeed does the girl.

Matthew's feelings refuse to be marshalled into any kind of order. He remains simultaneously shocked and sceptical. The girl's patter is practised and fluent: too practised, too fluent. And yet . . . And yet . . . There rises up within him an ancestral suspicion of indigence, of fecklessness—the teaching of his parents. Another voice counters that everything she says may well be true, that London is indeed littered with homeless people, that the social services are notoriously overstretched. He havers, flustered; the girl continues to plead. At last he digs into his pocket and puts all his loose change into her hand. She inspects it, thrusts it into a purse, and does not say thank you. He walks on. He glances back once, but cannot see her.

The child squats under a cart. It is summer. Her stomach is full, for once, and she is warm. Sunlight slants across her legs and arms through the spokes of a wheel. She picks up a straw and traces the pattern; absorbed, she makes white scratch marks on her skin, until she is distracted by the events of the street. She freezes while a dog pauses to eye her (she was bitten, once), but the dog cocks a leg, merely, and moves on. She is alert to the passage of carts and baskets, from which scavengings might fall. She watches intently as one of that other kind of people goes by, the kind that smell of money, a man with clean clothes, a stick and a top hat. She considers darting out to beg, in an instinctive response, but he is gone, and it is too late. She returns to her straw and her white scratch marks and sees with interest that the lines of sunlight have moved, they lie differently on her skin. And it comes to her in sudden wisdom that this is because the sun moves around the sky. She knows this because in the morning it shines through the window of the room in which they live, and in the evenings it has gone. The room forms itself within her head, bringing with it a whiff of distress, a signal from the bad time when she was ill, a whisper of pain and misery. She recognises that there was *then,* and there is *now,* and the mercy of the gulf between, and she pushes the signal away.

"Why are you picking things up and putting them down again all the time?" said Jane.

"I'm looking for a piece of paper I've lost."

"Here's a piece of paper."

"Thank you. It's not that one, I'm afraid."

She followed him around the flat, observing with kindly detachment. "Why do you want it?"

"It's got an important telephone number on it."

He sat down. Think. Think carefully. I rushed out immediately after Tony rang, didn't get back till nearly midnight, after the evening at the Richardsons. Went straight to bed. No one else has been in the flat. It should be on the desk where I usually dump mail, or in my briefcase, or just lying around. Or in the wastepaper basket. It is in none of those places.

Check once more, just in case.

"You've already looked there," said Jane.

"I know I have."

This morning I went to collect Jane at nine, the normal Saturday arrangement. A bit late, because I overslept. On the way back we went to Sainsbury's, and then dropped my washing off at the launderette.

He headed for the door. "Jane! Come. We're going back to the launderette."

She trotted obediently behind him. "Why?"

"Because I think that bit of paper is in the pocket of the trousers I put in the machine."

"The writing will have got washed off it," said Jane after a moment.

"Possibly."

Was it biro or tempo pen? Biro would probably be more tenacious. Please God may it have been biro. But by now the nice lady at the launderette will have unloaded my stuff and put it in the drier, noting that I have not returned, and being ever helpful.

As, indeed, she had. The drier, right now, was thumping and throbbing, panting forth hot air. "It's got cooked," said

Jane with interest. "I don't think you're going to be able to read the writing any more."

"Mmn," said Matthew.

The machine shuddered to a standstill. He opened the door, hauled out nicely toasted clothing. Fished in the pocket of his trousers and there, yes, was a folded scrap of paper, stained and wrinkled.

"You should have been more careful," said Jane censoriously. "If it was important."

"Yes," he agreed.

The writing is both bleached and blurred. The signature can still be made out, and the message. But the numbers . . . Is that a seven or a two? An eight or a three?

Well, all is not lost. One will simply have to try every possible permutation, at whatever cost in nuisance to others and humiliation to oneself.

And so they walk back to the flat, Matthew carrying the clean washing and with the battered piece of paper in his shirt pocket. They stop off at the stationer's for Jane to spend half her pocket money on some pencils she has had her eye on. Uplifted by this acquisition, she is in a buoyant and chatty mood as indeed, now, is Matthew. "It's good you found your bit of paper," says Jane, tucking her hand into his. "If you lose a person's telephone number you don't know where they are any more. Except" —the thought strikes her—"you could have looked them up in the telephone book, couldn't you?"

"I did," says Matthew. "This person isn't in the book. That was why the bit of paper was rather important."

"What did people do to find other people when they hadn't got telephone numbers?" she continues, struck by another thought.

"I suppose they very often lost each other," says Matthew.

They are walking past the shops, amid the Saturday crowds.

"How many people are there in the world?" demands Jane.

"I'm not sure. Millions and millions. Thousands of millions."

"How many are there in London?"

"Around eight million, give or take a few."

"Let's count how many of them I know," says Jane. And she recites a litany. Relatives, friends, neighbours. And the Indian people in Mum's corner shop and the lollipop lady and all the teachers in my school and the doctor and the receptionist at the surgery . . .

And people flow past them, a host of strangers, glimpsed for a moment and lost for ever. Swallowed by the city—gone, vanished as effectively as if they had died. The city unites and divides, with impartiality, with finality. Random circumstance flings people together—at work, at play—and separates them. Nowadays, technology imposes order—of a kind and up to a point. Telephones and telex reach into the darkness; machines talk to machines. But once . . . And Matthew is filled suddenly with a vision of the city as a place of terrifying haphazard loss and severance, of people circling in search of one another. Parents and children, friends, lovers. We have nothing but one another. He holds Jane's hand a little tighter as they cross the road; he touches, for an instant, the paper in his pocket.

"Mr Rutter would like to speak to you."

Before Matthew could react Rutter was on the line. "Good morning to you. Life treating you all right, I hope?"

Until this moment, it was. "What do you want?"

"A little chat, that's all. Somewhere we can talk comfortably. I'm prepared to come along to your place. Now I can't be fairer than that, can I?"

"No, thank you," said Matthew. "Look, I thought I made

it clear enough last time. I don't wish to talk to you. There is nothing whatsoever for us to talk about."

There was a short silence. When Rutter spoke again his tone had changed. No longer tolerant indulgence. "You're making a mistake, my friend. You really are. I've told you already, Glympton's aren't getting that Spitalfields site, I am. I'm doing you a favour, that's all. Trying to make things a bit easier for you. And there could be something in it for you as well, if you'd be a bit sensible."

Matthew said nothing. This, apparently, was interpreted as encouragement. Rutter continued: "Glympton's are rubbish. You don't want to be doing business with them anyway. Only a fool would do business with Glympton's, take my word for it. All you got to do is say you're not interested."

This man is mad, thought Matthew. Amoral *and* mad. I dare say it's a common combination. "Look," he said. "Since I seem to be talking to you, like it or not, I may as well get things straight. You are offering me a financial inducement to refuse to accept a Glympton Holdings brief for the Spitalfields site, which I have neither tendered for nor been offered, in the event that Glympton Holdings should succeed in securing the site, which hitherto they have not. Right?"

Rutter laughed. "If you want to put it like that, Mr Halland."

"But why?" said Matthew. "All Glympton's have to do is go to another firm of architects."

"Ah. I knew you was working for them."

"Oh, for God's sake!" Matthew exploded. He hung up. Three seconds later the phone rang. "We got cut off," said Rutter. "Sorry about that. Don't you worry your head about whys and wherefores. I know what I'm at, believe you me. Glympton's are silly buggers nosing in, that's all. They'll get what's coming to them. I don't stand for people messing me about. There's a lot of people in this world very sorry they got in my way, I can tell you, my friend. Anyone working for Glympton's is going to be sorry, you take it from me. So what I'd advise you, my friend, is . . ."

Matthew put the receiver down on his desk. It continued to crackle on. As soon as there was an intermission he picked it up: "I only have one thing to say. I have no connection whatsoever with either Glympton Holdings or the Spitalfields site. If you call me again I shall simply put the phone down. As many times as may be necessary. Goodbye."

He replaced the receiver. Silence. Continued silence. Well, that's that, let us hope. The fellow has to be given credit for crazed persistence, I suppose. So that is how people get rich.

With that bleached and foxed scrap of paper in front of him, he worked through the various possibilities. "I wonder if I could speak to Sarah Bridges . . . I'm so sorry. I wonder if I have the right number for Sarah Bridges . . . I'm so sorry." He encountered machines; he spoke to real people, who were patient or otherwise, according to temperament. Finally he achieved her answering machine. Her voice—noncommittal, of course, but pleasant, oh definitely pleasant. He said, "This is Matthew Halland. You very kindly sent me a note. I'll call again at some point, and hope to find you in."

"Not tonight," said Alice Cook. "Sorry. I've got something on. Actually Thursday may be tricky, too. I'll ring you, shall I?"

"We're going to be there for three whole weeks," said Jane. "And Mum's friend's coming for some of the time. You know, the nice one. Simon. And he knows how to sail boats and he's going to get us a boat and we're going to go sailing in it every day. Mum's going to get me a yellow life-jacket. And we're going to go fishing and he's going to teach me how."

"Sarah Bridges is not available at the moment. If you would like to leave a message please do so after the bleep."

London in high summer is a time of melancholy, not of celebration. The city becomes tawdry and stagnant, a receptacle for Coke tins and crisp packets. The grass in parks and squares is worn threadbare, down to dusty earth. The trees stand still and heavy. The sparkle has gone out of tubs and window boxes; the flowers begin to fade and die. The centre of town is awash with people who have nothing particular to do, drifting with backpacks and cameras. Elsewhere, the streets run with disaffected schoolchildren. The place has lost its sense of purpose. The days have no progression, it seems; time has ground to a halt, and people are without direction.

And Matthew decides that he will not after all go down to Devon to join the Whitworths at their cottage. He has not the stomach, just now, for a merry family holiday and, in that frame of mind, would not add to the gaiety of nations; the Whitworths are better off without him. He will stay in London, catch up with a backlog of work, and maybe take a day off here and there for his own purposes. He will go to the pictures; look about the place; read books. He has never been a person for whom solitude holds horrors. Loneliness and solitude are very different things, as he well knows.

It is not too bad, this fallow period. He takes in a couple of good films, enjoys a concert at the Festival Hall. He visits the galleries into which it is not possible to lure Jane. He misses her; tries not to think of the yellow life-jacket, this fishing tuition. On many evenings he sits reading in the flat, beside the open window, in the wing-back chair with battered red velvet upholstery. This chair bears the attritions of hard service:

a long stain down one arm where Susan slopped a glass of wine, a cigarette burn—perpetrator unknown—the ineradicable snail trails of Jane's sticky infant fingers. He tries to view it, these days, as simply a comfortable, convenient chair, and ignore these emotive scars; sometimes this works and sometimes it does not.

From the chair, on these August evenings, with the curtains undrawn, he can occasionally see the stars, when the miasma of the city permits. City stars are polluted—frailer creatures than the crisp brilliants that pepper country skies. Nevertheless, he can identify, can name names. He is surprised by how much survives of that boyhood craze of his. The map of the heavens is more familiar than he had realized. He fetches his binoculars; constellations and individuals leap into greater clarity. There is Mars, distinctly red, hanging low over St Pancras. And there, of course, is Polaris and good old Betelgeuse. Orion and Ursa Major. Could that be Cassiopeia? Perseus? He seeks out eventually one of his old astronomy books, smelling of damp, with his name in stilted schoolboy script.

Hercules, Taurus, Sagittarius. Mars, Venus, Pluto. The dead and dancing sky is mysteriously charted in languages which are no longer spoken; the graffiti of the stars, the imagined conjunctions of gas clouds billions of miles apart, commemorate the mythology of a departed people. The scientists of the twentieth century classify the stars by the letters of the Greek alphabet. The gods and heroes of ancient Greece are still going about their business above our heads, night after night. The world turns against the backdrop of this archaic reference system. The newspapers, this week, carry photographs of Neptune's moon, beamed across four billion kilometres by the travelling, ticking robot creature Voyager 2. Neptune's moon is named for Triton, the conch-blowing offspring of Poseidon and Amphitrite. It is as though these silent worlds of fire, ice and gas, whirling in their immeasurable distances of time and space, have for ever so disturbed the human imagination that they can only be approached by attaching to them the codes of a known system. They are the one stability in lives of flux, the only constant. They are inconceivable, and essential. They cannot be understood, and so must be labelled.

And Matthew, contemplating the city sky from his chair, his old *Astronomy for Beginners* in his hand ("From Mum and Dad, Christmas 1960") finds a curious solace. He tries to isolate and establish, to impose order on that glittering assembly; he watches the red and white lights of a plane track from east to west; he grapples for a while with the concept of distance. And he remembers that he did much the same thing, aged thirteen, in the back garden of his parents' house. With the same perplexity, the same amazement.

"Hello?"

"Is that Sarah Bridges?"

"It is."

"Ah," he said. Mildly panic-stricken, now. What am I doing? This is undoubtedly the most appalling mistake. "This is Matthew Halland. I've tried to get you a couple of times or so. I expect you've been away. I . . ."

"Yes. I have. Sorry. Holiday."

"Good one, I hope?"

"Yes, very. The Hebrides. I hadn't been there before."

"Wet?" enquired Matthew.

"Yes, quite wet."

That will do, on the Hebrides, for the time being, at any rate. "It was nice of you to drop me a line. I hope you didn't mind my leaving that message. I just wondered if . . ."

"Well," she said. "It was nice of you to buy me a sandwich."

"Oh, good heavens . . . My pleasure. I mean, anyone would have done the same."

"Not absolutely anyone," said Sarah Bridges.

"Well, plenty of people." No more of this. Get on with it. Actually the poor girl sounds as dubious as I feel. Also wondering what the hell she is doing, "I wondered if we could meet sometime and eat our sandwiches together. I mean, if you often lunch around there. Perhaps we could do a little better than a sandwich. Do you know that wine bar in Great Turnstile?"

She did indeed. And so it was arranged. Oh well, thought Matthew, the worst will be humiliation or embarrassment. Neither of them terminal conditions.

ELEVEN

In youth, of course, he had approached women with ease and without compunction. He had known all the rituals, then; so, too, did the women. You all knew where you were, from the first exchanged glances through overtures and manoeuvres to acceptance or rejection. It was an invigorating game with established moves, even if it occasionally ended in tears. And then there had been Susan and he had not played the game any more. He found promiscuity slightly mysterious. During all the years that he loved Susan he had not wanted to go to bed with anyone else. There had been the occasional frisson of sexual interest, of course, the recognition of someone attractive and desirable, but never anything compelling, disturbing, nothing that made him waver for an instant from the conviction that it was her he wanted, and no one else.

And in the end it had not been the feral whiff of infidelity that had spelt the end, but the simple death of love. Something he had never reckoned with. Death. Not a diminution or shift of emphasis, a levelling off with which one could have made do, to which one could have adjusted and lived on in a lesser way but tolerably. Not that, but a death so absolute that both knew they could no more spend the rest of their lives with one another than with some unreachable stranger.

And after that he had himself died for a while, or so it seemed. When at last he lifted his head again, and began to look around, Alice Cook had appeared. There had been no ritual, no overtures or manoeuvres, he simply found himself, by mutual agreement, having sex with Alice Cook once or twice a week. Their union had a curious innocence, it seemed to him, but also no history, and no substance.

"Why did you marry Mum, and not other people?" Jane had asked him once. Unnerved, he had stumbled through various answers. Because I happened to meet her. Because we found we had various tastes and interests in common. Because I fell in love with her. All of which reasons were true, and mutually dependent. He had seen Jane staring at him as he spoke, glimpsing perhaps the awful capriciousness of life, and he had quickly changed the subject. Not yet; she is only eight.

Approaching the wine bar, he was seized not by panic but self-contempt. The last time I did this sort of thing, he thought, I was about seventeen, and it turned out as unsatisfactorily as one could have expected. At my age, it is contemptible. Furthermore, I have embroiled this poor wretched young woman.

He was early. He found a table, ordered a drink, sat. When, twenty minutes after the appointed time, she still had not arrived, he knew that she had more sense than he did. He called the waitress, paid for his drink, and headed for the door.

Where he collided with her.

"I'm so sorry," she said. "I . . ."

"Not at all, I was just going to have a look . . ."

Back to the table. Return of the waitress. Sort out the matter of food and drink. All of which serves to construct a platform, a base, a tenuous sense of companionship.

"Actually," said Sarah Bridges. "I may as well be honest—I'd pretty well lost my nerve."

"I don't blame you." He checked himself in time—not appropriate to add, I nearly did the same myself.

"I haven't done this since I was about sixteen. And even then it was what my mother always told me not to do."

"Sensible woman," said Matthew.

The drinks arrived, creating a diversion. A chequered exchange about the Hebrides, to which Matthew had never been, which petered out. A silence which stretched, approached danger point. Both spoke at once.

"When you think about it," said Sarah Bridges. "The usual . . ."

"As a matter of fact," Matthew began. "I've always thought . . ."

She laughed. "Go on."

"No. Please . . ."

"I was only going to say that actually the usual ways you meet people—you know, at work or because you know someone in common or at a party or whatever—are pretty dodgy too, when you come to think about it. I mean, in one's mother's sense. Nobody comes tricked out with a guarantee and a list of character references. You have to learn to suss people out as you go along, and I suppose the thing is that if you've got any sense you get better at it as you get older." She gave him, at this moment, a cool and level look. Making the point, presumably. Her eyes were brown, he saw, with curious little green flecks.

"Oddly enough," said Matthew, "I was about to say much the same thing. I've always thought random association as promising—or as potentially disastrous—as anything else. One of my best friends is a man I met because we drove into each other on a roundabout."

"Whose fault was it?"

"His. Or so I maintain. We still argue about it occasionally."

"I like that," said Sarah Bridges. "But what an incredible piece of luck. The only people who've driven into me have been couriers on motorbikes, who might have been nice people I suppose but I never really got to find out, and a van driver who was absolutely horrid."

"It really arose because we discovered we both liked playing squash and hadn't got anyone to play with. I was on my way to a squash club at the time and . . ." Heavens, he thought, enough of this.

"I'm afraid I can't play squash."

"I've given it up now anyway."

"I don't do any sports," she said. Nailing her colours to the mast, evidently. "I rather like going for long walks, but that's all."

Matthew admitted to watching the occasional game of cricket. She gave a noncommittal nod; possibly awarding a black mark.

"Very occasional," said Matthew. "In search of fresh air as much as anything."

And here, now, was the food, supplying a further interval, a break for inspection and assessment. She wore a blue striped dress, Matthew now noted—no jewellery except a silver locket which sat neatly in the pit of her throat. Those wings of brown hair against the cheeks. He addressed himself sternly to his plate, caught out in a glance across the table.

"Is yours all right? I haven't been to this place for some time."

"Fine," she said. "It's a feast. I usually just have a sandwich. In my office, if it's raining."

Her office, it transpired, was in one of those little streets near the British Museum. She was deputy editor of a magazine for connoisseurs and collectors of furniture and *objets d'art*.

"I'm an architect," said Matthew.

"I know." A touch of reproof in her tone. "It says so on your card. What are you building at the moment?"

And so he told her. Cobham Square. Frobisher House. He mentioned the glass engraving. And, lo and behold! it turns out that she knows of Eva Burden, that last year she had to seek out photographs of her work to illustrate a series of articles on glass engraving past and present. A small piece of common ground has been pegged out, they are taming the great wilderness of each other's experience and concerns. They are no longer talking, quite, as total strangers.

"A year ago," said Sarah. "I could have told you all about the history of glass engraving techniques. When I was editing those articles I could have reeled off names and dates. And now I've forgotten almost all of it. That's the trouble with my job—I become an extremely temporary expert on one thing after another. Just now I know about bellarmines. Do you know what a bellarmine is?"

"No," said Matthew, lying. Because it was becoming more and more agreeable just to listen to her. Because listening you could also look, and learn. You could note that the right hand incisor tooth is slightly chipped (and what is the history of that?), learn that she has occasionally the very slightest hint of a stammer. That her eyebrows are neatly arched, that her fingers seem exceptionally long, that she uses her hands to emphasize a point.

"Are you really interested in all this?" She came to an abrupt halt, catching him out in mid-contemplation.

He said that he most certainly was.

"Hmn. I suspect you're just being polite. Frankly I'm not sure how interested *I* am. It's just that it happens all to be in my head at this moment. Which doesn't give me the right to inflict it on other people. Perhaps you should tell me what's in your head."

No, that would not be a good idea. If, indeed, it could be put into words at all. Adroitly, Matthew sidesteps.

"I could tell you about various things I'm bothered with just now which are in fact far less interesting than bellarmines, such as the distance between balusters of a staircase, and the price of sheet glass, but I don't think I will. On the other hand, if we're trading esoteric information I could possibly cap the bellarmines. I was thinking about dinosaurs on my way here. I came through Lincoln's Inn Fields."

"I often eat my sandwiches there," said Sarah.

"Oh, do you?"

"No dinosaurs in Lincoln's Inn Fields, surely?"

"Strictly speaking, no. But the Royal College of Surgeons was once the home of the Victorian palaeontologist Richard Owen and, such is the power of association, I can never walk past it without conjuring up dinosaurs. What was bothering me just now was that I couldn't remember if an ichthyosaurus is a swimming creature or a sloshing about in the swamps creature."

"I can't help you there, I'm afraid. I'm totally ignorant about dinosaurs. They don't rate very high with antique furniture connoisseurs. I could look it up for you—they've kitted us out with a terrific range of reference books." Matthew accepted the offer with enthusiasm.

"Ichthyosaurus. I hope I don't forget it. Actually, I've never heard of Richard Owen. Is that very ignorant?"

"Not in the least," said Matthew. "I only happen to because I took my daughter to the Natural History Museum last month." And thus arises the opportunity for various other cards to be laid discreetly, deftly upon the table. Matthew's domestic situation: Susan; Jane. Sarah's: unattached, hint of a liaison discontinued at some point in the recent past. But these matters are dropped, merely, upon the checked cloth, allowed to rest there briefly alongside the empty plates (Matthew realizes that he must, all this while, have been eating, without being conscious of so doing) and then whisked away before they can become portentous. This is not the moment.

She has a flat in Hackney. She plays the violin (badly) and sings in an amateur choir. She has firm opinions and takes account of an alternative point of view with her head slightly tilted, and an expression of faint severity. She is fatally susceptible to chocolate mousse; she drinks in moderation, she wears glasses for reading (fished from the maelstrom of the untidiest handbag Matthew has ever glimpsed). The sun, when it falls across her arm, lights up a fine pelt of golden hairs.

And suddenly the meal had wound to a close. They had finished their coffee. A brief tussle over the bill ("But I owe you a sandwich . . .") which Matthew managed to win. She glanced at her watch: "I shall have to . . ."

They were in the street. Why not, he suggested—casually, craftily—walk through Lincoln's Inn Fields? It's hardly out of your way. And so they did. Over the road and onto the path under the trees, among the great gnarled antediluvian feet of *Platanus X hispanica* Muenchh. And, walking beside her, under the shifting branches, over the brocaded sun and shadow of the grass, in the great green bowl of the square, Matthew experienced a surge of uplift, of anticipation, of well-being. Be careful, he told himself. Stop this. There is no reason, no justification. The whole place was lit up, it seemed—the sparkling buildings, the bright clothes of passers-by, the iridescent pigeons. He wanted to share with her his exuberance, to offer her the whole of it, to see it with her eyes and for her to look through his. He wanted, violently, to tread the world again with someone else.

They pause to inspect the memorial to Margaret Macdonald, who "took no rest from doing good." Sarah points out her favourite lunch-time bench, admits with a laugh to proprietorial indignation when others have reached it first.

They linger for a minute to watch the tennis players. And there, of course, is the Royal College of Surgeons. "Ichthyosaurus," she says. "Is that right?" It is indeed, Matthew replies. She moves away to throw a newspaper into a litter bin; a crowd of schoolchildren come jostling past, separating them. And Matthew waits, looking up at the windows of the Royal College.

He lays down his pen, and stares out at the trees, which he does not see. In his head are stones, bones and words. He takes up the pen again, and writes: ". . . a compensation for the want of horizontality of their tail fin was provided by the addition of a pair of hind paddles, which are not present in the whale tribe. The vertical fin was a more efficient organ in the rapid cleaving of the liquid element, when the ichthyosaurs were in pursuit of their prey, or escaping from an enemy . . ."

He becomes aware of a presence at his side, of a gentle pressure on his arm, of the chink of china. His wife has brought him a cup of tea. He sighs, and surfaces, leaving the ichthyosaur to cleave the Jurassic seas; he returns to 1858 and three-thirty of an August afternoon, in which his wife is trying to discuss with him the matter of the coal merchant's bill, and at what hour they should leave for the theatre, and invites approval of a purchased footstool. He considers the footstool, which is covered with a wool embroidered motif of entwined acanthus leaves. "Very nice, my dear," he says. He lays his hand upon his wife's, and feels her warmth, the blood rushing beneath her skin, the life of her.

The flock of schoolchildren has passed, and Matthew looks around for Sarah Bridges. He cannot see her. He scans the path in each direction; she is nowhere. What has happened? Surely she has not walked off—just like that? There has been some mistake. Those children . . . She must have thought he was heading for the road. He dashes to the pavement. Dashes back. Makes a tour of the tennis courts, returns to where he was before. Gazes in all directions.

She is gone. With nothing said, no arrangement made. Whether by accident or design he cannot know. Digested again by the city, which surges around him now, uncaring, pressing about its business. As must he, the afternoon half gone. And drained now of that brilliance, that promise. He crosses the square once more and makes for the tube station.

"We got back last night," says Jane. "We drove for hours and hours and we had lunch *and* tea at motorway places. I'm all brown. I caught five mackerels and a sort of flat fish." In the background, Matthew can hear Susan's heels click across the room; she speaks. "What? Mum says could you fetch me on Friday evening instead of Saturday because she's going to the theatre with Simon. We went sailing all day twice and had picnics on the boat and I helped pull the ropes." There is a fractional pause; Susan, perhaps, has spoken again. "Did you have a nice time on your holiday?"

He went to see his mother, at this hinge of the year, suspended between summer and autumn, with the days inching forward, cooling down, misting over. She led him immediately into the garden to pick the apples for her from the tree which he remembered as being, once, no taller than himself.

"When did you put this tree in, Mum?"

"Two years after we moved here. You're missing out those on that branch at the back. Mind, what I'll do with all these I don't know. Maybe you should take some for your lady friend."

He looked down at her, startled.

"You said last month there's a person you see."

"Ah. Yes. She's not really the type that would make chutney, I'm afraid."

"Then it'll have to be the neighbours."

He carried the baskets into the kitchen for her and sat at the table, helping to sort the fruit. "Put the wormy ones into that box. She's not the domestic type, then?"

"Nothing's going to come of it, Mum, if that's what you're wondering."

Her lips were pursed, as always when she was intent upon an issue. "I'll tell you something. A couple of years after your father died I thought of setting up with someone again. There's a man I know that comes to our church—nice fellow, widower. And he had it in mind, I could tell. I only had to give him an opening." She shot Matthew a canny glance. "You didn't know that, did you?"

"I certainly didn't, Mum." And why should he feel so shocked, perturbed, put out? What could have been more natural, more to be wished for?

"I'd nothing against him, and you're not looking for romance when you're sixty-eight. He'd have been company, someone to tell your troubles to, have a laugh with. But then the more I thought about it the more I came to think I'd be better off the way I was. It's not easy, adjusting yourself to another person. All the more when you're older, both of you." She shot him another look. "Put those bruised ones in with the wormy ones. Anyway, the point I'm making is, maybe we shouldn't be so set on all the world being paired off. You can be as miserable with someone else as on your own. But I dare say I don't need to be telling you that."

He said nothing, attending to the apples.

"Time was, if a woman was single, or a man either, come to that, people wondered what had gone wrong. Well, things have changed, as far as I can see, and about time too. I miss your father every day of my life, but I can manage on my own. If I can't have him I don't want someone else for the sake of it. I don't know why I'm telling you all this really. Just I wouldn't want to see you do something you might regret."

"What was his name?" Matthew asked, after a moment.

"Who? Oh, him. Trevor Stewart. And it's all water under the bridge. I see him from time to time. He drops in and cuts the grass for me every so often."

"Oh, does he? There's no need for that. I can cut the grass when I come over."

"You've got enough on your plate," said Mrs Halland crisply. "And he's the sort of man that needs something to fill his time with. I'm doing him a favour. Put the kettle on, will you—we've earned a cup of tea."

"Sarah Bridges is not available at the moment . . ."

He rang off, unnerved. Why should it be marginally worse to risk making a fool of yourself to a machine than to a human listener?

Graham Selway telephoned. "Good to see you the other day. You must drop by Spitalfields more often. Can I pick your brains for a moment?"

"Go ahead."

They discussed a conversion that Graham was currently working on. "Thanks a lot—that's a help. How's the city of the future? Incidentally there's some ugly business going on in connection with that site I took you to have a look at. Remember?"

"I remember," said Matthew.

"Apparently it's become a battleground between would-be developers. Principally Glympton's and some rather shady outfit run by a character called Rutter, who's apparently started operating in a big way of late. They've both been buying up

163

as hard as they can, Glympton's having the edge so far, or so the word goes. But Rutter acquired five or six strategically placed properties and has been busy winkling the tenants out, it seems—they're mostly Bengali sweatshop people. And a couple of them have been sticking—holding out. Presumably the poor things don't have anywhere else to go. Well, early this week there was a fire at one of these places, in the middle of the night. An awful business with a couple of children trapped in an upstairs room. They got one of them out, but a little boy was suffocated by the smoke. Ghastly. And the word going round is that it was an arson job. Police enquiries and all that, of course, but it doesn't look as though they'll be able to pin it on anyone. I'd hardly believe it myself, except that I've seen these bully boys about, collecting rents or whatever. Not people you'd want to tangle with. It makes the flesh creep, doesn't it? Matthew? You still there?"

"I'm still here," said Matthew. Graham's window must have been open; behind his voice could be heard a stream of song from one of those canaries. And then the rattle of a trolley over the cobblestones.

"You may have read about it. There was a paragraph in one of the papers."

"I think I did. I hadn't made the connection." Some brief news item—the overworked words stifling the reality: fire; child; death. "I've come across this man Rutter, as it happens."

"Have you really? Well, I should steer clear of him, if I were you. It's a rougher world than one realizes. Maybe they have a point—my more entrenched neighbours, with their gaslights and their panelling."

"Theirs seems to me a pretty fey view of the eighteenth century," said Matthew. "If they're after authenticity I hope they're also denying themselves such anachronisms as modern medical facilities and the various public services."

"Dear me. I'd forgotten what a no-nonsense fellow you

are. But you're quite right, of course. Long live the Health Service and the Metropolitan Police."

The conversation was concluded. Matthew put the phone down.

An overcrowded, dilapidated terrace house is indeed a fire trap. Faulty wiring, dangerous cooking facilities, careless inhabitants; it happens every day, up and down the country. Or, someone could lend a hand. Shove a handful of blazing paper through the letter box in the small hours and hope to strike lucky. Make off fast, and who can prove anything?

No, you'd hardly believe it. Except, he thought, that I do.

TWELVE

Matthew's street, in summer, burst into flower. Each façade began in May to bloom with window boxes and hanging baskets from which cascaded tongues of ivy, drifts of sparkling lobelia, bright torrents of fuchsia. Pots and tubs on doorsteps overflowed with petunias, geraniums, Busy Lizzie. The front of the local pub became a floral cliff—cloaked from top to bottom in an eruption of pink, scarlet, magenta, blue, silver, white and green. By midsummer the whole place was in rampant bloom, with only the occasional withered and fading frontage marking out a household away on holiday. Matthew, no gardener himself, appreciated this display, which seemed some act of defiance against rubbish-strewn pavements and polluted air. Sometimes, faced with a long day in the office, he would get up in good time and go for a brisk walk in the neighbouring streets and squares and then, in the clarity and emptiness of the early morning, this festive quality of the normally sober terraces was at its height. You moved through a garden.

It was on these occasions, with no one else around except postmen, paper boys with orange sacks and a few foraging dogs, that he had several times come across the wild-looking young man. Wearing jeans and a T-shirt with logo of a grinning cartoon face he strode down the centre of the road, shouting. Looking neither to right nor left, forging ahead, shouting at the closed houses, the empty streets. "We're going to fight, you know!" he shouted. "We're going to fight the fuckers! We'll get the fucking Giro! Fuckers!" He would turn a corner, and then five minutes later Matthew would meet up with him again, plunging on, hurling himself purposelessly, it seemed, across the city, empty-handed, shouting. And Matthew would continue on his way, chilled. What wretched, fouled-up life had he glimpsed? Amid the flowers.

And now in September the flowers were losing their glow. The young man was seen no more, lingering only as an image of disquiet, of unease, of the city's soft underbelly.

When Rutter telephoned Matthew was taken entirely un-awares. There were no preliminaries—no intermediary voice. Just that nasal tone, instantly recognized. "Mr Halland? I thought it was time we had another word. You ended up talking off the top of your head before, and that was silly. I thought you'd like to know things are progressing quite nicely down in Spitalfields. Far as I'm concerned, that is. I don't think Glympton's people are feeling very happy."

Matthew was silent. I should hang up, he thought. And then: no, that is exactly what I should not do.

"You still with me?"

"I'm here," said Matthew.

"Ah, so we're talking, are we? That's very sensible, my friend. Very sensible."

"What is the point of this phone call?"

"You want to know what's the point of this phone call? I make a lot of phone calls, Mr Halland. I'm a busy man. You don't get where I am by sitting on your arse wondering what to do next, you know. You want to get ahead in this world you move in before other people do. I'm everywhere, my friend, let me tell you. I've got eyes in the back of my head. I'm making this phone call because I think you may want to tell your friends at Glympton's how things stand. They may as well face facts. There's no way they can develop that site now without I sell them my properties, and I'm not doing that. There's no negotiation, far as that's concerned. But if they want to know what's good for them, then you tell them all they got to do is have a chat with me about a price on their holdings. We can come to an arrangement that'll be satisfactory all round."

"I see," said Matthew. "Satisfactory to all concerned."

"That's right."

"Except people like the unfortunate Bengali family who lost their child in a fire."

There was the briefest of pauses. "Ah, yes. Shame about that. But they've only got theirselves to thank for it, I'm afraid. They cook on open fires, you know. What can you expect?"

"This happened at three in the morning, I understand. Not a normal mealtime."

A more considerable pause. "What are you getting at, my friend?"

"It seems to me that this fire was arson. And that your henchmen may have had something to do with it. In other words, you."

"I don't think I care for that suggestion," said Rutter, slowly and in a new voice.

"Neither do I. In fact I would find it barely credible were it not for your remarks about your methods of dislodging recalcitrant tenants."

"What methods, Mr Halland? I don't think I know what you're talking about. I think maybe you've got a bit of a vivid imagination."

Matthew was silent for a moment. "In view of the Spitalfields fire, I intend to repeat to the police your comments about how you deal with uncooperative tenants."

"What comments? I don't think the police would be very interested in hearing stories about comments that wasn't ever made. They've got better things to do with their time, haven't they? You still there, Mr Halland? You've gone all quiet on me. Because there's another point I'm going to make and that is that I don't like people interfering in things that's none of their business. You can go and chat up the fucking police if that amuses you, my friend, but I wouldn't advise you to. You'd be wasting your time. You might even be doing yourself a bad turn. You wouldn't want my minders to be getting interested in you, would you?"

"That remark constitutes a threat."

"What remark, Mr Halland?"

"There's such a thing as the rule of law."

Rutter laughed. "Up to a point, my friend, up to a point. The law's what you make of it, far as I'm concerned. I've never had too much trouble with the law. You don't get anywhere in this world by pouncing around worrying about the law. I wouldn't be . . ."

Matthew slammed the receiver down. He was juddering, he realized, as though gripped by intense cold. This was what was meant by shaking with anger, then. A new experience, at this pitch. He sat staring at the phone for a few moments, then reached for the directory to search out the number of his local police station.

He was possessed, in the ensuing days, by the thought of Rutter. He told himself that most people are not like this, that such a man is an aberration, a sport, a freak. Most people are constrained by natural inclination or by social conditioning to moderate their greed and treat one another with a degree of charity. Everyone is preoccupied with self, but most learn, if only out of expediency, to temper the preoccupation and acknowledge the existence of others. He told himself all this, and continued to see Rutter in the innocent faces of passers-by, of the assistant in his newsagent, of a potential client. Rutter's language overlaid the anodyne exchanges of colleagues or of strangers. He saw that the man was simultaneously risible and appalling, contemptible and fearsome. The classic combination. And the world, apparently, accommodates such people. It furnishes them with means and opportunity. It prescribes their behaviour, and facilitates their progress. They know just how they stand and act accordingly.

When he was about nine years old, the playground of his school had been dominated by a pair of bullies and their satellites. These two, distinguished only by a quality of strident aggression and some sort of compulsive energy, operated a protection racket which determined whether or not others might occupy play space and be exempt from the kicks and thumps of the satellite force. Some children were able to buy peace and *Lebensraum* with sweets or comics; others—randomly selected, it seemed—were denied even that mercy and condemned to a fugitive life on the perimeter of the tarmac, loitering against the wire or skulking in the toilets in a pathetic attempt to survive the play periods unscathed. The teachers, Olympian figures exempt from this daily hell, were distantly aware of the situation and made occasional efforts to police the playground. When they did, the bullies played football decorously and the teachers were reassured in their belief that things weren't really that bad. As soon as they had gone, the bullies got back to business again. Matthew, one of those condemned to live on his wits and spend much of every day with thumping heart and sinking stomach, felt that he moved between two mutually exclusive worlds. Walking out of the school, heading for home, he entered a haven of order and justice. Here, if disagreeable things happened to you it was probably your own fault; you had been disobedient or cheeky or untruthful and deserved the ensuing disapproval. The hand of fate was another matter, but at least you had moral support—if you were ill or injured everyone was nice to you. But each morning he was faced with the prospect of moving back into the anarchic lawlessness of school. He saw the distinction, and longed to grow up.

"Is that Sarah Bridges?"

"Yes?"

"This is Matthew Halland. I . . . Well, I just wondered . . . I enjoyed our lunch the other day and then somehow we seemed to lose each other."

"Yes," she said. "We did."

"I lost sight of you for a moment and then you'd disappeared. I looked all over for you."

"Oh. I looked for you too, actually."

A pause, in which Matthew savoured the uprush of satisfaction. A simple misunderstanding. A mistake.

"Ichthyosauruses swim," said Sarah Bridges. "Swam, rather."

"What? Oh . . . Oh, I see. Thanks. I had a feeling they did. How clever of you to find out."

"No problem. I got quite absorbed."

"You've set my mind at rest. Thanks again." He took a breath. Continued boldly. "Could we meet again fairly soon?"

And she has no objection, it seems.

"So . . ." said Alice, beaming at him over a glass of mineral water spiked with lemon. "How are things with you?"

"Not bad," said Matthew guardedly. "Not bad on the whole." They were sitting at a table in the Covent Garden precinct in the early evening, a meeting arranged by Alice in a breezy and somewhat unexpected phone call: "Long time no see . . . Have you got an hour after work today? I'll be killing time before a theatre."

Alice was vibrant. There was no other word for it. She gleamed with good health—skin aglow, dark curls bubbling. Matthew studied her, with guilt and a touch of unease. "You're looking very well, Alice. Good holiday?"

"Holiday? Oh Christ, that was *ages* ago. I'd forgotten we hadn't seen each other for so long. It's *October,* Matthew."

"So it is . . . Honestly, I don't know what happens to the time. It always seems to be next week before you know where you are. I've been up to my eyes. Blackwall, Cobham Square, one thing and another. I rang you—more than once. And then there was . . ."

"Matthew," said Alice. "This is not recrimination time." She beamed again.

Matthew subsided. "Ah. So anyway . . ."

"The thing is," she continued. "I'm pregnant."

He stared. "Alice!"

"Don't worry, it's not yours."

He reached out, grabbed her hand. "Alice . . . I'm so glad for you. That's the best news in ages. Terrific!"

"Isn't it!" There she sat, exuding well-being. People flowed past. A string quartet was in action. The precinct pigeons picked up a living around the café tables.

"Who . . ." Matthew began delicately.

"A guy I've met. Well, obviously." She giggled.

"I hope . . ."

"We shall see. Maybe and maybe not. I'm crossing bridges as I get to them. Right now everything's good. He's all for it, too. The baby."

"I'm really glad, Alice. You've made my day."

"And what's new with you?"

"I can't compete. Nothing much. Work. I got further embroiled with that dreadful fellow I told you about."

"Him with the Rottweilers? Gosh—tell me."

She listened intently. "How absolutely ghastly. It's incredible. I mean, how can there be people like that? So what did the police say?"

"The police expressed cautious interest. The police don't go in for being either shocked or surprised. They—or rather he—shook his head thoughtfully from time to time and wrote things down. It's like being an adolescent in conversation with some worldly uncle who's seen it all and doesn't want to spoil your youthful illusions. They know all about people like Rutter. About Rutter specifically, I suspect."

"But what are they *doing*, then?"

"You may well ask. So did I. They were pursuing enquiries. They thanked me for my information."

"Of course they have to be able to *prove* it . . ."

"They do indeed. There's the rub."

"D'you think they were going to have him in and talk to him? The Rottweiler character."

"Hard to say."

"Well, I think it's horrific. If people can do that sort of thing and get away with it. It's scary. I mean, this isn't the middle ages."

But Alice was away in a private bubble of content. The vehemence of her speech, the vigour of her outrage—quite genuine, quite unforced—were at odds with her aura of roseate tranquillity. She looked as though at any moment she might gently levitate. And Matthew, infected by this, felt a rush of warmth. He leaned across the table and kissed her. "Whoops!" said Alice, giggling again. "Let's not get carried away . . . Help—look at the time! I'm meeting my bloke at seven."

It was darkening. They walked out into the evening streets: It had been raining; the cobbled expanse around the precinct shone black and gold. There was a smell of coffee—and flowers. They were passing the florist's stall, a rainbow in the city night. Matthew stopped and delved in his pocket. "Hey—what's this!" said Alice. He thrust red carnations into her arms: "It's for nothing—and everything."

A few minutes later, alone, Matthew stood at the side of Charing Cross Road, thinking of Alice's child, whom in all probability he would never know, but with whom he would have a tenuous link. He waited for a gap in the traffic, and saw lives as a web of connections, random and mysterious.

The child loiters on the edge of the known universe. She looks through the river of vehicles, past wheels and the legs of horses to the alien shore beyond—the streets and buildings that reach away into infinity. Behind her is the hub of things, the maze of alleys through which she can slip with ease and knowledge. She peers, curious and wary, into that nowhere outside.

A passing omnibus sprays water from the gutter and she darts backwards to the shelter of a wall. She squats alongside rubbish and a pile of old rags, watching the world go by, waiting for some opportunity to seize. The pile of rags twitches, and the child sees that it is inhabited. At its centre is a face, a face that is ridged and grooved and stubbled, from which a pair of bleary eyes gazes impassively. The child stares into these faded eyes, across a puddle of water in which she can see her own reflection—her face as grimy as the face that inhabits the rags, but different, she perceives, profoundly different. She glimpses, suddenly, the span of a lifetime, and its weight.

And then the bleary eyes close. The rags heave once, and start to snore. The child observes, and observes too that from one filthy fold there protrudes a hunk of bread. She considers taking this. She edges forward to do so, but all at once she hesitates, in the clutch of a sensation which she cannot identify. It is as though she were invaded by a stranger who has feelings that are not her feelings, responses that are not hers. And yet she has no choice but to defer to this stranger. The bread is there for the taking—she could snatch it up and be off, without fear of retribution. But she does not, and cannot. She sits there in the dirt, surprised and enlightened.

The next day Matthew found the windscreen of his car smashed. He did not think too much of this, attributing it to vandalism or a stone flung up by a passing vehicle, until he arrived home one evening the following week to be confronted by a pile of excrement on the mat inside his front door. Then he made the connection. He cleared up the mess, grimly, and telephoned the police, who were sympathetic and offered various practical recommendations. Matthew screwed up his letter box, arranged for the postman to leave his mail with a neighbour, and parked his car several streets away from the flat. He did these things in a condition of impotent rage. It was as though a furtive, dirty hand were reaching into his life. He found himself staring with suspicion at every unrecognized passer-by in his street.

Sarah Bridges leaned towards him, frowning slightly.
    "Sorry?"
    "I've made a mistake with this place," shouted Matthew. "I apologize. I hadn't realized it was like this."
    The restaurant rang with noise. It was a subterranean complex of converted cellars with whitewashed brick barrel vaulting and sawdust-strewn floors. Conversations, laughter and the clink of cutlery reverberated off the low ceilings, creating a pervasive clamour which virtually drowned out individual remarks. At the next table a gang of carousing financiers, average age apparently around twenty-five, punctuated raucous chat with collective bellows of mirth.
    Sarah smiled and said something which looked like "Never mind." Or possibly "It's fine." Or neither of those. The

occasion was moving in the direction of disaster. They were reaching the end of the meal, on a conversational course which proceeded in fits and starts, with interludes of misapprehension or defeated silence. Matthew felt as though they were vessels bleeping morse at each other through a blizzard of atmospherics. He sank into a dismal frustration.

". . . past failings?" enquired Sarah.

"Sorry? How will I make up for past failings?"

Earlier, he had caught her glancing at her watch. Now, thank heaven, she laughed. "I said, how are you getting on with your glass engraving?"

"Oh, that . . ." said Matthew in relief. "The preliminary sketches are ready, apparently. I'm going down to have a look at them on Thursday. Then she'll start on the real thing."

"Will you have some sort of unveiling ceremony? When it's in place."

"I really hadn't thought. It's a nice idea."

The financiers brayed in chorus once more. Sarah shrugged and smiled. Matthew resisted an urge to throw everything on the table at them, and summoned the waitress instead.

"Coffee?"

"I really must be back at the office by half past," said Sarah.

"Two coffees," he instructed the waitress. "And you might mention to our neighbours that they would benefit from a few lessons in restrained and considerate behaviour in public places."

"Sorry, sir?"

"Never mind. Two coffees, please. And the bill."

"Please let me pay this time," said Sarah Bridges.

"No. If anything, this place should pay us for coming here and acting as crowd."

The candle-lighting and the sawdust on the floor were presumably a confused attempt to hitch the place to its utilitarian past. In the shadowy recesses of further vaults too small even to accommodate a table or two, racks of wine bottles carried on the storage theme. Damp, rats and effluent had been ingeniously displaced by romantic murk.

The financiers departed in a horde, with a hideous racket of chair legs grinding on the stone floor. Matthew peered at the bill, put down some notes, and looked across at Sarah Bridges. "Well . . ." he said, glumly.

"Well . . . I'll have to go, I'm afraid. It's quarter past."

They emerged blinking into the daylight. "I'm sorry about that place," said Matthew. "One of my colleagues claimed it was good. His head shall roll."

"It wasn't *that* bad." She was poised for departure.

"So . . . Thank you for coming, anyway."

"Thank *you*."

"I'll give you a ring some time, shall I?"

"Yes, do," said Sarah Bridges. Dismissively? An absence of enthusiasm there, surely?

She smiled, he smiled. And then she was gone. Leaving him with the sour taste of anticlimax. Those who resist expectations are spared much. Forget it, he thought. Serves you right for unjustifiable optimism. Life isn't like that, as you well know. She was a mere illusion, in any case.

The leaves were falling. There was a bite to the air. Down at Blackwall, Frobisher House had roared up to its full height, a brilliant turquoise cliff sprung from the mud. In Cobham Square there were once again floors, and doors, and plastered walls. Matthew's drawing-board was occupied by the stark, neat outlines of buildings as yet unsanctioned, which might be snuffed out at this conception stage, or survive to climb also into the London skies. He worked as he had always done, with absorption and commitment, given over to the demands of some technical problem or the stimulus of an idea or an interesting solution. He moved from the isolation of pondering a new project to the give and take of site conferences or meetings with clients.

And in tandem with all this there ran the preoccupations of his own life, so that Jane, Susan, Sarah Bridges, Rutter, love, loss, indignation wove through the days. He would look about him at the ceaseless performance of the city, millions of people propelling the place forward in a fit of collective absence of mind—buying, selling, building, servicing, while concerned with more important things. Public life fuelled by private passions. The immortality of the whole ensured by the transience of the many.

He was awoken in the small hours by the telephone. When he answered the caller rang off. He went back to bed. Half an hour later the same thing happened again. He left the phone off the hook.

Returning from the corner shop, he saw that the man was still there, leaned up against a battered Ford, glancing occasionally along the street.

Matthew hesitated. He tucked his newspaper under his arm, took a firmer grip on the milk carton and bread loaf, and stepped forward. Level with the man, he stopped and swung round.

"What are you doing there?"

"What you mean—what am I doing? I'm waiting, aren't I?" A credible exhibition of mounting outrage.

"I think you or one of your chums put a brick through my car window," said Matthew. "Plus a couple of other idiocies. I think you're working for Rutter. So you'd better tell him that the police are onto it. And onto you too. Got that?"

And the outrage, now, is even more credibly overtaken by bewilderment, quickly chased by indignation. "Look, you're off your rocker, mate. I don't know what the hell you're talking about. I don't know no Rutter. I'm waiting for my wife to come out of the dentist's surgery. So just bloody well piss off and leave me alone, will you?"

And Matthew saw that he was speaking the truth. He gabbled a humiliated apology, and slunk back to the flat. Thus springs paranoia.

THIRTEEN

Matthew stood beside Eva Burden and considered the three sketches. A wash of sunshine flooded down onto them through the big window so that the paper was golden and the pencil lines seemed to ripple in the watery light.

"The middle one. I like them all, but that's the one."

"Good," said Eva Burden. "I hoped you'd say that. It would be my choice, but I always let the client have the last word."

"It's quite uncannily like what I had in mind. Except that I didn't really know what I had in mind."

She laughed. "My goodness, I wish everyone was so easy to please. My delightful vicars are always wanting more feathers to the angels' wings, or a nicer expression for the Virgin."

"I think it's perfect. The whale is absolutely right."

"What you are seeing, of course, is flat and dead. The real thing will have light—another dimension."

"I can't wait. It's going to be far too good for the building, I suspect."

"You shouldn't be so dismissive of your own work," said Eva severely.

"It's impossible to feel very proprietorial. That sort of thing is architecture by committee."

"I suppose so." She leaned over the sketch, frowning. "I still wonder if we shouldn't have had a human figure somewhere. Frobisher himself, maybe?"

"I think not. If anyone, it should have been the Eskimo."

"The Eskimo?"

"They brought one back. As a trophy."

"Poor fellow. An involuntary immigrant, like me. What happened to him?"

"He died, it seems. Almost at once."

They had believed that the captive would perish on the voyage, for he was grievously sick of a fever. They shut him in the hold and brought food and water to him, for it were well that he should survive as testimony of their landfall at *Meta Incognita*, and a proof of the savagery of that terrible place. And when at last the perilous journey was completed, and the ship safely berthed in the Thames, they brought the captive up and set him upon the wharf in his boat made of skins, as a spectacle for the populace. Many people came running, and were astonished by the savage, and indeed thought at first that he was some brutish monster, half man half fish, until the sailors pulled him from the boat and stood him upon his feet. Whereupon they marvelled at his features, and at his garments made of skins and furs, and mocked him that he would not speak.

For from this time on the captive was silent, who before had spoken and chanted in his own outlandish tongue and had learned some few words of English. He looked about him all ways, at the people and at the place, and when his eye fell upon some oxen that drew a wagon he shrank back and looked fit to faint from fright, whereupon the people mocked him the more. But speak he would not.

In the following days they set him upon a cart, with his boat, and brought him into the city and paraded him about the streets, for an entertainment and that the people of London might marvel at the resolution and feats of navigation of Martin Frobisher, and reflect upon the strangeness and barbarity of that empty quarter of the globe. The captive made no resistance, but suffered them to lead him about, and when the populace stared, and shouted, and made to touch him to see if he be flesh or no, he did not flinch but seemed like a man in a trance, as though his soul were elsewhere. But then all of a sudden he rose up, and stood, and began to sing in his own tongue. He looked upwards to the sky, and sang with a great voice, and shortly after that he expired and died. Which was a great annoyance to the admiral, who was minded to keep him for the rest of his natural life, as a token and a trophy.

"No," said Matthew. "I don't think a human presence would be appropriate. It's just right as it is."

He sees that he has left the world and come to a place which is nowhere, peopled with devils and monstrous beasts. And presently he is beyond fear, beyond despair; he no longer perceives this terrible nowhere nor hears the screaming of the devils. He goes away, deep into himself, back into the proper unity of man and space. He denies the sequence of days and weeks that have led him to this horror, and turns within to find what is true, and right. He summons up from the depths of his being the images of all that he knows—the land, the creatures, the people—and prays to them to draw him back. He refuses this nowhere, he rejects it, he turns away from the dictations of time and seeks within his own head the securities of place. First he sees a picture, many pictures. And after a while these pictures start to drown the unreality around him, and as they do so he begins to speak. He sings to the world of which he is a part, and from which he was snatched but to which he now returns. He sings, and celebrates the land, and thus he becomes a part of it once more.

"Right," said Eva Burden. "I shall get going, then. Let's have a drink to celebrate. White wine? Or are you a beer man?"

"White wine would be fine."

They stood at the window. The river gleamed in the dusk, the far bank a tier of lights, the bridges strung with jewels. A ferry passed, blazing like a fairground, throbbing with music.

"Parties," said Eva Burden. "This is not a serious river any more. It is for dancing and eating. It no longer leads anywhere—never mind to the Arctic."

"Even my eight-year-old daughter complained of the absence of real boats."

"Of course. It is a poor degraded thing, the river. In danger of losing its identity. Its suggestion of elsewhere. That bothers me quite a lot. Immigrant mentality, again. You worry about that for yourself. Until you discover that it can never be quenched—your own personal elsewhere. You are stuck with it—for better and for worse. For the rest of your life you will have an invisible point of reference, known only to you, making you different. Dear me—what is it about you that sets me off always talking about my origins! It's something I seldom do, believe me."

"Well, please don't stop. I find it enthralling."

"You're one of those who are naturally curious, that's what it is. One senses it. Those who are prepared to receive. You would have made a good immigrant yourself—success depends on perception and versatility. But for all the protective colouring you may take on, there will always be that secret elsewhere. Sometimes when I walk about this city I feel that one should see thousands of mirages—Caribbean islands and Indian villages and shimmering intense snatches of Turkey or Greece or Poland or wherever. The place is not just itself—it is a reflection of the rest of the globe. All of us who carry this cargo of private association. But here I go again . . . being obsessive. And in any case it's true of everyone, whether you come from Watford Junction or Hong Kong. You become part of the urban stew and add to it your own little bit of flavour."

"Some flavours are more pungent than others. I think you're entitled to pull rank. Speaking as one who grew up in Watford, or thereabouts. When I was young the most desirable attribute going was a foreign girlfriend."

"Really? You surprise me. I don't think that was the case in my day. Or maybe I failed to exploit the one natural advantage I had."

"Italian was best," said Matthew. "I imagine Sophia Loren had a lot to do with that. With French a close runner-up. German I think suggested intellectual potential which the average youth found daunting. Intense Scandinavians did well, presumably because they never said anything much."

"And what about you? What did you go for?"

"I was too diffident to try my luck very often. I aspired briefly to a Parisienne, but was much too callow for her, and soon got the push. I settled eventually for a girl from Gloucestershire."

"Your wife?"

"Not any more, I'm afraid."

Another carousing ferry passed in a blaze of light and sound. "I was married very briefly," said Eva. "Since then my relationships have been with women, and none of those very lasting. Perhaps that's another thing about immigrants—a tendency to remain alone."

"Come now—that's flatly contradicted by the facts. Most immigrants congregate, and breed vigorously. It's the natural, expedient thing to do."

She laughed. "I suppose you're right. It's just me. But don't get me wrong, I prefer it that way. I'm perfectly happy, after my fashion. Except for the problems that beset anyone. I've had another offer for this place. Fairy money. All those noughts. It makes me feel like a millionaire. Except of course that it would cost me almost as many noughts to buy a studio somewhere else. But I dare say I shall go. Soon these parts will be unrecognizable—a nowhere, like the river."

Driving away from Eva Burden's studio, Matthew carried with him the image of the glass engraving. He was startled by how closely her sketch realized his own idea—a ship that was not quaintly archaic nor over-stylized, the sense of vigour, of ingenuity and purpose. There was more creative satisfaction, he found, in having transmitted a concept to someone else than in the completion of a building. He considered this, as he picked his way west and north through the city, until the reflection was pushed aside by something else.

He had begun to think repeatedly of Sarah Bridges. The process, though, was not so much one of thought as of a protracted interruption of his proper concerns, an unrelenting assault upon the routine processes of the mind. She floated now from the crowds at an intersection, while he sat waiting for the lights to change, and smiled upon him until the traffic behind was blaring indignation. At other times her face superimposed itself upon his drawing-board, so that he sat in a trance, no work done. Her voice blotted out whole passages of conversations, like some sort of atmospheric interference, leaving him at a perpetual disadvantage. He lay awake at night, and when eventually he slept he experienced fervent dreams in which she did not feature but which seemed prompted by obsession.

He recognized the affliction, and greeted it with a mixture of apprehension and excitement. He had not expected ever to feel this way again, and did not know whether to laugh or cry.

He was at his desk in the office, starting to go through the mail.

"There's a parcel just come. Shall I open it?"

"Yes please, Debbie."

Half a minute later his secretary let out a shriek. He sprang to his feet, looked over her shoulder, and snatched the box from her.

He slammed through the door, out through the reception area and down the stairs. Before he dropped the lot into the dustbin he had time to observe that the rats were shrouded in clingfilm and neatly laid head to tail, like sardines in a tin, a curious piece of delicacy. Coming up the stairs again, he wondered fleetingly if they should have been preserved as evidence. No. His word, and Debbie's, would have to suffice.

The office was in an uproar. Debbie was being consoled by colleagues. The senior partners had emerged from their offices, and were standing around in bewilderment.

"I'm extremely sorry about that, Debbie. Are you all right?"

Debbie, stalwartly, declared herself quite recovered.

"Well, we've had the occasional disgruntled client in our time," said Tony Brace, "but I never thought anyone would go quite this far."

Someone else proposed that the supporters of the Prince of Wales had perhaps taken exception to the design of Frobisher House.

"That's not particularly amusing," snapped Matthew. He

had started to shake, he discovered. Tony put a hand on his arm and steered him into his office, where he listened with incredulity to Matthew's explanation.

"How many, Mr Halland?"

"I didn't count," said Matthew tersely. "Several."

"In a state of decomposition?" continued the policeman, sympathetically. It was a different one. Police Constable whatever was away on leave now. His successor was equally avuncular and unruffled.

"Yes."

"I'm sending a car round. If you could just tell the men which dustbin."

"Is that really necessary?"

"They'll have seen worse, don't you worry. And we need the wrappings."

"All right," said Matthew. Fat lot of good that'll do, he thought. Anonymous sheet of brown paper. Arbitrary postmark. Unidentifiable handwriting. The policeman was now giving advice about how to handle future mail items.

"And what do I do if it's a bomb next time?"

"I doubt that. Jokers like this usually stick to this sort of thing. It's kept at a nuisance level. Low-grade aggro rather than anything that's going to provoke a full-scale criminal investigation. That's invariably the case, in my experience. For your peace of mind."

Matthew sighed. "And for how long does it usually go on? In your experience."

"Till they get tired of it, or till something else takes their eye. They've not got long attention spans, people like this. They're like children, in one sense."

"They make all the children I've ever come across look like models of civilization. But I don't know why we keep

188

talking about "they". I've told you who's behind this. Have you people talked to this man Rutter?"

"I understand the response was much what might have been expected."

"And so?"

"We're pursuing the matter, Mr Halland."

"On a rather more important level," said Matthew. "What about the Spitalfields fire?"

There was a slight pause. "Ah. Yes. The last I heard, the boys down there aren't too sure on the arson angle. There's some evidence it may well have been accidental."

"Is that what you'd all prefer to think?"

Another pause. Affronted, this time. Or pained.

"All right. Forget I said that, if you'd rather. Thanks for your advice. I'll direct your men to the appropriate dustbin."

Matthew rang off. Debbie put her head round the door. "Coffee?"

"That would be very welcome, Debbie."

He went to the window and looked out at the complex grey expanse of this city in which people were engaged in doing unspeakable things to one another. Children were being beaten up, old ladies mugged. Men and women stuck knives in total strangers, or violated those they knew best. You were looking upon a landscape of secret carnage. Given which, it seemed a bit craven to be whining about a few dead rats, some shit and a broken windscreen—positively finicky, indeed. The problem was, of course, that you were looking also at a landscape in which coexisted a horde of people who knew little of one another, who rubbed shoulders in the streets, stared into one another's eyes in the tube, and saw nothing of each other's lives. Here was a place in which some were driven beyond the limits of endurance while others wondered how to spend their evening, in which one man admired the summer flowers while another walked the same streets howling his despair at shuttered houses. We react to what happens to us in terms of our expectations. Those who have not hitherto been exposed to jungle law tend to respond squeamishly when they get a taste of it. Out there, thousands live by quite other arrangements than polite behavioural codes favouring mutual consideration and fair play. The city has many points of view, and many climates. The official creed proscribes shoplifting, crashing the red lights and driving while under the influence. For many, these are accepted practices. Fraud, theft and homicide are outlawed, but remain a standard means to a livelihood for some. You could grow up assuming that the world would treat you well, or knowing that there wasn't a hope in hell that it would do any such thing.

Debbie returned with the coffee. "Tony told me about this man. I think it's shocking. How can they let people like that get away with it?"

"I wouldn't know, Debbie. Some sort of attempt is made to see that they don't, I suppose."

"God, when I opened that box . . . I mean, how does anyone come by a load of dead rats in the first place?"

"Evidently there are those for whom it's a standard commodity."

Each day he sat in front of the telephone, considered dialling Sarah Bridges' number, and did not do so. When at last he took the plunge he could not tell if her voice was welcoming or cool. Striking a note of casual camaraderie, or so he hoped, he suggested a meeting. She agreed. He put the phone down in a state of elation, and anxiety. He feared that she might have accepted out of boredom, or indifference.

All over London, the plane trees were losing their leaves. Pavements were littered with the flattened yellow shapes and over head the simplified branches hung out the black spheres of the seed pods against the white autumn skies. Matthew saw that time was passing and felt relief. He took Jane to St James's Park, where they fed importunate wildfowl and counted the different species. Jane, too, was preoccupied with the passage of time, for her own reasons.

"I'll be eight and a half next week."

"I know."

"Why don't people have half birthdays as well as whole ones?" she continued after a moment.

"Because their parents can't afford it," said Matthew promptly. "And it would make the real birthday less interesting."

"Something can't be interesting if you don't know it's ever going to happen."

"You know quite well when your birthday is. April."

She was silent for a few moments. "That's just a thing you say."

And he perceived for an instant the perpetual now of childhood, the interminable present from which, eventually, we escape and which we can never retrieve. We cohabit with these mysterious beings who occupy a different time-zone, who share our days and move with us through them, but whose vision is that of aliens—anarchic, uncorrupt and inconceivable. We talk to them in our language, impose on them our beliefs, and all the while they are in a state of original harmony with the physical world, knowing nothing and seeing everything. They roll with the planet, wake and sleep; their time is essential time, before it has become loaded with significance.

It was a day of wind, sending squalls across the lake, spinning the fallen leaves. Blowing Jane's hair across her face. There was an odd tacit agreement between Matthew and Susan that Jane's long hair should not be cut. Fair and fine, it reached now below her shoulder blades and was usually done in a plait or lifted up into a ponytail. Matthew was maladroit at both these operations and frequently wondered at his own reluctance to propose chopping it short. A primitive feeling perhaps that such an action would be to discard a part of her, to undervalue her process of growth, to reject the past. Jane herself appeared indifferent, except when the hair bothered her, as now.

"My hair's getting in my eyes."

"I'll tie it back."

"Plait it," she requested. "Please."

They sat down on a bench. "Tighter," said Jane. "You're doing it too loose."

"You know I'm not much good at this."

She considered. "You're good at other sorts of things."

"I hope so."

"Is everyone good at something?"

He saw the drift. Jane did not, so far, excel in any particular direction. She held her own at school, but did not shine; she was not athletic.

"Most people find out eventually what they like doing, and that's often what they're good at as well. Sometimes it takes a long time—not till they're grown up."

She was silent for a while, watching a park attendant sweeping up leaves from the paths. "And you can do things well or do them badly. That man's clearing up the leaves well, isn't he?"

Again, he perceived the train of thought. "Yes." The apt parental clichés trooped into his head; he picked his way past them. "Better than I could, I suspect." The plait was now done, for better or worse, and Jane's preoccupations had taken another sideways shunt.

"What are ducks good at?"

"They have to be good at being ducks—better at getting food than other ducks, or escaping from enemies."

"What happens if they don't?"

"They starve, or get killed. Unless they've got themselves a cushy meal-ticket like St James's Park."

"Is it still like that anywhere for people?"

Jane had been doing a project on prehistoric man at school; Matthew, knowing this, was able to interpret the question.

"Not exactly. Well, up to a point." Deep in what's left of the Brazilian rain-forests. In Brixton, or Whitechapel, or parts of Liverpool or Manchester or Bradford. He decided, cravenly, to wind up the conversation. "Look, I think we've had enough of this park. I want to go to Cobham Square to take a look at how they're getting on. I've been too busy to go there this week."

"It's Sunday. They won't be building it."

"That doesn't matter. I can still get in."

In Piccadilly she wanted to ride on the top of the bus, and in Regent Street she had to be downstairs, in the front seat. Everything matters; each decision is of moment. For those who live in essential time, every minute is equally weighted, as though it were the first or the last. Everything that happens is fresh, to be examined and assessed. Without the wisdoms and the tarnished vision of experience, each incident is ripe with threat or promise, nothing can be taken lightly, all that arrives is potent. Tragedy threatens when the front seat in the bus is occupied, but then the occupants get off at the next stop and the sun shines once more. A linguistic conundrum on an advertisement is succeeded by an unidentifiable species of dog, and that is swept aside by the splendour of a burst water main at Oxford Circus. Matthew, sharing these events in muted fashion, glimpsing the potential but unable to escape his own distracting commitment to the tyrannies of time, saw again that she lived differently, and unreachably. It is children alone who experience immediacy; the rest of us have lost the ability to inhabit the present and spend our time in anticipation and recollection.

At the bottom of Tottenham Court Road they abandoned the bus to walk the rest of the way. Here, Jane's attention was caught by a street trader from whom—after anguished indecision—she bought a green and pink plastic windmill. And then they struck out across country, past the British Museum, the Senate House, and so to the space and sobriety of Cobham Square, where Matthew's site was in shrouded silence, freed from the drills and the cement mixers.

"Are we going inside?"

"Yes. But you're to stay right by me. It's full of holes and leaking electricity."

There is an entrance door now, fitted up with locks to which he has the keys, and within there is space, a great echoing emptiness of airy floors, the shell of the 25,000 square feet of office accommodation that will launch this terrace into the next decade of use and prosperity. There are windows, the original windows looking onto the plane trees and the unlovely frontage of a Fifties block of flats erected to replace the blitzed south side of the square. There is the brick and stucco façade, there are the porticos and the Coade stone dressings, but within is space alone—new anonymous untroubled space, an acreage of untrodden floors, virgin planks laid upon newly sawn beams and steel joists fresh from the rolling-mill, walls on which the plaster is still damp, labyrinthine intestines of pipes and cables. The buildings have been stripped down to the bone, and are reborn. Somewhere behind that surface of new plaster the brick records the soot-stained spine of fireplaces; the stone staircase sweeps down where it was first installed. But that is all.

Matthew patrols, noting problems, checking what has been done and what has not, scrutinizing a reconstructed cornice, seeing the solution to a problem. He allows Jane to scratch her name and the date low down in one corner of a plastered wall. They stand together for a moment at the window and watch the life of the square—children playing, an old man reading on a bench. And then they leave. Matthew locks and double-locks, and they are out into the autumn afternoon again, into the dusty sunshine.

They walk to the corner, where the far side of the square leads onto a busy thoroughfare. They pause at the kerb. Jane is holding her windmill up to watch it spin.

A sudden gust snatches it from her hand. It flies into the road. And in one unconsidered panic-stricken movement she is after it. There is the blast of a horn, the screech of brakes; the white van swerves, blasting and screeching. It sweeps round her, it brushes her anorak, the wind of its passage lifts her hair. A woman gives a stifled cry; heads turn. The van is gone, and Matthew has pulled Jane back onto the pavement. He is trembling; his heart seems to thump his ribs. He stands clutching Jane's shoulder—now, this moment—and sees another moment, another life, streaming away into infinity. He lives, in that flash, the whole of it—her broken body, the ambulance, the hospital, the faces of strangers, tomorrow and tomorrow and tomorrow and the rest of life.

And then he is shouting at her: "How many times have I *told* you . . ." She stares at him in horror, at his strange raw face, and bursts into tears.

He puts his arm round her. "I'm sorry," he says. "It's all right. But . . ."

"I didn't mean to . . ." she wails.

"I know," he says. "I know. It's all right." And they cross the road, his arm tightly round her, as though she were ill, or he were.

FOURTEEN

These nights are twenty-four hours long, or one, or a few minutes. Time, like the city, is blown apart, wrenched into a shattered parody of itself. Jim leaves the square in twilight and returns at dawn. Sometimes, it is as though he had been gone an eternity; at others he is convinced that the world must have spun in some mad acceleration. On duty, at the warden's post, or tramping the streets, there is time as lethargic as the movement of limbs under water, inching onward in slow empty hours. And there is time displaced by action, when the helter-skelter demands of danger, anxiety, life, death, fire, water, the noise, the voices, the sights and smells are such that when at last you subside for a moment, take stock, hitch yourself to the natural continuities, you find that the furious sequence of events was telescoped into five minutes, or half an hour. In twelve hours nothing happens; in ten seconds, a street explodes into fire and dust.

And you cannot reach back, now, into the age before it all began. A few months ago. That time is behind glass, innocent and impregnable, as distant as the previous unblemished city, which seems some strange imagined incarnation of today's splintered, pockmarked, cratered, dusty, smoking labyrinth of distress. The place mutates each night. With each new day there is a new landscape—streets that have become a wasteland of rubble, into which whole houses have slid in a torrent of brick and matchstick timber, a yawning void where there was that pub, that shop, that café. He has to find new routes for his bike, to outwit the diversion signs, the bomb craters. He rounds a corner to see a carcass where yesterday there was a church, a boarded-up hole where last week he called on a friend. And rumour has it, always, that there is worse beyond. Down in Limehouse the Army trains for street-fighting in the ruins that were homes. In Poplar there is a UXB so large, so deep, so dangerous that a whole district is cordoned off. The Tower has had a direct hit. They got Battersea power station. The city has fragmented in another sense also; it has split up into a confederation of villages, within which people huddle, sniffing the acrid winds from elsewhere, guessing, hoping, waiting. Each day you remain unscathed is a day gained; the bomb that falls a mile away has not fallen on you.

"There's cloud coming up," says Mary. She is looking out of the window, as she does each evening before he leaves. He joins her and sees a bank of grey to the east.

"Good. Maybe we'll have a quiet night." Starlight is to be feared. The full moon most of all.

They stand for a moment. The child is out there in the square, playing with other children. Skipping. The parents watch the white twitch of the ropes in the twilight; they listen to the high thin sound of the accompanying chant. Then he turns to go.

"Tell her to come in, will you?"

He nods. He kisses his wife. He goes out of their door

and down the stairs, through the familiar strata of other people's landings, the whiff of their dinners, their prams and bins and bikes. He disentangles his own bike from the cluster in the hallway, puts his clips on, wheels it down the steps.

He calls to the child. She grins, and goes on skipping. He calls again, and this time sees her pull a face, wind up the rope, start to move towards the pavement. He waves. She waves.

And then he is on the bike and launched upon his navigation of the city, picking his way across boundaries, from one village to another, out of the relatively stable streets of his own area down through Coram's Fields, Gray's Inn, Holborn and into the devastated wastelands of the City. He rides fast, to beat the black-out and the ebbing light, whisking down unimpeded ways, selecting short cuts and avoiding known hazards. He passes through streets in which every building is skeletal, a symmetry of gaping glassless windows, and others where a single masonry façade stands amid the shells of shattered houses. There is a strange intimacy about these ruins— the staircases tripping down naked walls, the stark fireplaces, a column of washbasins, the pastel colours of wallpapers. You stare, record, and do not think too hard.

He sees a burnt-out bus with its nose in a crater, a tree from whose branches flaps clothing blown from the window display of a shattered shop. The city is full of such flukes and oddities. He stops to buy cigarettes and then again to push into the bright curtained fug of a pub for a quick half pint. Five minutes snatched from the night ahead, a stay of time in which to gossip, swap news, and then smack the glass down on the counter and out into the last grey glimmer of daylight and the final half mile to his post.

It is midnight before the sirens go, and they are starting their third hand of whist, and had thought to be settled in till morning. The first two hours are quiet; the throb of aircraft once, high, and then bangs and thuds, far off, down at the docks somewhere, and the sky lit for a while. He does the rounds, checks his shelters. Nothing to report. Back to the post for a cup of tea. Out again. He finds a drunk huddled in a doorway and hauls him to a shelter. The eastern sky is glowing now; there are fires down there, and he can hear the Woolwich guns. It is hotting up. He heads for the post again to see if there are any messages.

He hears aircraft. That slow insistent drumming. Getting louder, nearer, a whole bloody great wave of them, flying low. He ducks into an entrance, where he stands, peering out and up into the black sky that shows nothing but which roars and drums, louder and louder. They are right overhead.

The first of the sticks falls several streets away. Jim drops at once to the ground and lies with his hands clasped behind his head, waiting. He hears the second, nearer, a whoosh and a thud that leaves his ears ringing, but no slow groan of falling bricks and masonry—it has smashed harmlessly into the road. And even as he registers this the third is on its way—a whistle hurtling downward with such force that it is as though it did not fall but were sucked from the sky. There is an almighty bang, and then absolute silence. He lifts his head. His ears clear and he hears the long shudder of a building in collapse, and bricks pattering down. And at last silence again; a different silence.

He picks himself up and hurries down the street. There is broken glass everywhere, and rubble, and as he makes his way through, shining his torch to right and left, he sees gaping blown-out windows, pocked façades and, at last, the seat of the blast. The building on the corner is not there any more. It has compacted like a concertina; five stories have condensed into a pile of brick and timber out of which—as he swings the beam of the torch up and over—there rear twisted iron girders and the intact party walls at either side. The whole thing fumes with dust. There is a smell of gas. And underneath the lot is a cellar shelter in which, half an hour ago, he counted eight people.

The cellar has a reinforced ceiling. Chances are, they have survived. He shouts into the rubble, but can hear no reply. He heads for the post to report and to order out the Heavy Rescue, and sees on the way that the next street is cratered and that the first of the stick has demolished a derelict warehouse further on. At the post, the switchboard girls are in action already. Another warden has reported an incendiary fire and a suspected UXB. The whist cards lie on the table, beside half drunk mugs of tea.

He reports. Joan on the switchboard gets busy again.

"Our Heavy Rescue's out over in Spitalfields. They're going to log us next but it could be some time. They'll see if there's any can come in from Westminster."

He curses. "I smelt a gas leak. Call up a fire engine, too, and the casualty station. And keep at them, Joan."

He rounds up a couple of sub-wardens, and the three of them plunge out again. It is noisy everywhere now. The wave of planes has passed, but the city has flowered in their wake, dappled with fires, echoing with sirens and hooters.

As they reach the pile of rubble they see one side of it twitch and judder, settling. The sky is bright enough from reflected fires to see the structure of the debris, and they start gingerly to shift timbers and bricks, looking for a way in. Jim shouts again, and this time there is a muffled cry. Encouraged, excited, they burrow faster, they find the bottom of the stairs, which shields a black cave of dirt, dust and splintered timber, and Jim gets his head and shoulders through. He shines his torch. The rubble is looser here, there are tunnels and passages. And he can hear them now. Someone moaning, and a man's voice: "You going to get us out of here, mate?"

He tells the voice not to worry, to hang on. He is bright and calm, feeling no such thing. He has seen that there is a route down, twisting through timbers and blocks of masonry. He backs out to tell the others. "I can bring them out. Anyone that can move."

There is a reek of gas. Jim edges back into the hole, with the other men shining torches behind. He creeps into the smashed bowels of the building, under a girder, over splintered joists. It is quite quiet in here, except for the shifting of the rubble, which ticks and mutters around him, a continuous shudder of uneasy weight, settling, slipping, and all the time the light spatter of falling plaster, and a trickle of water from a broken pipe. And the someone down there underneath who is moaning.

He is tense with the expectation of a gas explosion. And he can smell scorching now, too. Somewhere, the rubble is smouldering. He keeps talking, to reassure those buried, to distract himself: "Have you out in a jiffy now, not to worry. Heavy Rescue blokes are coming along behind. Nice cup of char waiting for everyone at the wardens' post. Won't be long now."

And then he is into the corner of the cellar and sees that the ceiling has held up at one end but that it slopes down into a compacted ruin from which protrude a pair of legs, a hand, and a head, the face a shining mess of blood. He swings the beam of the torch away and finds a woman lying on the floor, grey with plaster, like the cast of a person. Dead. A man is slumped against the wall, who looks up, blinks in the torch-light, and groans. And someone else is moving towards him on hands and knees, and another is stirring under a fallen beam.

He brings them out, one at a time, the three men who can make it, guiding them up through the rubble, expecting every moment that the whole pile will shift, shunt, and seal them all down there. He comes out, gulps the air, and goes back in. Until they are all out, except the plaster woman, and the legs, the hand, the head.

He leans up against a wall, knackered. The ambulance has come, and gone. The firemen are hosing down. There is nothing more that he can do here, but for several minutes he stands, watching the black outlines of figures move to and fro against the mound of smoking shards. A building fragments into an inconsiderable heap of great density. Likewise, corpses always seem smaller than living people, but heavier.

It is well past dawn, and quite light, when at last he leaves the post. The All Clear went some while before, but there was checking of shelters to be done, and the night's log to be made up. So that when eventually he swings onto the saddle of his bike, and pushes off across the city again, it is raw, chill morning. The clouds have rolled over now, too late; there is a grey pall everywhere, and rain pouring down.

He senses that all is not right before even he turns into the square. Something reaches him as he rounds the corner: a charge in the air itself, a portent of change, of inexorable event. And there are too many people about; a fire-hose snaking along the pavement.

He comes into full view of the terrace, and sees. He sees what he has seen so many times but which now, here, is different. Unutterably different. The void where there should be a solidity; the confusion on the ground; the moving figures.

He approaches. They are concentrated around one particular point in the rubble—the black glistening firemen, the rescue squad. And then someone steps aside, and he sees. He sees that they are uncovering a child, the upright body of a child, the head tilted back as though looking up to the sky, the face and neck washed white by the pelting rain. A child. His child.

He stands there. He has become, it seems, nothing but a pair of eyes, seeing this. He knows only this here and now, this sight. And it comes to him, in a long moment, that there will never be a time when this has not been—the small cold statue of her there, and the rain falling, and the leaves piled up under the plane trees.

FIFTEEN

Matthew woke, in some time-less stretch of the night, to a profound sense of melancholy. He swam up from a dreamless sleep to absolute wakefulness, and lay there in the dark in deep unease. He felt himself tenuously inhabiting his body, poised beside an abyss. Nothing to be done, nothing, nothing. The pity of things. He stared into it, mourning. And then slowly the feeling ebbed and he began to hear the sounds of the London night. The rumble of an aircraft, an accelerating car, a sudden burst of laughter under the window, the tap of high heels on the pavement. He listened to the receding wail of a police siren, to a barking dog. He stepped back from the abyss, savoured the ground under his feet.

He went to the bathroom, returned, pulled the curtain aside and stood looking out into the street. Roosting cars, the dark frontage of the terrace opposite, with here and there the glow of a lit window, dustbins, rubbish skip, bike chained to a railing, and a single figure hurrying away in the distance. The alien but companionable world of others. He got back into bed, and waited for sleep, calm now but affected in some way he could not identify, as though there were some knowledge he had received and lost again.

There had been no more dead rats. Matthew's car remained intact. But he found himself irritatingly jumpy. He inspected his front door with suspicion each time he returned. He swung about at the sound of following footsteps. When the phone rang he would snatch off the receiver and hold it to his ear in silence until he heard the puzzled interrogation of a friend, a colleague, his mother.

It looked as though the bullies were losing interest in him, as predicted. In which case no doubt harassment was simply transferred elsewhere. He found himself thinking a great deal about Rutter, both in frustrated rage and a kind of detached interest. Cities will always favour people like him. They fatten on opportunity; they are spawned by the place, and then shape it to their own advantage. It seemed the supreme irony that their labours should so long outlast them, in terms of what is built and what is destroyed. And eventually, of course, history makes its own reassessments—ruthless greed becomes entrepreneurial skill, opportunism becomes farsightedness and acumen. The ravished landscapes and blighted lives, incapable of testimony, slide into oblivion. Finally, the statues are erected; the bold, visionary figures arise in bronze upon their plinths.

It was hard to imagine Rutter commemorated in bronze, or bestowing his name on streets and squares, but more startling re-interpretations of a man's endeavour are plentiful. As it was, it was easy to see him as an apt incarnation of the spirit of the times, licensed to do what he would by an official creed of self-advancement and economic adventurism. Those responsible did not, to be fair, have such as Rutter in mind—they simply created a promising environment. It would then seem curious, if not perverse, to penalize the growths most fervently responding.

He would think savagely of Rutter, as he drove to the office, or down to Blackwall. And then the thought would be overridden by the merciful vagaries of the attention, as he was distracted by a professional problem, by the dictation of his diary, by the teasing image of Sarah Bridges.

He waited for her outside the National Portrait Gallery, on a Sunday afternoon. The time and place were at her behest. She had hesitated in the face of his proposals—dinner, a walk by the river—and replied that in fact she had been intending to go to the Gallery to check up on a picture of Byron, in connection with the magazine. Possibly he might like to come with her? They could have tea somewhere afterwards. He wondered if he was being fobbed off.

And so he waited. Ill at ease. A touch apprehensive. Exhilarated. And so, ten minutes into anxiety time (she has changed her mind; there is a misunderstanding about where or when), he saw her, poised at the far side of the zebra crossing, head turned to assess the traffic, a gust of wind blowing her hair across her face.

The exchange of greetings. He scoured hers for a significant warmth, and could not find any. Friendly, cheerful, but, he felt, neutral.

The entry into the Gallery. The choice of a route. And now they are digested by the place, in that odd ambivalent state of those who are alone together in a crowd, conducting a dialogue and yet preoccupied by what they have come here to do. They have come to look at pictures. They look.

They go first to Byron, where Sarah satisfies herself that an unattributed illustration she has come across does indeed represent this portrait. Then, by previous agreement, they climb stairs and begin to wander through the Gallery, which Matthew has not visited for several years.

Under these circumstances, it is inevitable to drift apart, to come together for comment and discussion, to separate again. Matthew moves from one painting to another, through a pageant of reference and association, thoughts scudding through the head, seeing, watching, noting.

Eyes. The painted eyes upon the walls which return the gaze of the living eyes which pass before them. The painted eyes are old, young, blank, alert, but all have the serenity of their condition—caught at a single moment, endowed with an artificial permanence. The living eyes are lustrous, rheumy, fresh, jaded; they blink and peer, they steal glances from side to side, and across the room.

She is wearing pale trousers and a dark brown jacket. She has a way of standing with one foot at right angles to the other, like a ballet position.

Faces. Tudor faces, Restoration faces, eighteenth-century faces, Victorian faces. Faces forever hitched to their time, defined by dress and ornament, by the conditioned strokes of the painter's brush. Faces which prompt a thousand flickering unspoken responses from all these viewing eyes, the undreamed-of inheritors.

She is looking around now. Looking, it would seem, for him.

Take, for instance, the 375 faces which look out from "The Reformed House of Commons, 1833" by George Hayter, a remarkable gathering, a complacent thriving company in their wing collars, their high-buttoned waistcoats, the fettering garb of the day. Locked away there in their perpetual present, oblivious to the streaming narrative of subsequent event, which pours through Matthew's mind as he observes them.

And now she is at his side. "My goodness!" she says,

considering the picture. And then, "That, of course, is a splendid con. A fake."

"Fake?" enquires Matthew, turning to her, his mind no longer on the Reformed House of Commons.

"It's a moment that never was. He painted the individual portraits in his studio, so there was never a time when they were like that at all."

Matthew nods. He points out that of course there is a sense in which this is true of any portrait. What we see is the refinement of many things that the painter saw—expressions, emotions, manifestations of personality. Again, a form of invention. "Like when you try to remember someone's face," he goes on. "What you conjure up is an impression, which may be short on accuracy. For instance, I hadn't noticed your mole."

Her hand goes up to her cheekbone and touches—for an instant—the mole. She smiles. "But why should you?"

He does not reply. They continue to look at each other until, at the same instant, both break off unnerved. Matthew turns back for a last survey of the three hundred and seventy-five. Sarah says briskly. "On. We've hardly seen anything."

They pass through the Romantics again, where she hovers over Byron for a further minute. They go down the stairs, together now, and are plunged at once into the splendours and sobrieties of the nineteenth century. Matthew is halted by Gladstone and Disraeli, near life-size; Sarah roams ahead.

A portrait, of course, is also a relationship. Two people are involved. There are the eyes that look out, but there were also the eyes that observed and recorded. Disraeli gives an impression of ill-concealed boredom, commemorating perhaps a not entirely successful *entente* between painter and sitter.

She is no longer in sight. The room is bereft.

He wonders what she is looking at. What he sees and what she sees is the same, and unimaginably different. His

209

Disraeli is not hers. He thinks of all the images on these walls, lodging this afternoon in a hundred disparate heads. That earnest Japanese lady, the lanky Scandinavian youth, those noisy girls. And what does Sarah see when she looks at him, as she did just now?

She is beside him again, urgent. "I've found something special for you. Come."

She leads him to another room. "There!" she says. "Your ichthyosaurus man."

And there indeed is Richard Owen, fresh-faced and young. Not the whiskered head that accompanied the Chinese dinosaurs.

"So it is," says Matthew. He pays his respects. Then turns to Sarah. But what he says is not what he had intended; it springs reckless to the lips at some signal that he sees in her eyes. "I've been afraid you didn't really want to meet me today."

"Oh, but I did."

They stand in front of Richard Owen, whom they no longer see. Who has served his purpose, poor man. Until, again, they are unnerved, and step apart.

"And there's Darwin," says Sarah. "Looking like Lear."

She crosses the room to consider Darwin, while Matthew ponders an opened volume of *The Origin of Species,* displayed under glass along with *Past and Present, On Liberty, Culture and Anarchy.* Somehow, he is not able to give appropriate attention to the Victorian achievement.

They move on, in an unconsidered progress. Here is Macaulay, in his study, fingering his spectacles. "Actually," she says, "I was afraid you'd mind coming here. But I really did need to check up on Byron. I've not had a chance all week."

"I've been meaning to come here for ages."

Her smile. But living eyes are so charged that you have to look away, eventually. It is easier to meet the benign but judgmental gaze of Henry James, before whom they have now arrived.

"He looks like a person you'd love to have as an uncle," says Sarah.

"Do you have uncles?"

"Only one and I don't much care for him."

She has done with Henry James and gone ahead, which gives him a chance to look at her. That stance. The line of her nose. The mole. Her hair against her cheek. He is washed with desire so intense that for a moment he feels quite unstable. But desire is unexceptional, and can be falsely prompted. There is something more besides, as though some famished, starveling creature tottered to its feet and sniffed the air.

He catches up with her at Rupert Brooke. "There you are," she says. "I thought I'd lost you. You're still happy here?"

He is affronted, almost. He replies, at last, "I'm happier than I've been for rather a long time."

Someone behind them is restive. They are monopolizing Rupert Brooke. "Sorry," she says, and they proceed, together.

They have circled this floor of the Gallery and are meeting up once more with Thomas Hardy, Elizabeth Barrett Browning, Charles Kingsley. Both are aware of this, and entirely unconcerned. Sarah is talking now about her work. She is an authority on eighteenth-century French miniatures this week, she says. And cameos. She talks of these. And Matthew thinks about happiness. It occurs to him that this is rarely identified at the very moment of experience. He would like to share this thought with Sarah, but is prevented by not knowing how to put it, and by some superstitious inhibition. And by the miniatures and the cameos.

She stops. "I'm talking too much."

"That would be for me to say."

"But you wouldn't, would you?" The smile again. Teasing?

"No," says Matthew.

"We're back at Henry James."

"Why, so we are."

And have been, perhaps, for some while.

"This won't do," says Sarah. But they continue not to look at Henry James.

"What won't do?" asks Matthew, finally.

She waves at the walls, the pictures. "We're not taking things in."

"I am taking everything in," says Matthew.

She gives a curious little sigh. She touches his arm. "All the same . . ." she says.

He follows her, feeling still the print of her fingers on his sleeve.

She pauses. "Ah. Gwen John. Are you partial to Gwen John?"

"From now on, enormously."

And Sarah laughs. "You're not even trying."

"I give a solemn undertaking," says Matthew, "that I will come here on some future occasion, alone, and pay proper attention and respect to all that the place offers."

And even as he speaks he knows that this may well happen, but that for ever, now, come what may, Gwen John, Henry James and the rest will be enhanced. They will carry an indestructible freight of association. These moments are locked into their faces. These rooms will hold, for ever, this blaze of promise. Whatever the outcome.

"Do you think we should go, then?" she asks.

He is thinking, in fact, that he would like to stay here for ever, to settle down and live glowing in this good moment, immune from disillusion and distress. A craven thought.

"Perhaps we should."

They go slowly down the stairs up which they climbed an hour or so ago. Matthew knows that within that hour he has stepped from one state of being into another, from sickness to health, or possibly from tranquillity to dire peril, he neither knows nor cares.

They reach the bottom. They are exposed now to the blank collective gaze of the Royal Family. Sarah puts on the jacket which she has been carrying over her arm. Matthew helps her, his hand resting as he does so on her shoulder. He yearns for her now, both urgently and with total restraint. There is no hurry, no hurry at all. This will do. He can live on the riches of expectation.

He takes his hand from her shoulder, at last. She looks at him. Unwaveringly. And thus they stand, for ever, it seems, until she sighs again, and blinks. "So . . ." she says. "So there it is."

At twenty past three in the morning the moon had tilted right over the roof of the house and was spilling a parallelogram of pure white light upon the carpet. But insomnia was enjoyable. He lay with his hands folded behind his head, adrift, cruising from thought to sensation to fantasy, while the white shape on the carpet slid over to the wardrobe and began to climb the wall, and beyond the window the city roused itself into the distant roar of dawn.

"Is there always another day?" Jane had asked once, when he was putting her to bed, and he had reported the question to Susan, awed, and for a while, in good times, it had become a catch-phrase between them: "There's always another day." And then the image had turned sour, and they had ceased to use it. And now, once more, he found himself in a state to lie in glad anticipation of another day. And another, and another.

But Jane's question was ambivalent. She doubted, perhaps, the rising of the sun. An atavistic fear, and one with which to sympathize. We take for granted the comforts of reason. Maybe it is only children who preserve the complex

213

neuroses of the past, the threat of the supernatural, the fear of the millennium, the ultimate unreliability of the world. Nowadays, we worry about being unhappy, as soon as we are old enough to observe the priorities. It must have been simpler, if more nerve-racking, to dread the apocalypse.

And, thinking this, that not only will the sun rise but it will rise with a new significance, Matthew himself slips from rationality to anarchy. He leaves the prosaic terrain of his bedroom and begins to glide just beneath the surface of consciousness, that indefinite but crucial shift which frees the mind of constraints and sets it roaming in the strange country where everything is possible, where nothing surprises, where knowledge and memory are unfettered by the tame expectations of reason. This is the landscape of the psyche—a coded medley of allusions in which the private and the universal are inextricably entwined. Here the mind creates its own images, a brilliant mythic universe in which there is no chronology, in which the laws of nature are suspended. Here the narrator is the Creator, setting his own stage for the flickering, fragmented narrative of obsession and anxiety.

And here, indeed, is Matthew, standing at the edge of a great complex of gravel-pits, an archipelago of muddy lakes in which there wallow herds of antediluvian creatures, a Jurassic Noah's Ark, a lexicon of species, a thrashing slithering company of heads, humps, tails, flippers all boiling away there beneath his gaze.

He takes his companion's arm. "Observe the ichthyosaurus, my dear," he says. "You will note the use that the creature makes of the vertical fin."

She nods. She smiles. A wing of brown hair curves across her cheek. She lays her hand on his and he feels the fan of bone, and the warmth of her fingers.

On the far side of the gravel-pit is the skyline of a city, shining towers which rise from the muddy bank in crystal slabs

214

of turquoise, pink and gold. It becomes imperative to visit this city, and they advance across the water towards it, the saurian herds now vanished, a vessel of some kind sprung up beneath their feet. And the city too has dissolved and been reformed as cliffs of ice, opalescent gleaming façades among which they drift, watching the birds that wheel and turn in silver flocks against the icebergs. And now there is another vessel, brilliantly lit, a craft with open decks on which people are dancing; he sees the name upon the hull—*Rose*—and the baskets of flowers which swing from the canopies, and the crowds of dancers. He is alone now, and is himself once more, Matthew Halland, and he passes from the vessel, the seas, the ice cliffs and is walking in narrow streets, between canyons of grimy brick, the blank walls of buildings within which, somewhere, a child is calling. Jane. He is running now, frantic, in search of her. She is lost, imprisoned, endangered, and he cannot reach her. He rushes to and fro in these dark alleys, hearing her cries, distraught, and then the walls have melted away, and with them his distress, and he is walking calm down a great wide moonlit street, flanked by ruined buildings—the skeletal frames of houses, with gaping windows and a void beyond.

SIXTEEN

I understand the investigation is closed," said the policeman. "With a question mark still hanging around, if you take my meaning."

"I'm not sure that I do. You're saying that your people still think there may have been arson but they're not going to go on trying to find out who did it?"

"That's a bit of a crude way of putting it, if I may say so. And there does seem to be a distinct possibility of an accidental element, I gather."

"The possibility of an arson element seems to me distinctly stronger," said Matthew. "All things considered."

There was a fractional pause. "What I was ringing about, Mr Halland, was really to find out if you've been having any more trouble yourself."

"No. Not since the rats."

"Which is . . . let's see . . . just over a month?"

"I suppose so."

"I think we can probably take it you've been struck off the list," said the policeman. "But keep up the precautions for a while, just to be on the safe side."

"And what about Rutter?" enquired Matthew.

"We shall continue to take a strong interest in Mr Rutter, no question about that."

He visited his mother, who scrutinized him with such intensity that he found himself avoiding her eye, as though in guilt.

"You're looking well." Matthew understood that she was not talking about his health.

"I'm all right, Mum."

"Well," she said. "Whatever it is, it's done you a power of good. And not before time."

"I thought I'd make a bonfire in the garden while I'm here. You can hardly see it for dead leaves."

"All right, change the subject." She chuckled. "You never were one for confidences, were you? Come on then. There's newspaper under the sink."

Smoke streamed against the white November sky. Matthew stacked up the rubbish, enjoying himself. He dug the fork in, loosening the pile, and watched innocent flames creep around the spent growth of his mother's small territory. He thought of that other fire, and wondered how it is possible to be in a state of concurrent personal happiness and public disgust. Either this was the triumph of human nature, or its fatal flaw.

"How's that thing of yours, then, down in Docklands?"

"The building, do you mean? Not far off finished. They're laying the carpets and planting the trees. And the glass engraving's going to be put up over the main entrance next week. You remember I told you I found this person who's made an engraving of a ship?"

His mother nodded. After a moment she asked, "Is it her?"

"No. It's not her."

There was a silence. The bonfire spurted up, belched smoke, subsided.

"Better damp that down," said Mrs Halland. "I'll have the neighbours on at me. So the streets are paved with gold down there, are they?"

"I wouldn't say that. Mud, more like. Shall I take you for a tour some time?"

"No, thank you. I've seen pictures in the paper, that's quite enough for me. It's not a London I recognize, but then you could say that of a lot of the places, these days."

"That's a perennial complaint, I imagine."

"You've left your mark, anyway. How does that feel?"

"It's a pretty anonymous mark. Not one I'm specially proud of, either. I'll be glad to move on."

"Don't stoke that fire up any more. We'll go in now—it's starting to rain, anyway." As they moved towards the house she said, "Your father was bored with his work, you know, all his life."

"I rather thought he was. Poor Dad."

"But that's not to say he didn't do a good job. Of course he did. Conscientious, that was him. And he'd never really expected otherwise. People didn't. It's been different for you."

"I know."

On the back doorstep she paused, jerking her head at the fence. "Them next door. Young couple—nice enough. But do you know what he does for a living? Sells those machines they have in amusement arcades. A grown man."

"Maybe he's got no choice. These are hard times."

"There's always choice," she said sharply. "Your father's firm made biscuits. He turned down a position once with the football pool people. I'm not saying the world couldn't get by without biscuits, but it can get by without those machines that make flashing lights and silly noises."

"You're a hard woman," said Matthew.

She grinned. "I ask you, what's a fellow like that to say when he finds himself face to face with St Peter?"

"A lot of us may find ourselves stuck for the right phrase at that point."

"Sarah?"

"Yes," she said. "Hello."

"It's Matthew."

"I know."

"Is this too early?"

"No, not a bit."

"I wanted to catch you before you went to the office."

"You have—just."

"What are you doing?"

"Having breakfast. Opening my phone bill and two circulars. Looking out of the window."

"So am I. Looking out of mine. You are due north-east, by my reckoning. With three postal districts and a few million tons of brick and concrete in between."

"That's nothing," she said.

"And a few hundred thousand people. The first time I saw you, you vanished into them. For ever, apparently."

"Oh no—it was you who did that. I went back to the office and ate my sandwich."

"I'm sorry to be so subjective. But you were extinguished, as far as I was concerned. It's a viewpoint children understand. And now you're reduced to a voice."

"That sounds ethereal. In fact I'm rather sleazy in a dressing-gown, with toast crumbs and marmalade."

"What kind of marmalade?"

"Does it matter?"

"It seems to," he said. "But never mind."

"No trouble. It's Sainsbury's Chunky. And I've just realized something awful—it's after half past eight."

"I don't want to let you go."

"I'm not going far," she said.

Distance, like time, is inconstant. The house in which Susan and Jane live is two miles from Matthew's flat. Jane, when she returns there, is out of sight but on the same plane of existence. Susan is unreachable, as remote as though she were a thousand miles away or had stepped into another age. When Matthew mourns her, the person he mourns is not the woman who speaks to him from the front doorstep, or on the phone. It is not distance which separates us from others; space, like time, has its own elasticity.

Matthew, moving about the city in a state of heightened consciousness, is aware as never before of the fallacious nature of space. Sarah is right; she has not gone far, she never leaves him indeed, for she rides with him through the hours, a benign and distracting presence as he drives, works, eats, talks. But in his affliction, this heady detachment from the laws of nature in which the absent could be present and those he was with mere insistent shadows, he saw too how such contradictions are all around. There is no sequence in the city, no then and now, all is continuous. Equally, all is both immediate and inaccessible. Sitting in his car at a traffic light he listens to the anguished outpouring of an earthquake victim on the other side of the globe; his eyes meet for an instant those of an old woman crossing the road. He watches her—humped shoulders, legs warped by childhood rickets, tattered shopping trolley; a mysterious lifetime shimmers for an instant as she is lost from view, and the car is filled with that intimate distress in another continent.

And in his office, he is everywhere. He talks to Manchester, to Germany, argues with Reading and jokes with Cardiff. Twenty yards away, the people in the street are as remote as figures in a film—a panorama to engage the eye as he talks or thinks. In a haphazard moment he shares their space, but they are further from him than the glass manufacturer in the Ruhr to whom he talks, or Sarah Bridges, whose face and voice can steal into his head and obscure all that he sees or hears.

"It's Matthew."

"Oh, good," she said.

"I'm sorry. Tomorrow seems so far off."

"Yes. It's been this morning for days and days now."

"Are you busy?"

"Quite. It doesn't help. And you?"

"There was a board meeting. Now I'm on my way to Blackwall."

"Be careful," she said. "Don't let them drop things on you. Wear one of those helmets."

"Damn."

"What?"

"I'm in a call-box. I thought I had more change in the other pocket. It's saying fifteen . . . fourteen . . ."

"Oh dear. Can't you . . ."

"Eleven . . . ten . . . Now it's unstoppable."

"What is?" she said. "Why don't you . . ."

"Time. Seven . . . six."

"Try under the directories. Sometimes people put little hoards of ten pence pieces there and forget them."

"There aren't any directories. Only beer cans and fag ends. And what I wanted to tell you was . . .

. . . I love you," he said. To a void, an absence, the humming silence of the receiver.

*   *   *

Time and space are illusory, and the city itself absorbs and reflects, so that here and there, at crucial points, it is both the same and different. It is infused now with Sarah. Here, she walked away down the street, in her red jacket; there, she halted at a zebra crossing, with strands of hair blown across her cheek. The streets have taken her; she has become a part of their allusive babble, the insistent inescapable murmur that is unique to everyone, the myriad privacies of the public place. Whatever happens, she will be out there always, along with the shadow of Matthew's own well-being. He is leaving himself there too each day, and knows it. The allusions this time will be there, on that corner, beside that door, to taunt or sustain. Fleetingly, he thinks of this; unknowing, he greets that wiser incarnation of himself.

"That you, Len?" enquired Rutter, genially.

"No," said Matthew, after three seconds.

Rutter, too, hesitated. "Who's that, then? I know your voice, don't I?" There was a note of genuine perplexity.

Matthew, torn between fury and an equal perplexity, said, "What the hell are you after now?"

A pause. "I think that silly bastard's got me the wrong number. Sorry about this. Who *are* you, just for the record?"

"Matthew Halland."

"I thought I knew the voice. How are things with you, my friend? I was thinking of you the other day, down in Spitalfields. It is you that was all mixed up with those Glympton people, isn't it? I done a nice bit of business with them, in the end, but I dare say you know all about that. Mind, the buggers are going to come a cropper, but don't quote me. Spitalfields is a dead duck. That's not where the clever money's going today. Anyway, how's tricks? You still looking for a job?"

Either I'm losing my grip, thought Matthew, or he is. "I don't know what you're talking about."

"Wasn't it you that come to see me at the house about working for me?" said Rutter. "We got off on the wrong foot somehow, I remember. Pity, because I thought you was a clever sort of bloke, and they told me you done some good work. I can always find a vacancy for the right man. Tell you what, why don't you and me have another get together and see if we can't sort something out. What about a spot of lunch at L'Escargot?"

"Either you're even more depraved than I thought," exploded Matthew, "or you suffer from amnesia."

"Eh?"

"You heard."

"I was inviting you to lunch, my friend," said Rutter in an aggrieved voice. "I don't know what you're getting so upset about."

Matthew took a deep breath. "Look, you and I had a slight difference of opinion about your business methods. Remember? I accused you of involvement in the Spitalfields fire. Remember? I expressed my concern to the police, as I told you I would. Remember? Since when I have suffered various forms of harassment."

There was a pause. Rutter made an eruptive sound, a mixture evidently of enlightenment and amusement. "Now I see what you're at, my friend. I'm on your wavelength. There's been a misunderstanding. That's all fixed up, that Spitalfields nonsense. The fire was an accident but I've had the accountants give those people a payout. Just to show willing. They was very grateful. Anyway, we're pulling out of Spitalfields now I done this deal with Glympton's. So there's no problem any more. We got off on the wrong footing, you and me, and I'm sorry about that because I'm a man that likes to get along with people, know what I mean? Even if we're not going to do business I don't want you going off with the wrong idea about me. I'm a smart operator. I don't mess about, right? Some people might say I'm tough, and they wouldn't be too far out. I get what I want, Mr Halland. It's a good idea to bear that in mind. But I play fair. People that's sensible, that don't play silly buggers with me, find that they'll get a fair deal. Right?"

"No," said Matthew.

"Eh?"

"Never mind."

"You've been having some bother, you said? I've got every sympathy with you. There's a lot of villains about. Someone done over my new Roller last week while the bloody chauffeur was having a coffee—be off the road for a month, to get that paint-work right again. Deliberate, no question about that. And are the police interested? Are they hell." There was a disturbance in the background, a brief irritable exchange with someone else. "Sorry, I got to go," continued Rutter. "I got fifty people working for me but you still have to see to everything yourself. Anyway, it's been good to talk to you again, and thanks for calling. Cheerio."

His condition distorts awareness, Matthew finds. It is as though he were mildly drugged, with the vision clouded, so that sensation is the only clarity, and all else consigned to a muted background—Rutter, Blackwall, Cobham Square, the sequential demands of a day, the week. So this is what it is like to be elated. Happy. He remembers, now. And, doing so, he recognizes also the inborn hazard, the fatal innocence. He foresees a time from which he may look back uncomprehending at an illusion, a moment of unfounded expectation. He foresees and dismisses in the same instant. Life is instantaneous, or it would be unendurable, knowing what we know.

"It's me."

"I know," she said. "I knew before I picked the phone up. It rings in a particular way."

"Am I interrupting?"

"Definitely. Go right ahead and interrupt."

"What are you doing?"

"Proof-reading. How do you spell Hieronymus?"

"As in Bosch?"

"Exactly."

"With careless abandon, I should think," said Matthew.

"That's frivolous. They hire me to be scrupulous and accurate. Where are you?"

"On my way back from Blackwall. I've got plenty of change this time."

"Go on talking, then, while I go on spelling. How many m's in commemorate?"

"A fair number. What are you wearing?"

"Let's see . . . Black shirt. Blue skirt. Will that do?"

"I suppose it'll have to."

"Tomorrow," she said. "Tomorrow."

The condition, though, allows for much by way of dispassionate observation. The chronology of each day may be blurred, but the city is intensified, a cornucopia of incident, of image. He sees faces, gestures, the twist of a mouth, the gleam of an eye, the relentless amazing flow of humanity. He sees pigeon flocks wheeling silver against the white fluted columns of the British Museum. He sees great luminous clouds banked behind the forestry of Docklands cranes. He sees the yellow blaze of a dandelion pushing up between flagstones, the rainbow sheen of oil on a puddle, red ranks of chimney pots. The place is brilliant, and elusive; a quicksilver scene in which no sight nor sound is the same twice. It vanishes as soon as it appears, leaving only the indelible signals of the mind.

*   *   *

He stood with Eva Burden at the foot of the flight of steps leading up to the main entrance of Frobisher House. The glass engraving was in place, installed a few days earlier. The purpose of today's visit, at the behest of Sanderling's secretary, was some kind of informal ceremony of inspection and approval.

"I should be smarter," said Eva. She wore cotton trousers and an anorak. "I don't have ceremonial clothes."

"Not at all. I'm sorry to have let you in for this. It won't take long, I promise. These people move fast."

They considered the engraving. It occupied the panel above the large glass revolving doors, framed in a marble surround, and hung there as a delicate white tracery of light, an intricate ghost ship rocked upon the scrolls of phantom waves.

"It looks different this time," said Matthew. "Even better, if anything. Bolder."

"The light is different in the morning. I can only see details I wish I'd done otherwise, but that's always the case."

"Most of the people who walk in and out of there are never even going to notice it."

"Never mind, it's the spirit that counts. Have I got the expression right?"

"You have indeed. One of my mother's favourites. And entirely apt."

The building was complete, at ground level. Far above, at the summit of the glass column, cranes and pulleys still operated. There were walkways and flower beds laid out with shrubs. One of the old dockside cranes, painted marine blue, stood enshrined like a sculpture in the middle of a pedestrian precinct of brick paving and infant willow trees. The entrance to the complex was guarded by twin gatehouses manned by Cerberus figures in the form of uniformed security guards armed with walkie-talkie equipment. The automatic barriers swung open now to allow the entry of Sanderling's car. He stepped out, flanked by henchmen, and approached. Matthew introduced Eva.

Sanderling looked at her doubtfully, and held out a hand. "Good to meet you, Miss Burden." He turned his attention to the engraving, studying it for a full ten seconds. "Very nice. Super job." The thin smile gleamed in her direction for an instant, indicating benevolent patronage. "Clever the way you get the impression of light and shade. You're going to do us some decanters for the board room, aren't you?"

Eva inclined her head, indicating nothing in particular.

The group stood there, awkwardly. One of the henchmen referred to the stylized motifs of the sun and the points of the compass which occupied the lower corners of the engraving.

"Ah, yes," said Sanderling. "And the kite in the top corner. Is it a kite?"

"The Plough," said Eva. "Stars. For navigation."

"Of course. Very neat." A young woman holding a clipboard murmured in Sanderling's ear. He nodded. "I gather they've laid on a glass of something in the hospitality room. Shall I lead the way?"

The hospitality room consisted of a sweep of dark blue carpeting and a long polished table at one end of which were bottles of champagne sunk in a silver bucket and glasses on a tray. The exterior wall was entirely glass, affording a softly tinted view of the river.

"A bit bare," commented Sanderling. "I suppose the design people haven't got around to the art work yet. Any suggestions, Miss Burden?"

"You could make it a celebration of the Arctic," said Eva, after a moment. "Birds and animals. An Eskimo."

Sanderling looked bewildered, then nodded. "Nice idea. Can you make a note of that, Emma."

"No Eskimo," said Matthew.

Eva looked at him. "No, you're right."

Sanderling had moved over to the window and was identifying nearby developments and features on the far side of the river. Emma with the clipboard murmured once again and he glanced at his watch.

"We shall have to leave you, I'm afraid. Thanks so much for coming down, Miss Burden, and for your splendid effort on our behalf. Very good idea of Matthew's, that was." He glimmered again and made for the door, with the attendants in his wake, leaving Eva and Matthew alone with the champagne and the quilted expanse of the river.

"Another drink?" said Matthew.

"This isn't really my style, especially at twelve o'clock in the morning, but I suppose we may as well."

In the foreground, at the water's edge, was an old Thames barge, prinked and painted, the rust-coloured sail rolled up and new plastic covers stretched over the holds. In the distance, the City Airport hovercraft rushed east.

"So . . ." said Eva. "Do you wash your hands of this place now?"

"Heavens, no. Our responsibilities go on for quite a while yet. But in the sense that it ceases to be the dominant concern—yes."

"And what is the dominant concern?"

"Oh—a reconstruction we're doing at Cobham Square. A shopping precinct in Croydon. Offices in Finchley."

"And something else too, I would say."

"Sorry?"

She laughed. "You are glowing. Like a child with birthday and Christmas all rolled into one. I wonder what it is that happened since I saw you last."

"Ah," said Matthew. "I see. It's like that, is it?"

"It is indeed." She patted his arm. "Don't be embarrassed—you are a tonic. Good luck to you."

"Thanks. I think I need it. I'm rather conscious that expectation is deeply treacherous."

"Try not to be. It's all we have."

He moves about the city, doubling back and forth, navigating time and space. In Covent Garden there are no violets, but he hears Alice Cook tell him that she is pregnant, and buys her red carnations. The plane trees in Lincoln's Inn Fields rise up from the lake of their own leaves, but he sees an afternoon in June, shirtsleeves and Coke cans. In Cobham Square a white van sweeps around the corner, again and again, as he glimpses an abyss. He sees his scattered hours—irretrievable, enshrined.

"It's me."

"Thank goodness," she said. "I was beginning to panic."

"So was I. Traffic. A terrible insistent client. I was afraid you would have gone."

"Anyway . . . there you are."

"Here I am."

"Yesterday . . ." she said.

"I know. Yesterday."

"I can't quite believe in yesterday. I didn't imagine it, did I?"

"Oh, no," he said. "You didn't imagine it. Or if you did, then I did as well."

"That would be too much of a coincidence. It must have been real then."

"It must have been."

She sighed. "And now it's gone. Will it be like that again, ever?"

"Yes," he said. "Lots of times."

"Not *exactly*."

"Not exactly. Different."

"I want it to be now always."

"It will be," he said.

"I can hardly bear this. Just hearing you."

"Yes. It won't do. It won't do at all."

"But it's much better than nothing."

"True."

"You sound funny," she said, after a moment.

"Funny?"

"Where are you?"

"You know the phone box on the corner . . ."

"Oh," she said. "You don't mean . . ."

"Look out of the window," he said.

And he waits, poised at this instant of exquisite anticipation, until it topples on into the next, and he sees the shape of her framed there, and she speaks again, voice and presence fused in one moment of perfect grace, until that too is fled.

Night, once more. The child has woken. "I didn't know where I was," she says. "I was frightened. I thought 1 wasn't anywhere." He pulls back the curtain. "Look," he says. White clouds flowing across a blue-black sky, and the ice green quiver of a single star. The dark geometry of buildings, and the rhythmic jewelled flash of an aircraft tracking overhead. "There," he says. "You're here, I'm here."